PEST CEMETERY

SCOTT BELL

Unlocking New Worlds

For all the dogs and cats I have known. The truest friends
walk on four legs.

Chapter 1

October 15th

I parked the car and left the motor running. With a teaspoon of gas in the tank, the Mazda's engine bravely puttered on, farting little puffs of gray exhaust into the chilly night. Rain spat from a pewter sky, dotting my windshield between swipes of my sawtooth wipers. I had nowhere to go, no way to get there, and nothing to do when I arrived, so here I was.

At a cemetery. The end of the road, in more ways than one.

Washed in the wan light of my tired headlights, the Pottsville Shady Terraces cemetery office was constructed of reddish bricks—the color of dried blood—inset with two aged and weathered oak doors. Scabrous ivy scaled the building's exterior and choked the brick-and-mortar wall surrounding the graveyard. An iron gate to the left of the office was closed and padlocked—visiting hours 8:00 a.m. to 4:00 p.m., according to a gold-lettered sign—and beyond the gate, rows of mismatched headstones were visible through the bars, like jagged teeth sprouting from diseased gums.

Yes, I have an overactive imagination.

Cemeteries were ranked among my three least favorite places to be, right after bus-station restrooms and dinner parties with strangers. They made me uncomfortable, and in my core operating system, running away from uncomfortable situations was a feature, not a bug. The impulse to put the car in reverse and leave this place was strong.

However, the gas gauge read a quarter-minus empty, my wallet had long since collapsed into a black hole, and running away meant spending the night in a car with a damp dog and a tuna-addicted kitten. Ever try to sleep in the back seat of a drafty Mazda with a hyperactive husky and no cat litter for a poop factory that could excrete more waste than its entire body weight?

Short version: I needed a job, and I needed it right now, and the only job available for an itinerant college dropout in the vicinity of Pottsville, Pennsylvania, was one in a graveyard. The Mazda wasn't making it farther than the Pottsville city limits in any direction, not without gas.

I powered up my pay-by-minute phone and checked the Craigslist entry one last time: "Wanted. Cemetery caretaker. Flexible hours, room & board provided. Light groundskeeping, other duties as needed."

Other duties? Hmm.

Room and board cinched the deal for me. A place to stay—with a toilet I didn't have to beg a key for and a bed without a transmission hump—sounded pretty close to heaven. Sleeping in a cemetery would be fine as long as I wasn't sleeping *in* the cemetery, so to speak.

"Stay here," I told the unlikely pair sharing my car.

George side-eyed me, tongue lolling, panting his dog breath hard enough to fog the windows. A husky-coward mix, the two-year-old pup was all looks and no brains—he would be quite happy hanging in the car rather than risking exposure to a vicious squirrel or belligerent chipmunk or even a frisky sparrow. He ran from trouble so fast and so frequently I suspected he had French ancestry. He and I were a lot alike that way.

"Tabitha." I craned around and spoke to the tabby kitten who'd claimed the back seat. "Mistress of Death. Leave George alone, understand?" The killer powder puff remained curled in her blanket and ignored me, not even so much as twitching an ear.

"All right, Bradley." I twisted the key, and the engine died with a shuddering wheeze. "You got this. Just remember you can avoid being a screwup for entire minutes at a time, and six years of college was a choice, not a failure."

The car door squealed when I opened it.

A fat, cold raindrop hit me in the face.

Chapter 2

The guy on the phone had given me the code to a lockbox hanging from the doorknob. I worked the combination and opened the box, finding a pair of keys on a ring inside, which unlocked the door to a dark room. I patted the wall to flip the switch, and warm yellow light spilled from a pair of Tiffany lamps on side tables, revealing a reception room furnished with padded leather armchairs and a sofa. A coffee table arrayed with a selection of magazines occupied the space in front of the sofa. An archway on the far wall led to an unlit hall that suggested more rooms farther back.

A painting to the left of the arch drew my eye. I stepped over for a closer look. It was an Impressionist rendition of a cemetery, and the brass plaque read "Pottsville East Shady Terraces – 1959." The painting showed a daylight scene of a graveside ceremony set in the springtime, based on the profusion of green trees and flowery bushes. Mourners gathered in clumps around a casket, all dressed in black with dots of pigment indicating boutonnieres and handheld bouquets. The painting reminded me a little of Monet's *The Picnic* except the subject was a bit more macabre. As I studied the piece, my eyes swam, and for a brief instant, the people in the painting appeared to move, and the foliage was stirred as if by a phantom breeze. I blinked, and the dizziness passed. The painting remained a painting, as static as a Polaroid.

"Jeez," I muttered. "I must be hungrier than I thought."

"Hey," said a man's voice, making me jump. "Who are you?"

In a moment of confusion, I thought the words had come from the painting, but when I turned, a dapper fellow—that was how I thought of him: Dapper Fellow—stood in the open door. He had slicked-down black hair shot with gray and wore a two-piece suit like he'd been born in it. Narrow tie, Oxford lace-up shoes—all he needed was a snap-brim fedora, and he could have stepped out of a magazine ad from the age of black-and-white photos.

"I'm, ah, yeah... Sorry, I didn't know anyone would be here. I'm Langston," I stammered out. "Brad Langston. Here about the job. Ah, from Craigslist. I spoke with Mr. Chesterfield..."

"Sure, kid. I'm Stan Caputo." Caputo patted his pockets then frowned. "I keep forgetting. No smoking here."

There seemed to be nothing to say to that, so I kept my mouth shut. Avoidance of babbling was not among my superpowers, but I was working on it.

Caputo squinted. "You're younger than the last guy."

I kept myself from slumping in defeat only by an act of will. *Here comes the rejection.*

"What brought you here?" Caputo said. "I mean, why this job? Guy your age should be out on the career track, starting a family and whatnot, but a cemetery caretaker...? I don't get it."

My brain flooded with the litany of excuses I'd used to answer this type of question. *Trying to find my next opportunity. I'm figuring out what I want to do with my life. I'm between career stages...* All bullshit. Oddly enough, the truth popped out. "I've never really succeeded at anything like a real job, Mr. Caputo. I want to be a writer, but it's super hard to make a living at it. I need... well, frankly, I need the job because I'm broke." I shrugged. "This seems like a quiet place to work, and I'd do a good job for you."

"Oh, it's quiet all right. Dead quiet. Ha! And the job's dead easy... Dead quiet and dead easy. Oh man. I crack myself up sometimes. No, seriously, the job's easy-peasy. Something's broke, you fix it. You don't know how to fix it, you call somebody to come fix it." Caputo waved a hand as though brushing aside any worries. "Most of the time, you're keeping the grass cut and the weeds trimmed. You know how to mow a yard, right? And cut the weeds with the weed-chomper thing, okay? No chemicals, *capisce*? Chemicals soak down into the soil, and they stink."

"No problem, but..." *What the hell is a weed-chomper thing? A Weed Eater?*

"You pay the bills," Caputo continued without pausing, "replace the light bulbs, prune the rosebushes, lock and unlock the gate for visiting hours, and on those rare occasions there is a new stiff planted, you let the diggers in. They do all the heavy lifting *vis-à-vis* the dearly departed. You don't hafta dig no graves is what I'm saying."

I opened and closed my mouth, words having momentarily become lost in the jumble of questions clogging my brain.

"Back there"—Caputo pumped a finger at the hall through the arch—"is a business office with one o' them... whatchacallits? Computer thingies. The shyster, Chesterfield, has it set up. Every month, the endowment fund deposits money to the cemetery account, which is what you use to pay the bills with. There's a checkbook in the top desk drawer. You cut a check for yourself out of what's left over." Caputo winked. "That encourages... whatdotheycallit? Frugality. Even so, there's enough simoleons to make a decent living. Pay for your groceries and so on. Don't get no ideas, though, okay? Chesterfield comes around every once in a while and checks the books."

"I wouldn't... I mean—"

"Now, past the office is a small suite—a bedroom, a kitchen, a living room. It ain't much, but it's better 'n a poke in the eye. Chesterfield explain all that to ya?"

"Ah, yeah. Yes, he did."

"Good. You seem like a good kid, or maybe I just gotta soft heart." Caputo smirked. "They said it would kill me some day, can you believe it?"

"I, uh... have pets. A dog and a cat."

"Really?" Caputo raised his eyebrows. "Dogs are nice. That's fine. Just don't let the dog pee on the headstones. Headstones are important, kid. There's six hundred and forty-two graves out there. Some of them, sad to say, are lost to history cause the headstones are so worn out they've kind of melted away. Time, kid..." Up until now, Caputo had maintained a wiseguy expression, but for the first time since I'd met him, he seemed sad. "Time takes everything, eventually. Which is why we need a caretaker. Somebody to, you know, take care of things. Keep the earth from swallowing all the markers, right?"

"Right," I said when it appeared Caputo had finished speaking. "Right! Exactly. And how do I reach you? I mean, in case I need something? Are you like the boss, or what?"

"Oh no, not me. Consider me like an adviser. A friend in low places, as it were. Call Chesterfield if you need something. Most things, you can handle just fine on your own, and the shyster wrote out all the instructions after Arlo... left. Arlo was the last caretaker. Everything is on a piece of paper there, in the office."

"What happened to Arlo?"

Chapter 3

"Arlo?" Caputo looked away. "He, ah, he assumed another position. In a different cemetery. We lost touch after that."

"Do you have an email address or a Facebook page or something?"

"Naw, kid, sorry. I don't talk on the phone, let alone get into all that other jazz." He shrugged. "Trust me, you'll be okay. I'm sure nothing will happen to you."

Caputo stepped into the room and bowed with an arm extended, like a maître d' in a fancy restaurant. "Whyn't you go get your pals outta that car, huh? They're probably freezing their furry keisters off out there. Make yourself at home—stay the night. There's some canned goods in the pantry that Arlo left behind, or you can use the petty cash and run down to the grocery store and get something to eat. If in the morning you don't want the job, just tell Chesterfield, and he'll call it square."

"Uh, sure." I mustered up a tad more confidence than I felt. Truthfully, Caputo's version didn't exactly match up with the attorney I had spoken with, and the man seemed a little sketchy. And what did he mean by "I'm sure nothing will happen to you"?

Say what?

But what choice did I have? It was a place to sleep. I could spend the night and check things out in the morning and see if the situation looked any better. Things were pretty bad when a bed in a cemetery was your best alternative.

"Sounds like a plan. I'll be right back."

Full night had descended, and the fitful rain had dialed up to a drizzle. George hopped out of the car happily enough, dancing around my legs, tail wagging. He barked, and his breath plumed, which seemed to amaze him. He cocked his head at the steam rising around his muzzle then barked a few more times to watch his breath cloud around himself. Most huskies were drama queens, howling and complaining and carrying on about the littlest things. George was an exception to the rule. If brains were measured in gunpowder, he would not be able to light a spark, and pouring all the courage from his heart would leave space in a very small thimble. Fortunately for him, he was a gorgeous animal and happy in his goofy way, always ready to go somewhere new, as long as I led the way and kept the squirrels from getting too close.

Tabitha, on the other hand, was less interested in moving.

"Come on, kitty," I told her as I picked her claws loose from the blanket. "Let's go meet Mr. Caputo. Don't rip his face off, because we need this job."

I carried the kitten inside with George at my heels. My pet-gathering expedition had taken all of two minutes, and at no time was I out of sight of the office door. However, by the time I returned, Mr. Caputo was nowhere to be seen. I found the light switch for the hall and poked my nose in all the remaining rooms, which included an office, a janitor's closet, and the three-room suite mentioned by Caputo. They were all empty. The last room in the facility was the apartment's kitchen, which was where we found the rear exit. A safety chain hung across the doorframe, meaning it had been locked from inside and not disturbed.

"Huh. How'd he get out?" George looked up at the sound of my voice, his blue eyes mirroring my confusion. "That was weird. Dude just skipped without saying goodbye, so long, have a nice day, or nothing."

The black-and-white husky huffed an agreement and made a bee-line for the kitchen's pantry, where all the food was stored. Trust a dog to have his priorities right.

Chapter 4

A sound woke me in the deep middle of the night. I lay pretzeled between animals under stiff, bleach-scented sheets and a thick pile of blankets, warm and cozy but with a mildly urgent need to go pee. Tabitha was curled against my neck, and her long fur tickled my nose. In a rare moment of camaraderie, she had allowed George on the bed, so the husky sprawled across the bottom half, forcing my legs into a gymnast stretch.

The room was dark and quiet. Rain tapped at the window, sounding like a witch's fingernails, and chilly rivulets tracked silver paths along the panes. I watched the water drip for a moment, which only exacerbated my need to take a whiz. Burrowed into my warm cocoon, I didn't want to move. Plus, getting up meant disturbing Tabitha, who was a bit crabby at the best of times and was especially annoyed when her human servant interrupted her sleep.

It had been a long night getting settled into the new space. Miraculously, I had found canned tuna in the panty—a few months past the best-by date, but Tabitha hadn't minded—and some recent-vintage beef stew in a warehouse store's supersized can, which I shared with George. I had also turned up some musty-smelling tea bags and a jar of powdered coffee. Firing up the stove had been a challenge, as it dated from the Revolution or thereabouts and came equipped with burners that required a match and nerves of steel to light.

After eating, I had washed up in a sink with dual faucet knobs, one of which claimed to be for hot water. This started another adventure as I had to hunt down the water heater and pull up some YouTube instructions for lighting a pilot. I'd never done that before, so when the gas flames whooshed on just like the video showed, a great sense of accomplishment came with my singed fingers.

Stomach full, I had explored the rest of my new kingdom. The business office did in fact contain a "computer thingy," which in all honesty should have long ago been turned into a trash thingy. A blue folder lay on the desk next to a monstrous Compaq monitor. I opened it and found a business card embedded in the inner pocket. The name Maurice Chesterfield III, Esq. was embossed in raised script on the heavy stock. According to the card, Mr. Chesterfield was associated with the "shyster" firm of Creddick, Smith, and Madison. A phone and email address were listed on the card. It was Chesterfield who had interviewed me over the phone when I responded to the want ad, and the email address matched the one I had used to send a picture of my driver's license and a selfie of my face. George had photobombed the selfie, of course, as he always does.

The folder contained a stack of documents including a list of instructions for various tasks. I skimmed those then set them aside for later deciphering, except for the one explaining how to log onto the cemetery's online bank account. I was surprised to find a respectable sum had accrued in the three months since the last activity.

"Awfully trusting," I said to George, who had stayed close to my heels since dinner. "They're handing a lot of money to somebody they just hired without a reference or a background check." Icy-cold fingers brushed my neck, and I shivered at the chilly draft. There was an air gap somewhere that needed caulking. I powered off the computer. "Never mind, George. We may be screwups, but we're not thieves."

As I lay awake in the dark of the bedroom with October rain tapping at the glass, I remembered those icy fingers on my neck and shivered again. The noise that had originally woken me penetrated my foggy brain and made my hair tingle. From the adjacent room came the sound of voices followed by a canned laugh track. I remembered seeing a TV sitting in the living room—an old console model with a remote control so worn the text on the buttons were mere suggestions. Not being much of a TV person, I had left the set alone without bothering to see if it worked.

But obviously it did work. And somehow had turned itself on in the middle of the night.

A gust of windblown rain rattled the glass.

Chapter 5

I disentangled from the pet hotel and levered myself out of bed. Miracle of miracles, Tabitha only yawned a tongue-curling cat yawn, stretched, and tucked herself into the warm spot—no scratching, no complaints. George perked up and shot me a wide-eyed look of interest.

"We're not going for a walk," I told him, and he flopped back onto the bed.

The floor chilled my bare feet. I wore only thin cotton pajama pants. Goose bumps prickled my arms and shoulders, and from more than just the cold. Living next to a cemetery spooked me more than I cared to confess. I didn't believe in ghosts, but my imagination could supply enough scary stuff to stock a dozen nightmare situations. I'd seen a lot of horror movies where the plucky hero goes to check on the strange noise in the basement, only to get chopped into hamburger meat by the troll under the stairs. Earlier, standing near the computer, I'd passed off the icy brush across my neck as a stray draft flowing through a poorly sealed gap. I had refused to admit, even to myself, how much the sensation felt more like a chilly hand clamped around my neck than any draft I'd ever experienced.

I'm sure nothing will happen to you, Caputo had said.

I slipped across the tile floor and peeked through the crack of the door. Bluish light flickered across the living room walls, and the sound of the sitcom grew louder. From my narrow survey, the room seemed empty. I pushed open the door, ready for... well, not really ready for much of anything. I had no weapons, and my martial arts skill was limited to striking a kung fu pose and yelling, "Ha!" Had there been a TV watcher lounging on my couch or a spectral being eating ghost popcorn while catching up on reruns of *That '70s Show*, my defense against the dark arts would've been to pee myself and hope the intruder was allergic to urine.

The television was playing to an empty room.

As living rooms go, this one was about all I'd expected from a caretaker's apartment: worn but serviceable furniture, including a single easy chair, a sofa, some bookshelves heavily overrepresented with John Grisham titles, and of course, an old, console-style TV set.

The remote was on the sofa. *Did I leave it there when I went to bed? Or was it on top of the TV?* I didn't recall. I picked it up, figured out which button was the power, and switched off the set. Aston Kutcher died saying something funny. The room went dark.

I stuffed the remote down between the sofa cushions. Maybe Tabitha or George had walked across the device and sent a signal to turn on the TV. This had happened before with George. Covering the IR beam with sofa cushions should solve the problem. I quick marched my cold feet to the john, took care of the bladder issue, and rushed back to bed.

Tabitha reluctantly allowed me some space after I squeezed in. I scratched her chin by way of apology, which she graciously accepted as her due and forgave me my interruption of her rest. George settled against my legs, barely having woken. My eyes sagged closed, lulled by the rain speckling the window. The bed was cozy, just the right kind of warm in a quiet, winter-cool room with a husky foot warmer and a tiny kitten motor buzzing against my neck.

The self-activating television was a fluke. No doubt one of my fuzzy pals had walked on the remote, and since I had been really tired, it had just taken me a while to wake up to the noise. Nothing supernatural about it.

I was drifting off to sleep when the television turned itself back on.

Chapter 6

October 16th, Day 1

The rain had cleared by morning though the sky remained soggy and gray, which matched my mood perfectly. I escorted George out front and walked him down the hill along the cemetery wall, where he anointed telephone poles and mailboxes then stopped to leave a deposit on the grass parkway at the corner of the block. While I waited to use the plastic bag I had brought along for just this situation, I yawned and leaned against the rough brick perimeter wall.

The bricks shifted against my back with a crackling sound, and the wall lurched. I jerked upright to take my weight off it, averting by seconds a collapse that would have deposited me on my butt. Even so, the section I had leaned against showed a definite concavity, and closer examination revealed cracks running throughout the mortar as far as I could see in either direction. Inertia and ivy appeared to be the only things holding it up. The damage was extensive, and my layman opinion was the entire wall was truly screwed.

"Goofy TVs," I muttered. "Wobbly fences, dangerous appliances... Man, this place should be junkyard, not a graveyard."

George ignored my pondering and focused on his task. Once engaged in a poop, very little disturbed George or caused him to break his concentration.

I yawned again. I hadn't slept well. The hyperactive television had turned itself on three times during the night. The set was older than the Carter administration and probably had a short in the on-off switch rather than a pet-stomped remote as I'd first assumed. By the third time it happened, I was way, way over being freaked out by it. I settled things by pulling the plug from the wall, rendering it silent for the rest of the night. As far as I was concerned, it could stay that way. I rarely watched television anyway.

George finished his deposit, which I dutifully collected, and we headed back inside. After a breakfast of stale oatmeal for me and last night's leftovers for the critters, I carried my reconstituted instant coffee with me to tackle my new job. The office seemed like the best place to start. George tagged along at my heels. Tabitha ignored us. She was busy pushing a bowl around the floor with her nose, hunting the last scraps of tuna. I had already rigged her a litter box out of an old carton and some shredded newspaper, so everything was simply divine in the princess's little world—for now.

Correspondence overflowed in a basket on the desk. Included in the pile were various bills—power, water, gas—all overdue and stamped with bright warnings of imminent shutoff. The amounts had gotten pretty steep. The property tax bill alone was big enough to grab the cemetery's bank account by the balls and make it scream. Eight months' worth of bank statements were in the stack, un-opened. I found a similar stash stuffed in the top of the filing cabi-net—no files, just thrown in loose.

In the top desk drawer, I discovered the checkbook, a three-ring binder with tear-out checks, three to a page. Each check left behind a stub for recording the payee, date, and amount. The last check written was to the power company, dated three months previous. I flipped back through the old stubs and confirmed pretty quickly that whatever Arlo's talents might have been, bookkeeping wasn't one of them. My examination revealed that Arlo had written himself a pay-check—variously labeled as "pay," "wages," or the uniquely spelled "celery"—once a month, for an average of about two thousand dollars.

"Hey, George. Two K a month's not bad, right? Considering there's no rent to pay." George seemed happy with the deal, coming over for a head scratch.

The very first page of the attorney's notes dealt with the required documentation to add the next caretaker as a signer on the checking account. The documents were already filled out, with only the name left blank, so I wrote *Bank* on top of my to-do list. A to-do list seemed like the kind of thing a productive person would do, and I took some pride in my solid start. The word *Bank* looked a little lonely, so I added *Groceries* and *Gas* to give it some company. The pile of bills worried me, so I tacked on *Pay Bills* to the list, underlining for emphasis.

"Look, George." I showed the husky my list. "Progress."

George howl-barked in the language of his people, turned in a circle, and flopped on the floor.

In a drawer, I found a gray metal box labeled Petty Cash that contained ninety-two dollars and twenty-six cents along with a receipt from the hardware store for a garden-hose spray attachment that cost seven dollars and seventy-two cents with tax. It didn't take a lot of math skills to deduce the petty cash fund was supposed to equal one hundred dollars even, and there were two cents missing. I dug in the desk drawers but couldn't find the change I needed to bring the petty cash into balance. I tried my pockets and came up with lint. I almost wrote *Find two cents* on the to-do list, but that seemed juvenile, so I decided not to.

A meticulously hand-drawn map of the property was tacked to one wall, complete with rows of tiny numbered squares representing grave markers. The cemetery was bigger than I'd first envisioned, covering at least three or four city blocks. A few large rectangles dotted the map, and those had names instead of numbers. Family crypts?

Big money donors? I would have to go out later today and walk the property to see.

In the same drawer as the petty cash, I turned up a set of keys, each neatly labeled for its purpose—Office, Shed, Gate, and so on. I stuck the keys and petty cash in my pocket, along with the forms for the bank, and headed out to get started checking off items on my to-do list. Stuffing the petty cash in pocket made me a little uneasy. I planned to reimburse everything, including the missing two cents, but taking the money without telling anyone made me feel guilty.

"I need gas," I told George. "Or I won't make it to the bank. And tuna. We need that, or there's going to be trouble." I held my hand to the side of my face and whispered. "You know how she gets when there's no tuna."

George wuffed his agreement and waited for more wisdom from me—or a dog treat. He would be okay with that too.

I patted him on the head. "Stay here and guard the dead people, buddy. Back as soon as I can."

Before I jumped in my car, I unlocked the visitor's gate and got my first look at the Shady Terraces by light of day. There were no terraces though they had plenty of shade trees, or they would be shady in the summer. I wasn't much of a botanist—my best guess was oaks or elms, along with something that left behind a brown, prickly, ping-pong-ball-sized seed pod. Sweet gum, maybe? Dead leaves hung from the branches and carpeted the ground, and tangles of weeds, left over from summer growth, clogged the paths and choked the grave markers. Brittle ivy crusted the border wall and almost swallowed entire sections. Wild nests of overgrown rosebushes threatened to shred any unwary pedestrian on the footpaths.

I stepped inside the gate and shook my head. *What in the hell have I gotten myself into? This place is a disaster wrapped in despair. A real crap burrito.* Not only had Arlo dropped the financial reins almost a year ago, he had ignored the maintenance of the grounds just as long or longer. *Damn, Arlo, how lazy do you have to be not to mow?* Or maybe I had the situation all wrong. Maybe he had simply gotten tired or overwhelmed or ill and had been unable to do his job. Caputo had mentioned Arlo had taken another position in a different cemetery. Hopefully, it was someplace smaller, more manageable.

I wandered several rows deep into the cemetery, consciously avoiding stepping directly on graves wherever possible. It had always given me the willies, walking on a grave, knowing that underneath my feet a corpse moldered in a silk-lined casket. I always pictured the dead body as resembling the Crypt Keeper, that cackling, pun-loving monster from comics and movies, and my footsteps being the catalyst that woke him from his eternal rest. At which point, I pictured him reaching through the soil to grab my ankle.

I'm sure nothing will happen to you.

Yeah, I was good at keeping myself freaked out. "Plan for the worst and hope I live through it"—that was my motto.

I had spent a couple of summers in college working for a landscaping company, so while the extent of work seemed daunting, I had no qualms about being able to get it done. It would take months to do the job right and get the place back in shape. *But wait.* I pulled up short as a thought struck. *There's not a time limit, is there? I mean, who's going to complain if I don't get the whole place cleaned up in a day? The customers sure won't care.* I made a note on my to-do list: "Check out the lawn mower ASAP." If the Shady Terraces gardening equipment was as old and faulty as the computer and TV, I was in for a real uphill battle. *Can I afford to hire a lawn crew? Maybe take a lower salary?*

Even with help, it was going to take a ton of work to get this place put back right, financially as well as aesthetically. The grounds and outer wall would be months of manual labor, and the place needed a new computer, a filing system, a modern financial program like QuickBooks—the list was not endless, but it was long. *Who am I kidding?* I tucked my hands in my pants pockets and sighed. My shoulders slumped. I hadn't signed up for this. Shady Terraces needed a total redo, not a college-dropout wannabe writer, his trusty dog, and a diva kitten. This wasn't going to work. No way.

I turned and shuffled back to the car, zigzagging between the graves again. *Damn, I should call the attorney. But what do I say? Sorry, Mr. Chesterfield, I took your petty cash for gas and groceries, but I'm outta here?* That was wrong and probably illegal. I'd have to stay on for a few days, just enough to earn what I needed to move on. *And then...* And then I could reset to my default operational protocol and run.

After all, that's what I do best.

Chapter 7

Sunshine had burned through the clouds by the time I returned to the cemetery with a quarter tank of gas, sacks of groceries in the trunk—including a bag of scented kitty litter, which should make Her Highness happy—and a bunch of items checked off my to-do list. Adulting merit-badge achievement unlocked.

George helped me carry groceries from the car trunk to the kitchen. His idea of helping meant twining himself around my legs so that I stumbled as much as walked. I laid everything on the counter and returned to close the trunk.

"Oh, hello," said a cheery voice. "You're a pretty boy. Who're you, then?"

I shut the trunk lid and found George had abandoned me in favor of a new friend. He had surrendered without a fight, wriggling on the sidewalk with all four legs in the air, accepting a fierce tummy scratch from a woman about my age or a little younger in a padded US Post Office vest. A long braided streamer of her black hair fell over her shoulder.

"That's George," I said. "He didn't read the chapter in the dog manual about how to treat mailmen—er, ah, mailpeople. Postal people." *Smooth I am in ways of the Babble. Really, really smooth.* "Hi, I'm Brad? I'm the new, ah, caretaker? Of the cemetery?" Every sentence out of my mouth sounded like I was asking a question. I couldn't seem to stop.

"Sounds like you're not so sure." The woman straightened and regarded me with a quizzical look. She was handsome—or maybe striking—instead of pretty, with topaz skin and a toned figure. If I had to guess, I would say she could trace her roots to somewhere in the Middle East. She quirked an eyebrow. "Did you lose your memory? Head injury, maybe?"

"No, sorry." I twisted my mouth into a smile and stuck out my hand. "New to the job. First day and all."

"Saiera Khosani." The letter carrier shook my hand. Nice handshake. Brief, firm, businesslike. "And I have mail for you, Mr. Brad."

"All bills, I expect. Heh heh." My attempt at a chuckle faded and died, and the tightening of her smile suggested Saiera Khosani had maybe heard that line a time or two. I forged onward with "There seem to be a lot of them. Bills. For a cemetery, I mean. Who knew, right? Heh heh." George saved me from more babbling by leaning against Saiera's leg—she was wearing shorts despite the weather—and demanding more attention.

"Who's a good dog?" she cooed while she scrubbed his fur. "Who's a good boy? Such a handsome fellow you are!"

George agreed on all points, wagging his tail hard enough to create a breeze. The thought crossed my mind to ask Saiera if she'd like to come inside and meet Tabitha, but everything I thought of sounded like a come on... *Wanna see my kitty? Wink wink, nudge nudge.* The husky worked his new friend for all she was worth, wiggling and rolling around her ankles.

"He'll never give you up now," I said. "You're his best friend forever."

"Too bad, George." Saiera straightened and picked up her satchel. "I already have a fellow, and he would be very jealous if I brought you home." She reached into her sack and fished out a bundle of envelopes wrapped with a rubber band, which she handed to me.

"I, uh... Thanks. Maybe I'll... see you again?"

"I come by once a day, except on Sundays." Saiera clamped on a professional smile. "If you're still here tomorrow, you will see me when I bring the mail, yes?" She gave the husky one last head pat and strode away. I hung there with George for a moment, both of us watching her walk, though for very different reasons.

"Stop that." I nudged George so that he would look at me. "It's not nice to drool over a woman's butt."

George cocked his head in confusion.

"Oh, by the way." Saiera had turned around and was walking backward.

I thought for a dreadful second she had heard the comment about her butt. My face heated, and I tried to wipe away my guilty look.

"Be careful of the ghosts, Mr. Brad."

"Ghosts? What gho—Oh, you mean from the cemetery. Ha ha." If I was going to work in a graveyard, I guessed I was going to have to get used to some stale jokes, the same as letter carriers. "Yeah, well..."

Saiera stopped walking, her expression serious. "Shady Terraces has a reputation, Mr. Brad. You heard what happened to the last full-time caretaker, right?" She touched her nose and arched an eyebrow before spinning away and continuing her rounds. "Be careful!" she tossed over her shoulder.

AFTER A LUNCH OF COLD cuts and mayo on white bread with a side of potato chips, I cleaned up my dishes at the sink. A window at eye level provided a limited view directly into the graveyard. A brick path from the back door led to an outbuilding the size of a two-car garage with a pair of swinging doors facing the interior of the property. The outbuilding abutted the perimeter wall on the east side—if I recalled correctly, there was an alley just beyond the wall.

The office was tucked into the southeast corner of the almost-square grounds. Almost square because the opposite corner was cut away in a curve created by Sycamore Street.

"Hey, George, you want to take a walk?"

George hopped up and danced in a circle around my feet before I'd finished wiping my hands with a dish towel. "Walk" was one of the few concepts he grasped.

I pulled on a hoodie and had my hand on the kitchen doorknob, with George bumping my legs, when the phone rang from the office. I ran back to grab it.

"Uh, hello?" I realized I suddenly had no idea how I should answer a call. "Brad Langston... uh, Shady Terraces."

"Mr. Langston?" a deep male voice rumbled through the earpiece. "Maurice Chesterfield here. Since you answered the phone, I assume you are continuing on as the caretaker for the cemetery?"

"Mr. Chesterfield! Yes, thank you. I'm sorry, I forgot to call you." *Damn, damn, damn.* First day on the job, and I was already in trouble. "I got... I got busy getting, you know, getting started."

Silence hummed through the phone, saying as much as words might.

"I have a to-do list," I said. That sounded lame, so I added, "I went to the bank and filled out the forms. So I can sign checks."

"Very good, Mr. Langston."

"I—what? Oh. Thank you. And I was going to get started on paying these bills. There's... there's quite a bit overdue here."

"Yes, that was an unfortunate lapse on our part." Chesterfield had a rich, cultured baritone, like an Orson Welles or a James Earl Jones. I pictured him a big, hefty guy in a three-piece suit with maybe a watch chain hanging across the front. A cigar-smoking, country-club kind of guy. "An oversight on my part, I'm afraid. The bills should have been addressed by previous caretakers."

"You mean Arlo?"

"No, Mr. Weaver has been gone many months. We've had other candidates since his time though no one has so far been... reliable."

"Ah... I see." I didn't see at all. After a pause, I rushed to fill the silence. "There's a lot of things that are, you know, falling apart. Or need to be upgraded, I mean."

"Yes, I would agree. Do you have an assessment?"

"Well, the computer needs an upgrade, and the wall around the property is falling down, and there's a lot of work needed on the grounds. And I think the TV is busted."

"That has been reported by others." I thought I picked up a hint of something in Chesterfield's tone. Amusement? Sarcasm? "Please put together a memo of the capital expense items you believe are needed to bring the property up to snuff, along with cost estimates. I will present your requirements to the trustees, and we can perhaps appropriate the funds needed. No promises, Mr. Langston, but I will do my best."

"That'd be great. Hey, do you have Mr. Caputo's number?"

"Who?"

"Ah... Stan Caputo? Medium height, medium build. Slicked-back hair. Snappy dresser."

"I'm sorry, I don't know a Mr. Caputo."

George's howling bark echoed from the kitchen, telling me, *Get off the stupid phone, and let's go outside already.*

"You have a dog?"

"Uh, yes, sir. Mr. Caputo said it would be okay."

"Mr. Caputo...? No, never mind. It's fine. Just remember to clean up after him, please, and to be respectful of the grave markers."

"Got it. Absolutely."

"I will drive down from Pittsburgh in a day or so to meet you in person. Assuming you're still there, we will go over the most pressing needs at that time. In the meantime, please call me with any issues you feel are beyond your capacity to handle though I'm counting on you not to bother me with trivia. You're the man on the spot, and you are empowered to take care of the facility to the best of your ability. Good day, sir."

"I—oh," I said to a dead connection. I had wanted to tell him about the petty cash, but he hung up before I got the chance. So far, Chesterfield seemed to be a decent guy. Maybe this would work out okay.

George pranced in, howled at me, and trotted back out. He was quiet for a husky, but impatience with slow humans could make him very vocal.

"Okay, okay. Such a drama king." I grabbed my pad and pen and followed the dog to the back door. "We'll go outside, you big whiner. Just don't pee on a headstone, okay?"

TABITHA BOUNDED OUTSIDE after us then pulled up short when she discovered the ground was still wet. She wasn't sure how she felt about that and sat down to clean a muddy paw. George, in the meantime—

"George! No! Not on a tombstone, buddy. We discussed this, remember? C'mere, let me show you a nice tree."

Keeping him off the pretty white blocks that obviously required squirting with husky pee was going to be a problem.

I took off in a random direction, following a gravel footpath that ran parallel to the eastern wall. Recalling the map tacked to the office, three main paths ran through Shady Terraces, and from them branched numerous side paths, all of which looped back to main trails at some point. If you squinted just right, the view resembled a jigsaw puzzle, with each section containing rows of more or less evenly spaced graves. Roses grew from beds planted along the main paths, their overgrown canes swaying in the breeze and reaching out to eat me if I stepped too close.

A brown carpet of leaves squished underfoot as I walked. The day had turned cloudy bright with the temperature in the low fifties. A north wind rattled through the trees and pattered the ground with drops shaken from the branches. Tabitha kept up for a bit then started crying about being left to fend for herself. I picked her up and tucked her under my arm. Or I tried to, as Tabby rode her human servant one way: on his shoulder. If I moved too fast, pinprick claws would remind me to be careful of the kitty.

"I should rig a saddle on George for you, you little diva."

Tabitha purred her agreement. She could be very loving when she wanted something... like a shoulder ride.

"Young man! Young man!"

I spun around to see an old lady standing on the footpath. I had no idea where she'd come from—probably from one of the side paths though I hadn't seen her at the last intersection. In my defense, she was too short to ride the kiddie rides at Six Flags, so it was possible she'd been hidden behind a mushroom.

"Ma'am?"

"Do you see the state of these roses, young man?" Her question came out more of a demand. She pointed at the nearest tangle of thorny bushes rising from a central mass that belonged in the Little Shop of Horrors. "Do you see the condition they're in?"

I stepped closer, one hand balancing the tabby on my shoulder. "They're, uh... they're bad?"

"They are awful. Simply awful. Do you see this? Black spot. Black spot all over them." The little old lady pointed at some greenish-yellow leaves covered in black dots. She then motioned me closer. "And look under these leaves. No, under the leaves... just turn them over. Do you see those white things?"

"Uh, yes, I do. I think."

"Aphids." She spat the word as though it tasted bad. "Aphids everywhere."

"I guess aphids aren't good either."

The old woman fixed me with a look that suggested I was no smarter than George. At a pinch over a leprechaun in height, wearing a Sunday dress and a pillbox hat in a style that had gone out of fashion when Eisenhower was in office, the woman possessed an aura of command that seemed natural to matriarchs, royalty, and grandmothers everywhere. George appeared from wherever he'd been exploring, took one look at the fierce little woman, and ran off with his tail between his legs.

Coward.

"I'm sorry, ma'am," I said. "This is my first day on the job here as caretaker, and I'm just now getting a feel for everything that needs to be done. Any tips on how I should get rid of aphids and black spot?"

"Of course!"

Of course. Why couldn't I keep my mouth shut?

"I have no doubt you'll botch the job without supervision of a rosarian," she added. "Now, go get some gloves and a pair of pruning shears, and we'll get started."

"I, uh..."

"Oh, Martha," said a new voice from behind me.

I spun around, earning a prickle of claws in my shoulder from Tabitha.

A different old woman stood on the path behind me, somehow having approached in complete silence. This one also was dressed in her Sunday best though her style was more modern. "Don't listen to the wicked witch, Mr. Langston."

I blinked. "You know my name?"

"Of course," she said. "Stan told us who you are. I'm Gillian Fairweather, and the old crone there is Martha Perry."

"Wicked witch! Old crone!" snapped Mrs. Perry. "You need to mind that sharp tongue of yours, Jilly Fairweather!"

"Mr. Langston has only just arrived," Mrs. Fairweather continued. "He'll attend to the roses by and by, after he's had a chance to get his feet on the ground, I'm sure. Why, the weeds alone—"

"Don't you start with the weeds again," Mrs. Perry volleyed. "It's the roses—"

"The roses!" Mrs. Fairweather had edged closer, and what I'd first taken for an even temperament was being revealed as a false front over a strong-willed interior. "It will be months before the roses are even ready to bloom, you silly nit!"

I slipped out from between the women as the war of the roses escalated. Tabitha and I made our escape by sneaking one step away, then another, then another, until we were distant enough that I was sure they had forgotten me. The two women were still squabbling as I rounded a bend in the path and disappeared from sight.

"Jeez," I murmured to the tabby, "people here really take their cemetery maintenance seriously."

Tabitha meowed in my ear.

George reappeared soon after my encounter with the old ladies. His coat was spiky and damp from where he'd rolled in the wet leaves—some of which still clung to his backside. His tail swatted like a signalman waving a flag. The dog, at least, was having the time of his life.

I ventured deeper into the cemetery, following paths at random and finding the conditions growing worse, more overgrown, the paths rutted and filled with puddles. The farther away from the main entrance I walked, the older the dates on the grave markers grew, as well as more worn and harder to read. Near the back wall, a small copse of briar-choked trees grew in a nasty tangle.

I set Tabitha on a headstone and ambled closer to the tangle, bending over to get a better look. *Yep, sure enough, there are graves under all that mess. A big job ahead for the weed chomper.*

A flash of movement caught my eye.

I looked up, and a chill of surprise washed through me. A woman stood among the trees, seemingly immune to the briars and brambles. She was stunningly, achingly beautiful. A waterfall of ink-dark hair framed her Latin features and tumbled over her bare shoulders. She wore nothing at all, yet she didn't seem distressed by the cold. She just stood there, watching me with an expression of sadness, her full red lips twisted in a rictus of pain.

"Hey," I said. "Are you okay? Do you need help?" A stupid question maybe, but what does one say to a naked lady in the forest?

The woman said nothing. I might have mistaken her for a statue, were it not for the slender arms that reached out as if imploring me to help her. She seemed not at all concerned about her lack of clothing and made no attempt to cover herself.

"How'd you get in there?" I craned my neck, searching for—and not finding—a path into the miniature forest. Any attempt to reach the woman would require a serious effort to shove through the hip-high vines and bracken. The woman would be—should have *already* been—torn to shreds, yet her marble flesh was unmarked.

George had wandered off, and Tabitha was becoming vocal about being left behind. I glanced back, and she was stretching one paw toward the ground as though trying to decide if hopping down was within her ability.

When I looked back, the woman was gone.

Chapter 8

By the time I made it back to the front gate, clouds had gathered in ominous premonition of another storm system brewing in the north. I locked the gate without bothering to check if anyone else remained inside the grounds. Hopefully, Mrs. Fairweather and Mrs. Perry had taken their argument outside because I was in no mood to deal with them.

Truthfully, I was tired, damp, cold, and deeply, deeply freaked out.

I had spent at least an hour prowling around the tangle of trees where the woman had appeared, looking for where she'd gone. I had fought my way into the brambles and earned numerous scratches as a result. I had called out until I was hoarse. The woman did not reappear, nor did I find any evidence she had ever existed.

My digging around in the brush did uncover a breach in the perimeter, a place where she might have gained access to the graveyard. A tree growing near the wall had lost a limb, either from a storm or old age, and it had fallen on the wall, breaking down a big section. The woman might have stepped over the brick rubble and around the branches of the broken limb and escaped into the farmer's field beyond, but... nothing taller than a dandelion grew in the recently cultivated field. If she had run that way, I should have been able to see her. Hard to miss a naked woman running across a plowed field.

A ghost. The thought kept creeping back in, no matter how hard I tried to shove it away.

Look, approach this logically.

Logically. Sure.

I saw a naked woman in a cemetery in the late fall. The temperature is in the forties, so she wasn't out for a stroll. She didn't have a scratch on her, and she didn't say a word. And she flat disappeared. So what does that leave?

A ghost. I shivered.

Bullshit. Must have been a hallucination. Maybe the beef stew was older than I thought. I ate a bad bit of beef...

Aw damn. Now I sound like Ebenezer Scrooge.

Remember how that turned out? Ghosts. Plural.

While I had a little light left, I opened the shed behind the main house and surveyed the interior. As big as a two-car garage, the shed contained a multitude of lawn-care tools—everything from a riding mower to a variety of Weed eaters. I caught a strong whiff of gasoline, grass, and... salt. Bags and bags of rock salt were stacked on pallets in the middle of the floor, next to the lawn mower, enough salt to melt half the ice in Pennsylvania.

"We won't have to worry about frozen footpaths," I muttered.

I was happy to see a washer and dryer against the back wall. *Yay! No laundromats for me!* Pegged along both walls were shovels, rakes, hoes, a chain saw, and a wide selection of smaller hand tools. Lined up under these, a half-dozen toolboxes contained a jumble of me-chanic's tools from wrenches to ratchets to screwdrivers. There was no organization. Everything was piled in helter-skelter.

Another addition to my list: "organize tools."

I sniffed at the mess, snagged Tabitha away from the dead bug she had cornered, then closed and locked the shed. George waited by the back door of the apartment, looking like one soggy, tired pup.

After taking care of my furry pals, I warmed up a mug of soup and carried it back to the office. From the beginning, things had seemed a little off here at the Pottsville East Shady Terraces, and it was past time for some research. While the ancient PC wheezed to life, I dug through the files and found plenty of Arlo Weaver's handiwork. I could not find the names of any other caretakers in the files. Anyone taking the job after Arlo had apparently not stayed long enough to make an impression or to draw a paycheck for that matter.

Had they, too, seen the ghost of the woman in the forest?

I opened a browser window—Internet Explorer 8, for God's sake—and typed "Arlo Weaver" and "Shady Terraces" into a search engine. A mixed bag of junk hits came back, including offers to Shop Now for an Arlo Weaver or a woven rug or a home on a shady terraced lot. On the second page, near the bottom, a link took me to a news article from the *Pottsville Post-Dispatch*, dated January 15 of this year, almost ten months ago.

> Pottsville East police reported today the body of Arlo Weaver, 72, caretaker of Shady Terraces Cemetery, had been discovered by mourners visiting the gravesite of a loved one. It appeared that Mr. Weaver had been deceased for several days and was located in a remote part of the cemetery.
>
> "We saw the buzzards," said Mr. Walling, 42, who, along with his wife, had discovered the body and notified police. "We thought at first somebody might have been dug up, you know? All them buzzards. Then when we came closer, we found poor Arlo, laying facedown in the dirt."
>
> Police have not provided any details related to the cause of death, nor have they ruled out foul play.

And that was it.

I tried different combinations of search terms and slogged through page after slow-loading page of search results, all without another mention of Arlo Weaver's demise. What was it Caputo had said about Arlo? *Assumed another position in another cemetery?* I snorted. "Yeah, right. A horizontal position. Good one, Caputo. Real slick."

I made a note of the story's byline on my to-do list: "Go see Andy Gluck, staff reporter, *Pottsville Post*."

It was interesting and not a little disturbing that the long-term caretaker had died in the graveyard without explanation. Although at seventy-two years old, maybe it was not surprising. He could have easily keeled over while working outdoors. Heart attack, stroke, fallen over and clonked his head on a stone—anything was possible.

But the police had not ruled out foul play. *Come on, Brad. Ten months ago? And not a blip in the paper since then? Hardly likely to be murder unless the cops here are the Keystone variety.*

After carrying a fresh mug of tomato soup into the apartment's living room, I turned on the electric space heater. Space heaters caught fire like a California forest, and I hated to use them. But the apartment's central heat put out only a weak stream of lukewarm air, and my nose was dripping from the chill. Comfort won over safety.

There were no windows in the living room, but I could hear the faint patter of rain or sleet striking the roof. I found an early Robert Parker novel among the paperbacks and settled on the couch with my soup and my yawning kitten. George curled up on the rug in front of the heater's glowing coils.

It was close to midnight, at the halfway point of Spenser's adventures, when my eyes started to droop. The room was cozy and quiet. George huffed and rolled over in his sleep, and Tabitha's paws dream-twitched.

I hit the pause button on my life and took stock. I was warm. I had a full belly. Both my cat and my dog were content. I was inside, out of the elements, with a chance to earn some money and get back into my writing. No doubt there was a big job in front of me, enough solid work to last for months. On the bright side, I had no boss, no time clock, and almost complete autonomy. Everything at that moment was almost as perfect as I could imagine it.

"So what if I saw a ghost?" I said to the empty room. "It's a cemetery, right? Bound to be a ghost or two." *And besides, at least my ghost was a hot chick with no clothes. Could be worse, right?*

On the chair next to me, a young Black man popped into existence.

He appeared fully formed, solid and material—no fade in, weak-ass translucence here, no sir. The boy wore a nice suit that didn't seem to fit him very well, along with an expression common to teenagers everywhere: disdain for anyone older than twenty.

"Yo, man," he said. "You gonna plug the TV back in or what?"

I VAULTED UPRIGHT, sending Tabitha flying, and yelled, "Jesus Christ!"

"No, man." The apparition rolled his eyes. "He ain't due for a while yet. I'm Delmont."

George had bolted around the corner of the couch beside me. From this position of relative safety, he let off a stream of husky howling that sounded like he was the incarnation of Cerberus unchained and he would bring hell to your front door, free of charge. Tabitha had bowed up in the middle of the floor and stalked, stiff-legged and sideways, toward Delmont the Ghost. *Unleash the Kitten*, I thought and wanted to giggle like an idiot.

I had heard the phrase "hair standing on end" but had never experienced the sensation until that moment. Every square inch of my skin, from scalp to toe, felt electrified and two sizes too small. There was a taste on the back of my tongue like I'd swallowed a roll of pennies.

And I very, very desperately wanted to pee.

"Chillax, man," Delmont said. "I'm a ghost, not a zombie. I ain't here to eat your brains or nothing. Wouldn't be more'n a chicken nugget there, no way."

A ghost is smack-talking me. Another giggle burbled up my throat, and I clamped it down with an effort. I had no idea why I was reacting with an insane desire to laugh like a hyena in the face of the supernatural. Was that a normal fear reaction? *Ha! I laugh in the face of danger, for I am a lunatic.*

"I... I... I..."

"Dude," Delmont said, "you sound like a car trying to start. Listen up here, Ichabod. It's real simple. I like to come up in here and watch some TV now and then. I can get it turned on myself—it takes a bit, but I can do it. What I need from you is to keep it plugged in. You with me?" The ghost held his palms up, emphasizing how simple it was. "Us spectral beings and shit, we have limits. I can bang a cupboard or rattle a chain, but sticking in a power plug? Huh-uh. That be beyond my current skill set, so to speak."

While Delmont spoke, Tabitha had stalked closer, a miniature fuzzy monster, poised to attack. She was crabby from being woken, and Tabitha had nothing but distilled contempt for strangers of any kind, even midnight visitors from beyond the grave. Before I could stop her, she pounced on Delmont's ankle... or tried to. The tabby kitten rolled through the spot she had intended to savage as though it wasn't there. It was like she fell through a holographic projection. She popped to her feet with a confused-kitty expression. Tabitha attacked again, bounding and slapping and gyrating around the strange visitor's foot.

"Tabitha, stop it," I scolded. I had no idea what Delmont might do, and I didn't want to find out. "Stop biting the ghost!"

"That's all right," Delmont said. "She ain't hurting nothing."

He lifted his foot, and Tabitha leaped after it. She caught nothing, her attack again thwarted by there being no substance to Delmont's body, and fell back to the floor. Her tail swished, and she glared daggers at the young—but dead—man in the chair. Her butt wiggled for traction, and a menacing growl issued from deep in her belly.

My legs unlocked, and I managed to scoop up the little fuzzball before she renewed her attack. "I'm sorry. Tabitha doesn't have a retreat gene in her DNA." I frowned at George, who had stopped howling and was peeking sheepishly around the corner of the sofa. "Unlike some people I could name, who are double-chromosomed for it."

Fascination had started to take the place of fear. Delmont seemed like a decent guy, and whatever his corporeal status might be, he had given me no reason to believe he intended any harm. That by no means meant I was ready to sit down and relax. I carried Tabitha to the far side of the room without turning my back on my surprise visitor. George stayed close by my heels.

I worked up a breath and tried to speak intelligently. "How are you...? How is it you can...? How can I see...?"

"Look here, Doctor How, I ain't here to play twenty questions. Just plug the TV back in, and we cool. Right now, it's about time for some *Fresh Prince*. You good with that? Cause I can go bang some pots and whatnot if you'd rather..."

"No, no. No pots, please." I put Tabitha down before she transformed into a Tasmanian devil.

She raced for the bedroom, and George figured she had a good plan and followed.

"How old are...? When did you, ah...? When was it that, ah...?"

"When did I croak? Is that what you asking me?"

"Yes. When did you... pass away?"

Delmont leaned back in his overlarge suit, sighed and looked away. His face was pitted and bumpy with acne. *Now that's depressing. Pimples last forever. Even death can't cure them.* "Nineteen ninety-four. Car wreck on my sixteenth birthday."

"Wow. That sucks."

"Like an industrial vacuum." Delmont hitched his chin toward the back wall. "I'm out there, eighth row, sixth from the left. Delmont Riggins, 1978 to 1994. Taken too soon."

The space heater pinged from heated metal, and sleet rattled against the roof. Delmont Riggins said nothing else, and truthfully, I couldn't think of a single topic of conversation right then. How do you make small talk with a ghost?

"How's the weather where you're from?"

"Dark and cold, with a chance of worms, thank you."

"How've you been feeling lately?"

"A little stiff and dehydrated. Thanks for asking."

I walked over, plugged the TV back in, and switched it on.

Chapter 9

October 17th, Day 2

I woke a little after six in the morning, curled into a corner of the sofa, with an infomercial playing on the television. Delmont Riggins was gone, which led me to my inevitable self-doubt. Was it all a dream? Had somebody slipped me an LSD roofie? Or did I have a brain tumor the size of a baseball squeezing my cerebral cortex and causing Technicolor, Dolby Surround Sound hallucinations?

If it *had* been real, then at some point, I had fallen asleep despite a ghost in my living room binge-watching Syfy-channel reruns of *Supernatural*. And wasn't there some irony in that choice? Delmont had rocked back in his seat and cackled hysterically at an episode featuring a ghost.

George lifted his head from my lap. At some point, he had abandoned his fear and come back to the living room. Tabitha remained in hiding, no doubt sulking about her inability to slaughter the intruder with her razor-like claws.

Before brewing coffee, brushing my teeth, or even taking a whiz, I pulled on my shoes, grabbed my coat, and barged through the back door. The sleet from last night had left everything coated in a glass-like layer of ice. Given the predicted temperature, I expected the ice would melt before noon, but for the moment, the world appeared to be a sculpture of pure crystal. Waterford trees and Swarovski bushes.

And treacherous footing. I nearly fell and busted my ass three times before I found the row of headstones I wanted.

My breath plumed when I spoke. "Eight rows... Now, six over. One, two..." I counted as I walked, glancing at the names engraved in granite and encased in glassy ice. *Ferguson, Southon, Walters, Rusch...* "Five... six..."

Riggins. Delmont Riggins, August 14, 1978 to August 14, 1994.

"Taken too soon," I read from the inscription. Then I added under my breath, "Holy Jesus on toast."

For my hallucination theory to hold water, I would need to have had prior knowledge of Delmont's information, yet in all my wandering about the grounds yesterday, I had never passed this exact spot or read this exact grave marker. No way could I have known a sixteen-year-old boy named Delmont Riggins was buried here, so no way could I have conjured up a midnight fantasy involving this exact information. Could I have passed by this spot, seen the gravestone, and recorded the name and date and inscription while under the influence of a baseball-sized tumor and blocked out the memory?

"C'mon, Brad." I sighed and huddled deeper in my coat. "Now you're reaching."

And seeing ghosts is not *reaching?*

I scanned the surroundings, a little unnerved by the silence of the place—or lack of human noise, to be more specific. Shady Terraces was located on the far edge of Pottsville East—the dead end of town, so to speak—so there was little vehicle traffic along the roads bordering the cemetery. Beyond town, on the far side of the Terraces, lay nothing but farmland and forest, including some Amish communities, if I remembered correctly.

Icy branches danced in the breeze like brittle wind chimes. Half a dozen crows fluttered from distant trees, their mournful voices rasping out, "Caw caw caw." I watched the black birds for a time, soaking in the cold reality of living in a graveyard that was, um, haunted?...

by at least two ghosts. And if there were two... how many more were there?

I turned to go back and nearly ran into Mrs. Perry, who was standing in the path, wearing the same dress as the day before and with her expression fixed in the same disapproving glare.

"Young man, I have a bone to pick with you."

"Mrs. P-Perry. Sorry, I-I-I didn't know anyone was here already. Wait... I didn't unlock the gate yet. How did you...?"

Same dress as yesterday... Oh no, I locked her in overnight!

The prune-faced old lady marched up and stuck a finger in my face, and I braced for a tongue-lashing about having left an old woman out in the cold all night. "These roses are still unattended. It's a disgrace. A total disgrace."

"I'm so sorry... What? The roses? I, uh... It's, ahh..."

"Do you have a speech impediment, boy? Stand up straight. Stop slouching. You look like something the cat dragged in. Did you sleep in those clothes? I have to say, young man, I'm very disappointed in you so far."

"I get that a lot," I admitted. "But it's only been—"

"Stop whining, sonny." Rheumy blue eyes regarded me from point-blank range, reflecting a deep disapproval in what they saw. "I want to know when you plan to take care of these roses. They're a disgrace. A disgrace. Humph."

"Martha! Stop browbeatin' the kid," Stan Caputo said. "He's only been here a day."

I goggled at the sudden appearance of the dapper man. It was like he had come out of nowhere... *Oh no.* I reached out and tried to touch Mrs. Perry on the shoulder. My hand passed through her body as easily as cutting through smoke.

The old lady squawked and jumped back. "Eek! Keep your hands to yourself, you lecherous creature. I won't be groped by anyone, least of all a runny-nosed vagabond!"

"I'm s-s-sorry," I stuttered. My insides had turned to quicksand, and my legs wanted to fold up under me.

"You do that way too often!" Mrs. Perry snapped.

I blinked like a semaphore. "What? I do what—"

"Apologize. You apologize so much you sound like a broken record."

"I'm sorry, I..."

"Martha." Caputo stepped between us and faced the old lady. "Leave the kid alone, okay? This one shows promise. He can *see* us. I don't want him to run off like the last half dozen. Capisce?"

"Well, he should—"

Caputo used a firmer tone. "Martha. Please. I'm serious here."

Mrs. Perry humphed again and vanished. Just. Vanished.

Hail Mary, full of grace. Mom had worked hard to get religion to take root in me, but my field had been rocky and infertile. Now, after having met a few ghosts, the Holy Spirit was waist high and growing fast.

"Siddown, kid," Caputo said, not unkindly, "before you fall down." He ushered me to a tall, sturdy headstone—Phillip Rusch's, to be exact—and I tucked my coat over my butt to keep the ice from soaking through my jeans. I did it automatically, without thinking. I would have sat in a bucket of ice water at that moment and not noticed.

I squinted up at Caputo, who seemed as solid as a living person. "I take you're a..."

"Stanley Caputo," he said with a grin. "Nineteen oh one to nineteen thirty-seven. Tried to rob the bank over in Pottsville and ran into a stakeout instead. Somebody dimed us, and that, as they say, was that."

I rubbed my eyes with my palms then blinked them clear. I sniffed then swiped at my nose with a sleeve. My mind refused to engage. Here was my chance to talk to a once live bank robber from the thirties, and I could think of absolutely nothing to say.

Caputo pointed at a crow who had settled a few rows away. "They say a flock of crows is called a murder. What do they call just one crow? Attempted murder! Ha ha! Get it?"

I smiled weakly. "Yeah, I think I saw that on a meme."

"A meme? What the hell's a meme?"

"It's... Sorry, never mind." Explain the internet to a dead gangster? *I don't think so.* "Look, Mr. Caputo. What's the deal here? I've never knowingly seen a... a ghost in my life, and now they—you—are everywhere."

"Brad... Can I call you Brad? Okay, you can call me Stan, deal?" The thin man patted his pockets and came up empty. "Damn, what I wouldn't give for a smoke. Okay, Brad, here's the dope, or as much as I got. I never been buried anywhere else, so I can't say for sure, but best I can tell, Shady Terraces is... unusual. Don't ask me why, okay? I don't know. Could be the ground is sacred, could be Pottsville ain't paid their afterlife taxes and they won't take nobody else from here, or could be"—he waggled his fingers and made his voice sound spooky—"the veil between the living and the dead is thin here." He snorted and dropped his hands. "There's this dame buried a few rows over, name of Clara, died of a drug overdose in nineteen seventy-two. She's alla time going on about spirits and karma and reincarnation and shit. You'll meet her if you stick around. She's the one who yaks about the veil between the living and the dead alla time. Point being, I'm not buying any of that nonsense. We're here because we're here. Why worry about the whys?"

"Huh. I always heard ghosts would hang around because they had unfinished business." I didn't mention I'd heard that last night on *Supernatural.* "That if they resolve whatever it is, they... cross over."

"Unfinished business? Nah, not me. Although, come to think of it, I wouldn't mind kicking that fed in the nuts. The one who shot me. Rat bastard."

"Oh. Yeah, I can see that. But how can you talk? I mean, you don't have lungs, right?"

"Look, kid. Brad. I don't have much time out here, okay? It takes a real effort of will to appear out here—to take shape, if you get my meaning. Especially in daylight. So I don't got a lotta time is what I'm saying. Here's a couple of tips: one, there are ways to keep us outta your life. I'll explain that in a minute; two, very, very few people can see us. Arlo could, but nobody since then... until you."

"Lucky me."

"Three, none of us can hurt you, capisce? With a real strong push, maybe I can knock over a can of beer, spill it in your lap, or bang a door shut if I really work at it. You're not in any danger—ah, except for... Well, there's one thing. It's bad, and it's coming. You need to... Oh, hell. Sorry, Brad, I can't hold it. Here I go—"

And with that, Stan popped out of existence.

"No, wait!" I jumped up and turned a full circle. No other beings, real or spectral, were around. "Damn it."

So many things I wanted to know. What did he mean by "It's bad, and it's coming"? That sounded like an important piece of information to just leave hanging. Then how about explaining how I could keep ghosts out of my life? That'd be nice. And while we're at it, what was it like, being dead? Was there a bright light? What did ghosts do when not scaring the piss out of me? Hang out in a spectral Starbucks?

And let's not forget: you still don't know what happened to Arlo. And who was the nude woman, and why did she look so sad?

The wind clattered through the trees. I shivered from the cold.

Just the cold and nothing more.

The murder of crows cawed and flushed into the sky, taking flight and wheeling away.

I DEBATED PACKING THE car and heading for the next job, wherever and whatever that might be. Maybe the Amish needed a farmhand. Shoveling manure had to be better than sharing a cemetery with visitors from the afterlife, right? I could easily throw everything I had in the car and be on my way in under an hour. Tabitha might miss her new litter box, but she would adjust, and George didn't seem to mind where he was as long as he had a place to hide when dastardly squirrels threatened to beat him up and steal his lunch money.

So just go already.

Only... I sensed within myself an odd reluctance to give up. I was not a particularly brave person. The idea of the incorporeal dead popping into my life without warning gave me the shakes, and my body had buzzed with terror more than once in the last twenty-four hours. Couple that with my history of underperformance in difficult situations and my reflexive, knee-jerk abandonment of challenges, and the obvious solution was to take off like a bottle rocket.

Good plan. Let's get to it. Failure is an option.

But... I'm tired of failure.

Could it be that simple? Or had discovering the supernatural world piqued a dormant curiosity that needed satisfying? I mean, damn... How many people got the chance to converse with the dead? For real. And maybe one dead person in particular had caught my attention, a heartbreakingly beautiful, infinitely sad ghost of the clothing-optional type. For more than the obvious hormonal reasons, she—pardon the pun—had haunted my waking dreams as if beseeching me to find her and ease her pain.

Ouch. That sounded lame, even to the king of lameness.

I glanced at the sun, now peeking above the trees. *And speaking of pain...* It was after seven o'clock. Tabitha would be scratching around her bowl for tuna about now. If she didn't find any, she might start eating George.

"Okay, Brad," I said aloud. "Suck it up. When the going gets tough, the useless and cowardly go feed the kitty."

THE WEATHER WAS NOT conducive to lawn work, so after breakfast and a shower, I tackled the office instead. With no training as an accountant or bookkeeper, I didn't know the right or wrong way to organize a business office. I could, however, recognize a mess when I saw it, and this place qualified as a first-class disaster.

Since I now had the banking passwords, I went online and set up payments for all the overdue bills, keeping a manual tally of the remaining funds in the account. The bottom line was a dismal two-hundred dollars and eighteen cents. The next deposit from the trust wasn't due for another two weeks, so there was no chance I was getting paid until then. Two hundred bucks wouldn't get me very far.

I then searched for and downloaded some freeware to manage finances, which included a check-writing and tracking function along with budgeting and other features I found utterly incomprehensible. It promised to take a while to download, given the wheezy old computer's limitations—oh my God, it was like watching old movies where 56k-baud modems connected to the internet—so I passed the time by starting on the two-drawer file cabinet. By starting, I mean I dumped everything on the floor. Ages worth of old statements, invoices, and receipts rained out, along with a menu for a Chinese restaurant, numerous door hanger circulars, a map of Virginia, and a twenty-year-old German pornographic magazine. The junk went in the trash, and I pushed the rest into a pile against the wall for later sorting although the Chinese menu triggered a yearning for sweet-and-sour chicken, so I set that aside.

At the bottom of the filing cabinet, I found an unopened box of hanging file folders. Speaking to the ghost of Arlo, who for all I knew was hanging around somewhere close by, I said, "Even I know throwing the papers on top of the folders is not the same as filing."

The finance program had finished downloading, so I went back to the computer. After watching the tutorials, running through the help function, and taking another trip to YouTube, I learned how to set up the cemetery's financials. For the next few hours, I dutifully entered information and amounts and payments until I had a reasonable facsimile of an up-to-date check register. When I sat up and stretched, my spine crackled like cellophane.

"Oh wow," I said. "What time is it?"

Almost four. I had somehow worked through lunch and deep into the afternoon, and while losing myself in the clerical work of organizing the cemetery finances, I had almost been able to forget about ghosts. Except, of course, for Lady Godiva from the briar patch. Her face—and yes, her body—had imposed itself on my thoughts more than once. Repeatedly playing back the scene from the previous day had convinced me of something else, something I barely wanted to admit. The look in her eyes meant she needed...

"Rescuing," I said to George as he padded into the office. The dog woofed to remind me it had been hours since he had gone outside. "But why is she naked?"

All the other ghosts had worn... Well, I guess call it "funeral attire." I could make an educated guess Delmont, Caputo, and the two old women, Mrs. Perry and Mrs. Fairweather, were appearing in the clothes in which they'd been buried. So if I boarded that logic train, it would inevitably lead me to conclude the mystery woman had been buried in nothing at all.

"Who does that, George? Who buries people in the nude? What if she was…"

A nasty thought broke out of the dungeon deep in my hindbrain where it had been rattling around. I didn't want to say it aloud, not even to George, but the question sank its hooks into my conscious mind and refused to go away.

What if she had been murdered?

Chapter 10

The bell over the outer office door jingled, and a female voice called out, "Hellooo! Mail's here."

Saiera Khosani appeared in the office doorway before I could get up from behind the desk. Today, she wore slacks instead of shorts but had on the same puffy vest with the USPS logo. A brown leather mailbag weighed down her shoulder, giving her a lopsided look. She dropped the bag on the floor and knelt to greet George, who had already assumed the position and was on his back, wriggling in pleasure.

"Hello, George," she cooed. "Who's a handsome boy? Huh?"

I had another chance to study Saiera as she scratched the dog's belly. She was average height and weight, with a modest figure, from what I could tell—a lot was hidden by the padded jacket. She had a wide mouth, a prominent nose, and conspicuous cheekbones, which confirmed my earlier impression of a strong face more than a pretty one though her dark eyes under heavy brows gave her an exotic look. She had left her hair unbraided today, and it did a lot to soften her features.

"You only read it for the articles?" Saiera asked.

"Huh?" I followed her gaze to the trash can, on top of which lay the porn magazine. My face warmed like I'd stuck it in an oven. "Oh! No, that's not..."

Saiera plucked the magazine from the trash and flipped through a few pages. She paused and said with a lifted eyebrow, "I'm impressed. Very limber."

"I was cleaning out—"

"Uh-huh." The magazine crackled as she flicked through more pages. Her eyebrows climbed her forehead. "Oh my. I've never done *that* before."

"It was in the filing cabinet." *Done what?* I wanted to look but didn't dare.

Saiera cocked her head as she studied a particular image. She grimaced. "That doesn't look fun at all."

If my face heated any further, it would burst into flame.

Saiera tossed the magazine back where she'd found it and scanned the room with a bemused expression. "It looks like an Office Depot exploded in here."

"Yeah, it's a mess." Keeping my eyes firmly away from the trash can, I went on to explain Arlo's filing process, the state of the checkbook, the overdue bills, how George liked to have his ears scratched, and how the ice made it seem a better idea to work inside, and I was on the verge of telling her about Delmont and the TV incident when I realized I was babbling and shut up.

"Wow," she said when I wound down. "I think my Aunt Leona has finally met her match."

"Huh?"

"Do you have any tea in this place?"

"Tea?"

"Yes, tea." Saiera mimed sipping from a cup. "To drink. It's cold outside, and I was hoping to bum a cup of tea from you before heading back out."

"Oh, sure. It's a bit stale. I went to the store last night, but I didn't have enough cash to stock up on everything. I just got enough to get by for a couple of days, you know. Dog food. Tuna. Can never run out of tuna. And... anyway, come on back to the kitchen. For tea." *Jesus, Brad, shut up.* Apparently, I could speak with ghosts just fine—living women, however, triggered a word tsunami.

Saiera followed me to the kitchen and sat at the table. George flopped at her feet and gazed at her with adoring eyes. He loved anyone who would scratch his tummy, but he seemed especially enamored of the hawkeyed letter carrier.

I lit the burner on the stove without crisping my eyebrows and set the kettle on to boil. I winced at the breakfast dishes in the sink but decided it was best to ignore them rather than calling attention to the mess by cleaning it up. I busied myself with finding the tea and rinsing out a pair of cups—they'd been in the cabinet for months and were covered in dust.

"I have milk," I said. "But no sugar."

"Black is fine. And who is this?"

Tabitha had appeared in the doorway, crying about something wrong in her cat-centered universe.

"Watch out for that one. She doesn't like strang—" My mouth fell open because the tabby kitten trotted over and climbed Saiera's leg as if they were old pals. She butted her head into the woman's hand and bowed up for a petting. "Strangers."

"Don't worry, I'm good with cats. She's just a little doll, isn't she? Did you adopt her, or was it the other way around?"

"I rescued her from a dumpster a couple of weeks ago, out back of the place I worked for a bit. She was crying loud enough to wake the dead." I winced at the unintended irony. "Somebody had thrown out a sack of kittens, and Tabitha was the only one still alive."

"Oh my God. How cruel!" She lifted Tabitha so they were nose to nose. "You're a little fighter, aren't ya?"

"The soul of a warrior in a Beanie Baby body."

We talked about cats and dogs while the kettle boiled, and I found my reflexive babbling easing under the influence of the same spell affecting George and Tabitha. Saiera seemed to be able to charm animals of all kinds, including nerd-beasts, cowardly dogs, and murderous tabbies.

I poured hot water in a cup and dropped in a tea bag for my guest then made myself an instant coffee. The dried coffee was as old as the Aztecs, tasted like burned socks, and had to be chipped out of the jar, but bad coffee was better than no coffee.

Saiera blew across her mug. "So. Everything's okay here?"

My ears pricked at her tone, which sounded a tiny bit too casual. "Okay? Uh, yeah. Sure. What do you mean?"

"Well..." She sipped and winced at the taste. "I've been on this route for a couple of years now. Ever since Arlo..."

"Died. Yeah, I read about that."

"Yes, since Arlo died, I've seen a half dozen people try out for the caretaker job. No one has lasted more than one night. Some were gone so fast all I saw was a dust cloud, as if something had... I don't know. Chased them off?"

"Hmm." *I'll bet that something was named Mrs. Perry.*

"And you're... different," Saiera said. "The others seemed, ah, I don't want to say *lazy*, but I got the impression they took this job either to hide out or to goof off. You act like it's something else... I mean, the way you're tackling the office work... Plus, you're younger than all the other people who have been through here."

I thought I detected a faint blush creeping up Saiera's neck though she seemed so self-possessed it was hard to imagine her embarrassed at anything.

"I want to be a writer," I blurted, surprising myself. I almost never told anyone about my dream, and now I'd mentioned it twice in the space of two days. "And this place seemed like the perfect day job while I practice writing." I waved a hand around. "Food. A place to stay. Easy work... Ha! I'm kidding. Forget that last part. I didn't realize what a mess the place was when I signed on, but, ah..." I shrugged.

"Caring for the final resting place of people's relatives is honorable work. I am sure the souls of the departed appreciate your doing a good job." Saiera smiled. "I hope you manage to stick around."

"I'll be here for a while yet." *And I have nowhere else to go.* I didn't say it aloud, but my thought seemed to hang in the air between us. I cleared my throat and added, "Will you... Would you like to come by again? Uh, for tea, I mean."

"Sure." Saiera raised her mug then grimaced and set it back on the table without drinking. "But next time, let me bring the tea."

STAN CAPUTO POPPED into existence as I escorted Saiera to the front door. He appeared in the lobby, seated on the sofa, one dapper knee crossed over the other. I flinched when he materialized, but Saiera missed it as she was headed for the door and had her back to me.

"Saiera Khosani," Caputo crooned. "Oh man, I love this broad."

I goggled at the ghost. "Stan!"

Saiera stood by the door with a quizzical expression. She followed my gaze to the sofa, and her frown deepened. "Did you say something, Brad?"

"She can't see or hear me," Stan said. "More's the pity 'cause I'd sure like to see her. Outta dat uniform, if you know what I mean."

"I... uh, no. Sorry. I... stubbed my toe is all."

Stan leered and waggled his eyebrows. "You should *stub* her. I could sell tickets to that."

"Thank you for the tea," Saiera said.

"You're wel—"

"Ask her to stay for a sandwich," Stan chimed in. "A meatball surprise."

"Stop it," I hissed.

Saiera blinked. "Excuse me?"

"Not you," I said, glaring at the ghost on the sofa. "I was... I was thinking of the office work. That's enough for one day."

"O-okay." Her bottom lip pursed in a frown.

"Sorry, bad habit. Talking to myself. I've been hanging out with George and Tabitha too long."

"Sure," Saiera said though she didn't sound sure at all. "Okay. Be seeing you."

I whirled on Stan as soon as Saiera had closed the door. "Nice job, dead mobster guy. Another woman I'll never see again."

The ghost waved a dismissive hand. "Don't worry about it, kid. She's into you. She'll be back."

"There's no way... Wait. What? She's into me?"

"Sure, sure. I never seen that broad with her hair down, and look-it, she shows up for cuppa tea." Stan put on a prissy expression, stuck a pinkie out, and sipped from an imaginary cup. "Yeah, tea my ass."

"Well... okay then. But, man, hit the brakes on the sexual innuendo, okay? You're not helping the cause."

"Yeah, you're right." Stan shrugged, palms up. "I get carried away at times. What can I say? Brother, I ain't had my ashes hauled since 1936. It's been a while."

"And what if..." I said, but Stan popped out, and I was talking to dead air. I had started to ask, "What if things had progressed to the intimate stage? Would I have an audience of the undead cheering me on? Or offering performance tips?"

"Ew." I shuddered. "Sex critiques, I don't need. Okay, so no fooling around at the Shady Terraces, Brad. Not that it was likely anyway, but now? Never, never, never going to happen."

I LET GEORGE OUT THE back door then followed him around, playing poop police until he ran dry. We wandered randomly for a time though I was not surprised when I found myself drawn to the wooded grove where I had seen the woman. The sun was dropping toward the horizon, and golden light slanted through the trees.

"Hello," I called out then glanced around to make sure no one was watching me make an ass out of myself.

A light breeze rattled the branches. No one appeared, living or dead. A bright-red cardinal burst from the ground cover near our feet, spooking George. The husky ran a safe distance away and barked at it.

I circled to the right, following the tree line to where the brick wall had collapsed. George trotted over the debris and into the field beyond, nose down and tail wagging. I picked my way across the rubble and followed him. My mind was occupied with thoughts about ghost behavior. Specifically, would a hole in the wall allow them to wander out? If they could get out, why hadn't they? Maybe the spirits were tied to the geography of the grounds, or they were limited to a certain distance from their remains. Something kept them close to Shady Terraces. Otherwise, boredom alone would have prompted them to wander off into the wider world.

Damn. I need to find a ghost expert. I kicked a dirt clod and sent it spinning away then laughed at myself. *Need a ghost expert? Who you gonna call?*

A gunshot cracked out, loud and close.

The stunning sound jerked me out of my head. I had wandered deep into the field, close to a two-story farmhouse at the far edge of the cleared land. A man in stained overalls and a plaid shirt marched toward me, a pump shotgun held across his body. He racked the slide, and a red shell popped out and spun away. George bolted past me, headed for home at the speed of a flying dog.

"Hey, you!" the man yelled. "Get off my land!"

I stopped in my tracks, and my hands balled into fists. "Did you just shoot at my dog?"

"That was a warning shot, boy. Next time I aim to hit." The man stalked up and treated me to a closer view of his bitter expression. He had the flinty face of a hellfire-and-brimstone preacher, chiseled from a core of self-righteousness and weathered by hostile winds. Though not a tall man, his shadow of personal menace loomed over me, threatening imminent violence. I read his eyes, and what they said was "I want to kill you."

I backed up a step. Fear threatened to crowd out my temper as the realization sank in that this man could very easily make good on the promise in his eyes.

"Look, I'm sorry. I'm the new caretaker over at—"

"I don't give a rat's dried fart who you are. Get the hell off my land."

"Going, going. Sorry for the intrusion." I backed up some more, palms out, until I willed myself to turn my back and walk away. My neck and shoulders tightened into a knot of tension as I quick-marched away from the farmer, and all the while, a thought kept playing through my mind: *Is this how Arlo died?*

THE DAY HAD GROWN SHORT and the shadows long by the time I made it back to the office apartment. George was huddled by the back door, his ears down, looking entirely miserable. He perked up when I let him inside. I cracked a can of stinky dog food and ladled a double helping into his bowl. While he ate, I toweled him dry and inspected his fur for punctures or scratches from running through the brush. I found none of either.

"Phew," I said. "Wet dog. You need a bath."

I threw the towel in the laundry basket then washed my hands. I paced from room to room, picking things up and putting them down. I went to the office and looked at my to-do list then walked back to the kitchen and forgot what the list said to do. I switched on the lights in the living room then went back to the office and stared at the pile of documents on the floor. I thought about making dinner. I thought about making a cup of coffee. I thought about curling up under the blanket on my bed and going to sleep.

In the living room, Tabitha sat atop a bookshelf like a fuzzy bookend. She batted at me as I walked by, trying to get me to play. I let her attack the Hand Monster for a few minutes, until her pinprick claws turned savage and the Hand Monster was forced to retire from the field of battle.

"You're a vicious beast, Tabby." I sucked a bead of blood from my knuckle. "Maybe I should sic you on the crazy old bastard with the shotgun, huh? I'll bet you wouldn't back down, would you?"

The quiet in the apartment, which had felt so cozy last night, had turned oppressive. I needed something more than my own brooding thoughts to distract me from the encounter with the bitter farmer and his pump-action boom stick. I needed some other humans even if they were only waiters at a Chinese restaurant or clerks at a convenience store. It was time to see what the town of Pottsville East had to offer in the way of nightlife.

I grabbed my coat and my keys and headed for the Mazda.

"See you later, Tabitha. Watch out for the ghosts while I'm gone." I turned on the TV in case Delmont popped up, then I departed the dead for the land of the living.

Chapter 11

My headlights washed the bricks in yellow light as I pulled into the Shady Terraces lot after nine p.m. When I switched off the engine and climbed out of the car, I craned my head back and gaped at the night sky, brilliant with stars. The air was crisp and cold. A passing jet droned, a thin rumble from far away.

I belched sweet-and-sour chicken into the night. My contribution to the atmosphere.

The gate to the cemetery hung open.

"Ah hell. Did I forget to lock that?"

I trudged over to close it with my shoulders slumped. In the grand scheme of things, leaving the gate unlocked rated as a barely noticeable blip on the failure scale. For me, though, it was another example of the type of careless mistake I made all too often. Rarely a day passed that some boneheaded thing I did—or failed to do—led to calamities suitable for a Three Stooges episode, like the time I locked my keys in the car and missed showing up as best man at my friend's wedding—with the couple's rings in my pocket. Or the time I'd set my alarm to six p.m. instead of six a.m. and slept through not one but two final exams. And of course, my all-time biggest screwup, leaving the bread in the toaster oven, which set the fire that destroyed... well, everything.

I reached for the gate to pull it closed and stopped short, hand paused in midair. Visible past two dozen or more rows of headstones, from somewhere deep in the graveyard, a greenish light glowed—not the ruddy orange of a fire, thank God, but the sickly pale green of a sinus infection. A late-night visitor with a green lantern? Grave robbers operating under a tarp?

What fresh graveyard hell is this?

I groaned and muttered a curse. The Chinese food in my stomach roiled and sent a shot of acid up my throat. Tempting as it was to simply call the cops and let them handle it, I was the one who had left the gate open. It was my responsibility to go see who was on the grounds this late and what they were up to. Maybe they were just late-night mourners, out to pay their respects to long-dead Uncle Jacob and Aunt Mary.

On a frosty cold night in October.

In a cemetery haunted by more ghosts than a Scooby-Doo marathon.

Yeah, sure.

The grass crunched underfoot, having refrozen after the sun went down. My breath huffed like a steam engine pulling up a steep grade, and I tasted egg roll on the back of my tongue. If the graveyard had been spooky in the middle of the day, with the sun out and crows cawing, it had turned downright unnerving under a crescent moon and a glittering canopy of stars. As unnerving as a tax audit or no Wi-Fi signal. I navigated rows of silent, hulking grave markers and ducked under the brooding branches of winter-bare trees. Thorny rosebushes caught at my jacket. I imagined hearing Mrs. Perry squawk, *"I told you to trim them!"*

The glow brightened as I approached, illuminating a side path like an invitation to a gala grand opening of an all-you-can-eat buffet at Hannibal Lector's café.

There was no sound. The jet had long passed, leaving behind an emptiness that pressed in as though I was underwater. My ears ached for natural sounds, something beyond the rasp of my breathing and the crunch of wet gravel under my feet. The sense I was the only living thing left on the planet crawled up my insides and settled in for a long winter's nap.

The path doglegged through a pair of turns and ended at the source of the glowing green light.

Several small buildings dotted the grounds, crypts—or mausoleums, I guessed they were called. Most resembled small Greek temples with twin columns flanking a central door. Some had ornate carvings above the lintel, typically including a name engraved in a deep, bold font. Many of the doors appeared to be made of bronze or a similar alloy and had glass panes for easy viewing of the interior, should one be so inclined

The crypt at the end of the path was nothing like those.

This crypt had only one side, a brick-and-mortar wall set into the slope of a hill, the top of which was twelve feet high. There was no way to judge the size of the interior, as the earth sloped away on either side, and the rear was lost in darkness. A pair of twin doors yawned open in the center of the brick wall, and from the guts of the crypt pulsed the sickly light that bathed the path and the surrounding stones in fluorescent green.

A deep and profound terror squeezed my heart and iced me as solid as the bottom of a freezer.

I had never pictured hell having a green tinge, but if this wasn't the gates to the afterlife and the glowing fire within that of everlasting damnation, then the devil's decorator should be fired. I wanted to run away. I wanted to close my eyes. I wanted to pee myself.

I could do nothing but stand there, a mouse before a snake.

A figure coalesced. Materialized? It grew distinct as it stepped out of the glow and through the crypt doors. I squinted and realized the figure was that of a short woman, covered in a simple cotton dress. At first, I thought the backlight had cast her features in darkness, then I realized she was a Black woman with coal-dark skin. What I at first took to be a Medusa's head resolved into a mass of hair that appeared to have been cut with a chain saw. She had bulbous eyes, a flat nose, and flaring lips. Short, middle-aged, and edging toward chunky, the woman was no one's idea of a demon escaped from hell but rather resembled a typecast servant from a 1930's black-and-white movie of life on a Southern plantation.

Except this one was a little crazy around the edges and perhaps prone to murder the plantation owners with a kitchen knife and feed their bodies to the hogs.

"G'way, boy," she croaked in a voice soaked in venom. Her golf-ball eyes flared wide, and she made a shooing gesture with a clawed hand. "Leave dis place, and doan come back. Or else..."

My feet were stuck to the ground, and my throat was clamped shut. I could neither move nor speak. For all that outward immobility, my heart was slamming a heavy metal beat, and I trembled with shuddering vibrations from head to toe. This was no Stan Caputo or Mrs. Perry. This was no Delmont. This woman, risen from the crypt, had not popped in for a few episodes of *Charmed* or to complain about the state of the roses.

This one was the real deal—a full-on bloodfest-massacre, monster-coming-out-from-under-the-bed, midnight-knock-from-the-Grim-Reaper kind of deal.

She was six feet away—

Then she was in my face, nose to nose, having zipped forward in the space between heartbeats.

"If you doan leave now," the woman crooned in a sing-song voice, "I will peel you like a grape and wear your skin as a coat. Such fine, fine skin..." Her ragged nails, grubby and torn, traced down my cheek. It felt like slugs crawling over my skin, trailing wet, cold slime. Her hypnotic voice dropped to a whisper. Her voice smelled of earthworms and things found under rotten wood. "Oh, Pippah could cut on you for hours, my sweet. You would bleed and bleed until you beg fo' yo' mama, boy. I would cut yo' man-thing off and fry it up with some fatback and collards. Mm-hmm, I sho' would..."

The smell of the grave flowed around her like an aura, a choking odor of putrid flesh left unburied and heating under a summer sun. I looked into the crone's eyes and saw nothing but evil steeped in blood, not an absence of soul but a soul stained so black with foul deeds that no redemption in this life or the next could scrub a spot clean.

The woman leaned close, and I knew she was going to claw my face off. Instead, she shrieked, "Run, boy! Go!"

I ran.

Faster than a deer. Faster than George after a dropped pizza. A Bradley Langston lightning bolt of electrified terror, I tore through rosebushes. I hurdled headstones. I dove under tree limbs. I ran and ran and ran and didn't stop running until I crashed into the back door of the apartment, winning Olympic Gold in the Terror Two Hundred. My key chattered into the lock, and I threw open the door then banged it closed behind me. I put my back against it and sobbed for breath.

A harsh cackle of laughter echoed through the trees and died when I closed the door.

George pranced into the kitchen, barking his head off. He danced around my trembling legs, excited and worried and howling his husky song of distress. As I reached to touch him, my hand shook so hard I couldn't make contact. I sat down and put my arms around him instead. My face was wet—sweat, snot, or tears, I wasn't sure. Maybe all three.

I don't know how long I sat there—more than a minute but less than an hour.

When I looked back through the window in the door, the glow was gone.

OCTOBER 18TH, DAY 3

Morning found my car packed and ready to go.

I didn't recall making the decision to leave, but by the time my brain caught up with my body, I had stripped the sheets off the bed and thrown them in the washer, taken out the trash, and dumped all the perishables out of the refrigerator. Preparations to depart the premises forthwith, post haste, and right-the-hell-now were almost complete.

I had made the bed with fresh sheets and was zapping the kitchen counters with a wad of paper towels soaked in Lysol when the sun peeked over the trees and hit the window with a beam of orange flame. The light snapped me out of the funk into which I'd fallen after the Wicked Witch of the Crypt had chased me out of the graveyard. I paused and blinked.

Robert Heinlein once wrote, "When the ship lifts, all bills are paid. No regrets." My Mazda was not a rocket ship, and my regrets numbered in the double digits, and the only paid bills were those I had made current on behalf of the Pottsville East Shady Terraces. That small task constituted my singular accomplishment as caretaker. *Yay, me.*

Mrs. Perry was going to have to wait a bit longer to get the roses trimmed—likewise, Mrs. Fairweather's weeds. Delmont would be watching TV alone for a while. I was trading two days of half-assed work and a couple of nights of toe-curling terror for ninety dollars in petty cash, some groceries, and a bag of kitty litter. Of the original amount, I had eight dollars and seventy-six cents left in my pocket.

"Seems fair," I told George.

George spoke only when he was upset or scared. Out of character for his normally quiet nature, he had been howling about one thing or another ever since I had started packing. At the moment, the dog flapped his tail on the floor and bayed his wolfish howl. Tabitha chased his wagging tail, rolling on the floor and batting at it, oblivious to anything that didn't involve her.

The front-door buzzer rang, sending George in a sprint for the bedroom. Tabitha chased after him.

I wiped my hands and walked to the lobby, half expecting, half hoping, half dreading to see Saiera standing on the porch with a bag of mail and a wide-lipped smile. Instead, what I found was a Black man in his midthirties, wearing a suit and tie that I suspected cost more than my Mazda, and with a leather satchel dangling from a shoulder strap.

"Uh... can I help you?" I asked.

"Good morning. Mr. Langston, I presume? I'm Maurice Chesterfield, of Creddick, Smith."

"I, uh, wow..." I took his extended hand, expecting mine to be crushed.

Though we were the same height, approaching six feet tall, my upper body was shaped like the letter *I*, whereas Chesterfield's was built like a *V*. From the top of his gleaming bald head to the polished Oxford wingtips on his feet, Maurice Chesterfield exuded power, elegance, and pure alpha male dominance.

When he smiled, a gold tooth flashed from a grill of otherwise perfect white teeth. "May I... come in?"

"Huh? Oh yeah. Sure. Sorry—a little out of it this morning." I stepped aside. The lobby seemed to shrink as Chesterfield entered. "Would you like some, uh, coffee?"

"That would be very welcome, thank you."

I led the attorney through the hall back to the kitchen. He paused at the open office door, and I turned to see what had caught his attention then remembered. *Ah hell. I forgot about the filing cabinet mess.*

"I was going to go through that," I said. "Um, later today. Probably."

"I see."

His comment unlocked my tongue, and I spilled my guts about the petty cash, the checkbook, the financial software, and the bills I had paid, and I might have gotten all the way to the porn magazine in the trash can had Chesterfield not stopped me with a raised palm.

"That's fine, Mr. Langston. I am very satisfied you have things well in hand."

When I had chipped some dried instant coffee into a pair of mugs and set the kettle on the burner, I joined Chesterfield at the table. The polished and razor-crisp Maurice Chesterfield looked as out of place in the dingy little kitchen as a prince at a garage sale, though he seemed relaxed and quite happy to be there. Clearly, he was someone comfortable with who he was and what he could do.

"The cemetery business is unique, Mr. Langston," he began.

"You can say that again," I muttered.

His gold-toothed smile flashed on and off. "As a business model, I mean. Private cemeteries are required to set aside a part of the proceeds from each sale of a plot to fund an endowment. The endowment is managed so that the cemetery might be maintained, for all intents and purposes, in perpetuity. The land is owned by the business and yet is only profitable as long as there are plots to sell. Once a cemetery has reached capacity, so to speak, the only continuing source of income is the interest on the endowed fund or, in some cases, long-term care annuities sold by the cemetery business. Shady Terraces has no long-term care annuities and is currently funded solely through the sale of plots. A survey conducted by my firm six years ago indicated there was space for about another two or three hundred burials."

"Huh?" I had gotten lost in the sound of the attorney's voice. He had such a distinguished, cultured voice, it was like listening to butter melt. "Oh, wow, that's a lot. I had no idea there was that much room."

"The trend today much favors cremation over internment, so we expect plots to be available for some time to come."

The kettle whistled, and I busied myself pouring hot water over lumpy, dried blocks and setting out the sugar bowl. "There's no milk. Sorry. It's best if you stir it up a bunch too."

Chesterfield eyeballed the black-and-tan mess in his cup. "I believe I'll let it cool a bit."

"The hotter it is, the less you taste it. You were saying something about a lot of room for... ah, future clients."

"Yes, indeed. This is not what makes Shady Terraces unique, however..."

When he paused, I leaned forward, and my body tensed. I thought for sure he was going to mention the infestation of ghosts haunting the place. I found myself holding my breath.

"Shady Terraces," Chesterfield said, "was endowed by the original landowner, Mr. Ezra Satterwaite. Not only did Mr. Satterwaite set aside the land from his personal holdings, he was a state senator and was responsible for the passage of Pennsylvania laws that make it impossible for any township to annex any undeveloped part of the property. Thus, according to state law, Shady Terraces must remain a cemetery for essentially the rest of time."

"So you mean no digging up bodies to make way for a shopping mall."

"Exactly."

The Ghostly Gang will be happy.

I must have looked underwhelmed because Chesterfield cleared his throat and continued. "I say this to you to lay the background for a larger picture. The firm has been somewhat... conservative in its approach to managing the funds for the endowment. We have accumulated a significant sum, and we see a long future of profitable growth for the cemetery... *if*—he held up a finger to pause me though I had said nothing—"if, Mr. Langston, the property is cared for properly. In this regard, I feel we have neglected our duty."

I double blinked. "I'm not sure I'm following you."

"We need someone committed to the job, Mr. Langston, and we have been less than diligent in making it happen. Arlo Weaver performed well enough, but since his passing, the firm has... let things slide." Chesterfield shifted in his seat and examined his coffee. He had not touched it so far. Some of his ultra-stiff manner slid away. He chuckled. "Truth? My boss said if I don't get somebody in place, forthwith, it's my ass out the door."

"Oh. Okay. Well, see, the thing is—"

"I'm prepared to offer you a job. With a salary." Chesterfield named a salary figure double what I'd expected to collect ad hoc from the leftover monthly funds. "A W-2 job with health benefits and a 401k match of three percent."

I goggled, and my jaw dropped. "I... I, uh..."

Chesterfield sagged a little, and his super-buttoned-up persona slipped another notch. "Man, I'm really hurting here. I really screwed up on this one. Dropped the ball and dropped it big time. I thought... well, it's a cemetery, you know? What the hell could go wrong?"

"Oh, you wouldn't believe—"

"You're my best hope to salvage this situation, Mr. Langston."

"Call me Brad." I kept my eyes on the floor and sipped my coffee, which tasted as bad as I felt, bitter and nasty. How was I supposed to tell the guy a ghost had scared the hell out of me last night, and I wanted to be about twelve zip codes in any direction away from here? I couldn't even think up a convincing lie. *Uh, my aunt's dying, and she needs me. I'm allergic to granite. George has his heart set on the Iditarod this year.*

Bleh. I sucked at making stuff up on the fly and under pressure.

The thought of a real job and real money crept into my head like a mousetrap baited with a cheeseburger and a milkshake. *More than*

I've ever made in my life. With bennies! All I had to do was stay away from an evil spirit that wanted to peel me alive and wear my skin for a coat. Not to mention what she wanted to do to my—

"Brad? Mr. Langston?"

"Hmm?" I blinked and realized that Chesterfield had been speaking while my mind wandered. I played back the memory and caught up with the conversation.

"You think you could free up some money for repairs as well?" I asked. "For the wall and whatnot?"

"Yes," Chesterfield said. "It's past time we invested in some capital improvements. Have you had a chance to create a list of necessary expenses?"

"No, sorry," I mumbled. "Well... I started it..."

"My apologies. I didn't mean to rush you. Of course, take your time and do it right." Chesterfield stood and offered his hand. "Thank you for bailing me out, Brad. You may have saved my career."

I shook his extended hand out of reflex. "But I haven't—"

"I'll email you the paperwork to get you started as a full-time employee. It would be best if you can establish your own bank account so we can direct deposit. And the email will include all the information on the company health plan, dental, vision, and so on. Thanks again, Brad. Good luck."

Chesterfield headed for the front door at a brisk pace. My mouth moved, but no sound came out. Again, I was rooted to the spot, this time with indecision. *"Wait!"* I wanted to say. *"I didn't say I was taking the job! I need to think about it."*

I jumped up and scooted for the front door, but by the time I reached it, Chesterfield was in his black Mercedes Benz and driving away.

Chapter 12

Andy Gluck, staff reporter for the *Pottsville Post-Dispatch*, appeared to have swollen several sizes since his byline photo had been taken. I met him at the Route 66 Diner at ten o'clock in the morning, the same day that Chesterfield had offered me the full-time caretaker job. I was showered and shaved, but I hadn't slept a wink since I woke up on the couch yesterday morning. The sensation of Pippah's slimy fingers caressing my cheek remained imprinted on my skin as if etched there by an invisible acid. The hateful, hellish burning of her black eyes appeared on my closed eyelids, snapping me awake every time I began to drift off.

A waitress dropped a plate. The resounding clatter-crash shot through my nerve endings with the power of a stormy lightning bolt. My skin jumped with the shock.

After I got settled in the booth, Gluck lifted his chins and asked, "You're buying, right?"

The diner was on Pennsylvania Highway 68 instead of the iconic Route 66 of story and song, but otherwise, the place was true to its roots, with Formica tables, squeaky plastic upholstery, and laminated menus featuring the best of American heart-attack cuisine. The reporter filled one side of a booth next to the front window.

Jabba the Hutt is strong with this one.

"Yeah, sure," I told him, cringing inside.

On the phone, Gluck had asked the same question, so I took the precaution of stopping by the bank and cashing a check to replenish petty cash. At the time, I figured a hundred dollars would be suffi-cient, but as I looked at Gluck's girth, doubts began to creep in. A hundred bucks might get us through appetizers.

The waitress stopped at our table with a full Bunn carafe of cof-fee. She was well past her best-by date, and her hand shook when she poured. Stragglers of gray hair had escaped the confinement of her scrunchie. Coffee threatened to spill into my crotch when she lifted the pot.

"What can I get ya?" she asked in a quavering voice.

"The All-American, Judith," Gluck said, "with wheat toast, sausage links, and three over easy."

"Cereal with milk," I said when Judith looked at me. "And keep the coffee coming."

"So what's this about, amigo?" Gluck asked after Judith had tot-tered away to terrify another customer. "You're the new guy at the cemetery, you said. Took Arlo's job, right? Arlo Weaver?"

"That's right. I'm curious... How did he die?"

"Shotgun blast to the chest. Boom. Right here." Gluck thumped his prodigious body, and his man boobs jiggled. "They said he died instantly. Tore his heart to shreds. Not sure how instant that is, but hey..."

"The cops ever figure out who did it?"

"Nope. Unsolved to this day. Spooky, huh?"

You don't know the half of it.

A shotgun, huh? I had seen a shotgun lately, wielded by a refugee from *Hell's Rejects*. "Do you know who the guy is, lives behind the Terraces in the two-story farmhouse?"

"You mean Vic Tarwater? Face like a strip mine? Attitude of a bear with his balls in a vice?"

"That's the guy."

"Stay away from that shithouse rat." Gluck's chins wobbled when he shook his head. "He is a troubled man, and you spell that with a capital crazy-as-fuck."

"Yeah, true that. I wandered onto his land, and the guy braced me. With a shotgun."

"Real history of violence, that guy. But he has an alibi for the time that Weaver died. Not a great alibi—says he was visiting his brother in DuBois, and the brother backs him up. Ah!"

Judith appeared with a tray, from which she delivered to Gluck a plate of eggs, hash browns, and sausage links, a plate of wheat toast, a bowl of butter packets, and another bowl of jelly packets. In front of me, she placed a bowl with a box of Wheaties laid inside and a pint carton of milk. My breakfast looked lost and forlorn next to the feast laid before the reporter. My stomach growled when the smell of eggs and sausage wafted to my nose.

"Anybody else, uh…" I paused, trying to think how to ask about the nude woman who had appeared in the graveyard. "Any other crimes I should know about? At the cemetery?"

"What?" Gluck stuffed a forkful of breakfast goodness in his mouth then spoke around the mass. "You mean like vandalism? That kind of thing?"

"No, I was thinking of more serious-type crimes." I attempted a nonchalant chuckle. "I'm kind of on my own out there. Wondered if crime was a problem out that way. Any, uh, missing person cases, abductions, that type of thing?"

Gluck paused in the middle of a wheat-toast wipe of his plate. His eyes narrowed. "Wait a minute. What are you into, Langston? What's going on out there at the graveyard?"

I had managed to awaken the reporter's latent instinct for news. I now saw that it was a mistake to underestimate Gluck's intelligence because of his appearance. He might look like he would eat Tokyo for breakfast, but he wasn't stupid.

"Um, no, nothing's going on, I swear. I'm just curious, is all. You would be, too, living next to a bunch of dead people. You ever been in a graveyard at night, Mr. Gluck? All those dead bodies underground, hands folded across their chests, eye sockets empty, bare teeth and maggots and worms and—"

"Jesus Christ! Enough already." Yellow egg yolk dripped from Gluck's toast and plopped into his plate. His face had drained from ruddy red to pukey pink. "You're a weirdo, Langston. Class A certifiable."

"Who else would work in a cemetery?" I crunched my cereal and said nothing for minute. Then I asked, "Ever heard of a woman named Pippah? Or Pepper, maybe? Buried up at Shady Terraces?"

Gluck gave me a fishy stare then shook his head. "Nah, nothing. Rings no bells."

My progress into the two big mysteries of the cemetery—the nude-woman ghost and the freaky, scary old Black-woman ghost—was essentially nil minus nothing. I had no leads on the first and only a name croaked by a crazy spectral apparition for the latter.

"Okay, one last question," I said. "Where can I pick up a book on the care and feeding of roses?"

A SOULLESS RECTANGLE of seventies' utilitarian design, the Pottsville library hunkered in the middle of an indifferently tended lawn and would be shaded by elms and oaks in the summer, when leaves covered the trees, but now seemed more of a sullen bunker surrounded by gangly trolls whose long, blackened, and glistening fingers loomed over the approaches.

I ducked under the tree limbs and hurried up the path to the portico covering the library entrance. Condensation pearled on the black-tinted front doors—the only glass in the building—and dampened the metal handle.

I stuck my hand in my pocket to dry it and crossed the lobby. On one side, knee-high bookshelves corralled three kiddie tables and a gaggle of tiny orange chairs. A strong smell of crayons filled the air. On the other side, tall bookcases featured a selection of "New Release" fiction and nonfiction titles. Rows of bookshelves filled the rest of the library. *Duh.* The checkout and information desk anchored the middle like a circular fortress, which protected a copy machine—twenty-five cents per copy—and a pushcart full of books.

A punk rock grandma, her white hair frosted with green highlights and her face sporting a half-dozen piercings, including ears, nostril, and lower lip, goggled at my approach through a thick pair of pink plastic-framed glasses. She kept her snowman-shaped upper body concealed by a blouse made of something stretchy and printed with a riot of orchids. I couldn't see below the desk, and I didn't care to speculate on what might be covering the rest of her. Tucked in the crook of the woman's arm was a dingy-white poodle-terrier mix with mean eyes and overflowing drool whiskers. The mutt growled as I reached the counter, baring its upper lip and glaring hate daggers at me. The woman squinted through her magnifying-glass lenses.

"Who's this then? Oh, dearie me, he's a cutie, Harrison. Hush your noise, now, and be nice to the young man." She spoke with an accent that I placed as either London or nearby. To me, she said, "Hello, ducks. Wot's a handsome lad like you doing in a place like this, hey?"

"Nice dog," I said with Oscar-worthy fake sincerity. "Harrison? Is that his name?"

I extended a tentative hand, only to snatch it back when the ill-tempered mutt snapped at me. Harrison yipped as though his raggedly tail was being twisted into a pretzel, his entire body convulsing with each bark.

The woman cooed at the tyrant and produced a dog biscuit from a hidden source under the counter. She set the dog on the floor to enjoy his treat, bending over to present me with a view of a wide swath of bold fabric covering her back.

An engraved plaque sat next to the checkout station: "In Gratitude for Forty Years of Service, Senior Librarian, Thelma Entwistle."

"Hi, I'm Brad Langston," I said as the librarian's myopic gaze returned to me.

My words doomed me to hell. I had entered the lair of a gossip demon, and by speaking, I had made myself powerless to escape.

For thirty minutes, Thelma Entwistle kept me pinned at the counter, hectoring me with questions, opinions, observations, diatribes, dissertations, gossip, fake news, dubious facts, and outright slander on topics ranging from Scottish terriers to the Supreme Court of the United States, from a rumor about the Pottsville City Council's misuse of funds to which was better, Coke or Pepsi. Thelma was a Coke gal. My eyes glazed over in awe. I only needed to add a rare "Uh-huh" or "Wow" to keep the tide flowing. It was akin to miraculous.

I have met my spirit guide to the World of Babble.

In a pause for breath, as Harrison tugged at his mistress's Rayon pant leg and growled for more treats, I stuck in the sentence "I'm looking for a book on roses, how to take care of them—"

"Roses! Whyn't you say so, love!" And, boom, she was off again. A torrent of words flowed freely, which started at roses and wandered at random along the stream of consciousness, meandering past strawberries, strawberries and cream, strawberries and champagne at Wimbledon, who was better, Nadal or Federer—Nadal was Thelma's choice as Federer was Swiss, you know, and "the Swiss just don't have the passion that Spaniards do"—and reached a fork in the trail with "Spaniards make the best lovers, of course." She threw in a wink. "What about you, Brad?"

"Huh?"

"What about you? Any Spanish in your blood?"

"Um. No."

Thelma arched a suggestive eyebrow. "Pity. Well, beggars can't be choosers, they say. Follow me."

A beeping sound erupted from the vicinity of the librarian's buttocks, and she swooped back from the counter. I blinked, and my brain caught up to the fact Thelma rode an electric scooter. Up until that moment, her prodigious body, combined with the counter, had concealed the machine from view. She zoomed the thing around in a K-turn, surprising Harrison, who had to dodge to avoid being squashed in the sudden change of direction, and then motored away through a gap in the circular desk. "Follow me, Bradley! Tallyho!" The dog jumped in Thelma's lap and glared at me from around her elbow.

I tagged along behind as she NASCAR'd her scooter around the aisles and snagged volumes out of the stacks without pausing to examine titles. She loaded me up with three books on the care and feeding of roses, one book on organic insect control, a book on compost heaps—I'd never realized how much there was to know about compost—and, I discovered later, a thin volume of poetry about roses.

On the way back to the desk—"You must have a library card, bucko!"—the title of a book hooked my eyes and pulled me to a stop. Thelma cruised on, trailing sentences and the vague scent of lilacs while I stopped to cock my head and confirm my initial impression.

"*Becoming a Paranormal Investigator*," I read, muttering the words aloud. Next to that book was one called *Plague of Poltergeists*, and next to that was *Ghost Tales of Pennsylvania*. As I traced my way along the shelf, I found a dozen titles related to the paranormal, ghosts, and the afterlife, all apparently nonfiction and none by Stephen King or Robert McCammon.

Cool. Maybe one of these has some answers about the restless undead at Shady Terraces.

I plucked out four that looked promising, including the one about becoming a paranormal investigator and *Ghost Tales of Pennsylvania*. I added to my stack a book called *What to Do if You Live in a Haunted House* and a thin little volume titled *Speculations about the Afterlife*.

Thelma's magnified eyes widened even farther when I piled my selections at the checkout station. "Oy, that's a tall stack now, innit? Oh my, I do like a man who likes to read. I need you to fill out this application for a library card, please. Do you read alone, love, or is there, um, someone who..."

My neck heated at the same rate my stomach contracted. My breakfast of champions threatened revolt.

Divert, Brad, or otherwise this lady will have her knickers off before you can say "Geneva Convention."

I had a question I was dying to ask. I had held back as Thelma's chatter-starter didn't need much of a trigger, and with my books in hand, I had a good excuse to escape. Up until this point, I had been the only patron of the Pottsville Library, so I was a sitting duck. If I offered a conversational topic, she could very well keep me pinned to the mat with a flood of opinions, all flavored with East Ender innuendo. *She's the head librarian, though. Been around forty years. Loves to gossip. If anyone knows, she would...*

"Thelma, have you ever heard of anyone named Pippah? Black lady. Midforties, maybe?"

The librarian's eyes, as big as baseballs up to that point, seemed to shrink behind her glasses. The application in her extended hand quivered in midair. "Who, dearie?"

"Ah, I may have the name wrong. Pippah? Maybe Pepper?"

"And where would you have heard that name, now?"

Harrison leapt into his momma's lap and bared his teeth at me again. His wet muzzle dripped. Our precarious state of detente appeared in jeopardy.

"Oh, I…" *Now, how do I tell her Pippah appeared to me in the graveyard and taunted me with dismemberment?* "Just a story I heard. From Saiera. Khosani. The mailma—uh, postal… letter carrier."

Thelma tittered. "Now, Braddie, me love, I wouldn't believe anything a Traveler like that witch Khosani tells you. They love to tell their tales, they do. She's a witch too. Very untrustworthy bunch, witches are."

I blinked. "A Traveler?"

"A gypsy, dear. Biggest con artists in the world, they are."

"Saiera Khosani is a gypsy?"

"And a witch."

"Right."

"You know the song, don't you? By Cher? 'Tramps and Thieves'? You're too young to remember, of course, but she was married to a man named Sonny. Sonny Bono. He got himself elected to Congress after they broke up. Poor man died in a ski accident, he did. Plowed himself right into a tree. Skiing is dangerous, you know? Eighth most dangerous sport in the world, they say. I played sports in my younger days. I was quite the striker, I was, and could *score* at will…" Batted eyelashes accompanied her assertion.

"It's good to have a skill." I sighed and reached for a pen. "Hand me that application, would you?"

Maybe somewhere in my stack of books there would be an answer on how to get Pippah out of my life and return the cemetery to its normal level of weirdness.

Harrison barked at me in high yips.

It sounded a lot like laughter.

Chapter 13

It was past lunch by the time I escaped the clutches of Thelma Entwistle, having gotten nothing more out of her about Pippah. I stopped for lunch at the same Chinese place I had eaten the night before—a dingy storefront restaurant in a strip mall, squeezed between an income tax prep store and a laundromat. The Buddha-like woman who had taken my order last night waited for me to arrive at the counter before pushing herself reluctantly off her stool.

"Order?" she barked.

Since I had money in my pocket, I splurged on wonton soup and a pair of hot, greasy egg rolls to go with my Happy Trio stir-fry. I found a seat at a table while the Hispanic guy in the kitchen set to work on my order. The restaurant had been busier at dinner, more than half full of patrons. Today, by comparison, other than an older Asian couple at a table in the back, I had the place to myself.

I pecked through my pile of ghost books, dipping and skimming rather than settling in and studying any particular work. My food came. I read while I ate, using the edge of my plastic tray to help keep the book pinned open in front of me. The old couple left. Other people entered, ordered, and found tables. I barely noticed. By the time I came up for air, the last scraps of rice on my plate had dried and hardened to stone. I had scanned multiple chapters, skipped some, and read others in detail. My conclusions?

Man, these people are seriously weird.

There was, like, an entire cottage industry of paranormal experts, investigators, and aficionados with a technical jargon and a myriad of pseudoscientific tools to measure their interactions with the denizens of the afterlife. At times, their efforts struck me as comical and at other times as reasonably impressive. The tools of the trade included electronic voice phenomena recorders, electromagnetic force meters—some with light scales to indicate signal strength, called KII EMF meters—infrared cameras, digital video recorders, and something called a Mel-meter that combined several of the above-noted functions.

A paranormal investigations team—and it was always a team, because who wants to go to spooky places to hunt ghosts all alone?—would strategically deploy gear throughout a haunted structure at night—always at night, duh, because *ghosts*—then start launching questions into the air. "Who is here? What is your name? Will you contact us?"

Responses would come in the form of the EMF readers' flashing lights, barely audible voices, cold spots, and strange, disconnected sounds. No one, not a one, mentioned an apparition popping into existence for a few hours of syndicated TV or to complain about the state of the roses.

Or come to think of it, threatened to peel their skin off with a fileting knife.

"You finish?" barked a voice at my ear.

I jumped so hard the table rattled, and my book snapped closed. I twisted in my seat and found the counter woman standing at my shoulder, holding her hand out for my dishes. With her mouth carved in a perpetual frown and her hooded eyes set in a broad face, she bore an unfortunate resemblance to a bullfrog and smelled faintly of cooking oil and garlic.

"Yes, thank you. I'm done."

I was certainly finished with lunch. Was I finished at Shady Terraces? Waffling around a decision was nothing new for me. I had straddled the fence of indecision so often I should have scars on my man parts. I had postponed the decision after Chesterfield's visit as the lure of money and security tempted me like a siren's song, dragging me closer to the rocks of disaster should Pippah's threat become more real than promised. I could very easily picture that crazy old woman using her spectral strength to strap me to an altar in some dank mausoleum, fog trailing around the floor and rats wiggling around my feet, the she-demon herself poised above me with a gleaming blade of surgical steel clutched in her decayed, skeletal fingers...

Overactive imagination, I know.

The pile of paranormal books on the table taunted me.

Ghosts.

Real ghosts.

Walking, talking denizens of the afterlife. Living proof—well, okay, *not-living* proof—that the essence of a human being could remain after the body had ceased to function. Proof of a soul? Or some other electromagnetic force that soaked into the fabric of the world, like a scent saturated into a well-worn shirt that remained long after the wearer took it off?

One thing the paranormal investigators seemed to agree upon: ghosts were people, too, though disembodied. Once-living people with hopes and dreams and loves and losses, who were the same people they had always been, for good or bad, just existing in a different state of being, like water turned to fog.

Or Chinese food turned to gas. I stifled a belch, gathered my books, and left.

SOMEONE HAD PARKED a nearly new Nissan Altima near the open gates to the cemetery. I pulled up a few spots away and switched off my engine. A white-haired couple emerged from the cemetery, hand in hand, and approached the car. The gentleman held the door for the woman, nodded politely to me, and circled around to the driver's side of the Toyota. He got in, the car cranked up, and they pulled away in a crackle of parking lot grit.

I was pretty sure they weren't ghosts.

I left my books in the front seat when I climbed out of the Mazda. The sun was out, the day was bright, and there was something I needed to do with daylight overhead. In my fear and panic the night before, I had failed to take note of—or didn't see—the name on the crypt from which the evil hag had emerged. One thing all my ghost books seemed to agree upon was that it was important to understand the history of a haunted structure. The texts agreed that the "signal strength" of Pippah's ghost should be diminished in the light of day, giving me the opportunity to approach her crypt without fear of reprisal. The experts claimed knowing the past would give me an edge on the present. Assuming, that is, the paranormal investigators were correct, and if Pippah wasn't some special kind of spectral being that defied the norm...

And if, and if, and if...

"If *ifs* and *buts* were candy and nuts," I muttered, "then... something something I can't remember."

I sniffed up a fortifying lungful of air and blew it out. I hitched up my pants, adjusted my hoodie so it would sit right on my shoulders, and walked through the Shady Terraces gates. I deliberately avoided going through the apartment, which would have meant getting sidetracked by George, who by now was probably chewing the toilet paper roll to shreds out of boredom. No, it was not nice of me to ignore the dog. Yes, I felt guilty because of it. I did it anyway because if I didn't, I might lose my nerve altogether.

Finding my way back to Pippah's crypt proved much harder than it should have. Nothing was as I remembered it. Paths that I'd followed the previous night appeared different in the light of day, and without a sickly green glow, I had only hazy memory to guide me. I inspected every hill along every path I tried, expecting at any minute to stumble upon one where the side had been cut away and a brick wall erected. Instead, I found the same rows of short, medium, and tall headstones aligned in neat rows, broken up by trees, underbrush, and bucolic paths long since overgrown by rampant rosebushes and hirsute holly.

At some point, I realized I had gone the wrong way, but rather than admit defeat and turn back, I continued onward, toward the rear of the property. It was some time before I admitted to myself where my feet were taking me. I disengaged my brain and let my emotions carry me forward, past silent granite monuments to past lives, faded bouquets and tattered rings of plastic flowers marking memories of loved ones passed from this earth. My feet kicked up scattered leaves and stepped over fallen branches. A pair of squirrels circled their way up a tree, tracing an arching bough before leaping, one after the other, to the next closest limb. I drifted without an obvious goal though the conclusion was inevitable. I reached the tangle of heavy-growth forest where I'd first seen her...

And there she stood.

Stock-still, framed between a pair of trees, as though waiting on a photographer to record her image for a collection of artistic nudes, stood the woman who had invaded my subconscious and taken root there, disturbing my dreams and distracting me with the memory of her mournful expression.

"Hello," I tried.

She returned my words with a sad smile. One slender hand lifted and beckoned me closer. When I approached, she turned and melted deeper into the forest, pausing only to ensure I followed before continuing on. How could I not follow her? Though it wasn't politically correct these days, I harbored a strong chivalric impulse. Women no longer needed the protection of a man, nor wished for it, according to the popular culture of my generation, and in public, among my peers, I sneered at the outmoded notion that men and women were different and each had roles to play suited to their biology. Women had no need for a man to stand in the way of danger, to take the enemy's bullet, or give up his place on the life raft so that the child bearer might live on. *"What kind of patriarchal bullshit is this?"* we asked each other and toasted our hipness, secure in our superiority.

But deep down, I believed a man needed to stand for something—something important. And the most important thing to stand for was the notion that the strong protect the weak, that survival of the species depended on the notion of women and children first, and that in a world full of predators, someone had to protect the gentle members of the herd. Not that I had ever accomplished any protecting of the weak and innocent—on the contrary, in fact. But I was convinced someone had hurt the woman in the forest, whose slender figure I followed through, over, and around a twisting path into a tangled forest. A predator had taken her. Maybe she was a strong, confident woman, able to fully care for herself but, in a moment of weakness, had fallen victim to someone stronger, meaner, and without remorse. When she needed a protector, no one had been there. We had failed her, and by extension, that meant I had failed her. Was I building a sandcastle out of half-formed assumptions and wild imagination? Of course I was. But the more I thought about it, the more right it felt. Someone had hurt this woman, and I meant to find out who it was and bring them to justice.

Or so I told myself right before I tripped over a root and face-planted into a mushy pile of leaves. I said a few really foul words in various combinations. When I looked up, the woman stood over me, a faint smile pricking the corners of her mouth.

"Yeah, I'm quite the clown," I told her. "Probably not what you were looking for in the way of knights in shining armor."

She shrugged, and I forced myself to look away. The view of her body from ground level was way more interesting than it should have been, given the likely condition of the woman's actual body. Necrophilia's not just for vampire lovers.

I stood and brushed myself off. When I looked up, the woman had crossed a small open area and stood on the other side of a mound of debris—limbs, leaves, and tangled brush. She caught my eye, pointed at the ground at her feet, and disappeared.

"What?" I asked the empty air. "That's it? Not a 'Hi, how are you? How's your day been?' Just 'Come here and take a look at this mess of weeds.'"

I stepped over for a closer look. A black strip of rope poked through the leafy debris. "Oh," I said. "Oh hell."

With my toe, I scraped away the top layer of brush and realized the rope wasn't a rope at all but rather the strap of a black purse. I pinched the strap with two fingers and pulled it loose from its shallow grave. I was a long way from an expert on women's handbags, but even I could tell the purse was a decent bag of good leather, though due to rain and weather, it had deteriorated to a sad shape. The faux-gold overlay fittings had flaked and rusted, turning the color of moldy bread. The bag itself was no bigger than a Junior League football, and the black leather was cracked and curling. The bit I had originally mistaken for a rope was in similar condition and had broken loose at one side, leaving an arm's-length black strap that put me in mind of a hangman's rope.

I popped the clasp then froze, belatedly remembering to consider things like fingerprints and DNA and all the magical tools of forensic science by which criminals are caught and innocent ne'er-do-wells are framed for a crime they didn't commit. I was running a real danger of tampering with evidence... although, given the state of bag and its long exposure to the elements, the chance of anything remaining of forensic value hovered lower than beetle dung.

"Screw it," I said and proceeded to examine the inside of the purse.

I plucked out the wallet first and popped the tab that held it closed. I thumbed the identification from the leather slot it was buried in. It clung to the sides, and I had to force it free from the slot that held it. The face that peered out of the Kansas driver's license was the same one I had seen standing over me moments before, smiling at my clumsiness. She had the same slight smile curling her lips as though we shared a secret known only to her and me and the nameless photographer at the Kansas DMV office.

"Espinoza," I read. "Maria del Consuelo Hinajosa Espinoza. Huh. Helluva name." I decided on the spot that she liked to be called Consuelo. She'd been born in April, three years after me, so assuming she was still alive—which I didn't—then Consuelo would be about twenty-three. The license would expire in two years, and it listed an address in Overland Park, Kansas. "You're a long way from home, Consuelo," I told the empty air. "Not in Kansas anymore."

The wallet contained sixteen dollars in loose bills, a Visa and a pair of gas station credit cards, a library card for Overland Park, a Starbucks gift card, and half a dozen slips of paper, receipts from gas stations and restaurants. I stood there in the cool dark of the forest, the low winter sun slicing through the branches, and flipped through the receipts. From them I reconstructed an eastward journey... St. Louis, Indianapolis, Columbus... one stop in Pittsburgh for gas and a Big Mac, then... nothing. All of the receipts were dated around mid-August of the previous year, the most recent being fourteen months old.

I returned to the purse and picked through the contents, feeling vaguely guilty about invading Consuelo Hinajosa Espinoza's privacy but determined to learn all I could about the young lady, who was now probably fourteen months dead and now manifesting in my cemetery as a sad specter asking for succor. Besides the wallet, I found a comb, a brush, some makeup junk, a crumpled pack of tissues, eight cents in loose change, and—

"Ah-ha!"

Attached to a lanyard was a student ID card for Syracuse University, featuring a slightly older version of Consuelo Espinoza, one who bore the same enigmatic smile and knowing brown eyes. I didn't need a junior-detective decoder ring to figure out Consuelo lived in Kansas but went to school in Syracuse, in upstate New York. A mid-August trip meant a return to school for the fall semester, driving from her home in Kansas all the way to Pittsburgh, where she turned north, probably along I-79 on the way to I-uh... something I couldn't remember—the interstate that ran alongside Lake Erie from east to west. For reasons unknown, Consuelo had pulled off the interstate and ventured along the back roads of Pennsylvania until somehow arriving at Pottsville.

"From whence," I said to her picture, "you traveled no farther."

I tucked everything back in the purse as carefully as I could then coiled the strap around it to tie everything together. I tucked the package under my arm and turned to head back to the apartment, deciding at that moment that finding Pippah's mausoleum could wait until I unraveled more of Consuelo's mystery.

Some irregularity in the pile of brush at my feet snagged my attention. I leaned in for a closer look and jumped back like a startled rabbit. I had no idea what I meant to say, but my startled exclamation came out "Gitz!"

The yellowed, skeletal remains of a human hand peeked from the twisted mass of broken branches and dead leaves.

Chapter 14

Yellow police tape hung limp, strung from tree to tree like a macabre Christmas decoration. A parade of uniformed and plainclothes personnel ant-marched from the front gates to Consuelo Hinajosa Espinoza's impromptu grave site. I had no doubt that hers were the skeletal remains hidden among the bracken in the forest... though calling this patch of trees a forest was straining the definition. I wanted to call it a copse, but that sounded too much like corpse, and my writer brain conjured up nothing but bad titles for noir detective novels. The Corpse in the Copse. Cinnamon Corpse in Cemetery Copse. Consuelo's Copse.

A thicket? It could be a thicket.

I was glad I had gone to the office and taken care of George and Tabitha before calling the cops. George had been practically crossing his legs he needed to pee so badly, and Tabitha was raising the roof about her bowl being empty. The discovery of Consuelo's remains had hit me hard. I merely opened the door and waved George outside, not even the least concerned where he took care of his business.

And now I was waiting, butt perched on a tombstone—Pvt. Jonathon Verbeek, 1912 to 1941—for the Pottsville Police to finish their business. The sun settled toward the horizon, and the cops had fired up a generator and hung portable lights around the center of the copse—*thicket!*—so they could see what they were doing. Their shadows capered through the trees as they worked.

Maybe grove *would work better than* thicket.

A pair of well-fed white guys in windbreakers emerged from the grove and approached me. I had watched them duck under the outlying branches, traipsing back and forth, from the moment the first officer had started stringing crime scene tape until now. By their body language and self-important frowns, I gathered they were Pottsville PD detectives. They confirmed this by flashing credentials at me that said Detective in bold print.

"I'm Detective Swanson," said the sandy-haired guy with the keg belly. He hitched his thumb at the dark-haired guy with a barrel belly. "This is Detective Czerniak."

I nodded a greeting at them. The first cop on the scene had taken my information and had no doubt passed it along to the detectives. Czerniak flipped open a notebook and made a point of clicking his Parker Paper Mate pen. The detective had a 1970s porno mustache to go with his wire-frame glasses and multidial wristwatch.

"How did you happen to discover the body, Mr. Langston?" Swanson asked. Czerniak poised his pen in anticipation of my witty response.

I shifted on my granite seat, and grit crackled under my butt. "I was surveying the property, seeing what needed to be done. This... thicket... seemed overgrown, so I wanted a closer look. I found the purse, then I noticed... the hand."

"And you thought... what?" said Swanson. The shorter, fair-haired detective looked more like a high school football coach than a police officer. All he lacked was a whistle dangling from a cord around his neck.

"I thought, 'Oh hell, a woman's been murdered and dumped here.' What else would I think?"

"It's a cemetery," Czerniak chipped in. "It's fulla dead bodies."

"Not stashed in brush piles, they're not," I said. "We frown on that in the cemetery business." As if I knew anything about the cemetery business. For all knew, there might be a cut-rate plan that involved thickets and brush piles.

"Still," Swanson said. "Could be somebody might've"—he levitated a hand at eye level—"floated to the surface, right? Wind and rain and whatnot? Regurgitated by the earth, so to say. Why think this a victim of a crime?"

"Seriously?"

"Humor me."

"I found a woman's purse with a broken strap next to a skeleton hidden in a thicket at the back of a graveyard. Seemed kind of obvious to me."

"Why'd you think it was a woman?"

"Um, the purse..."

"You take anything?" Czerniak asked. "From the purse?"

"No. Of course not." I crossed my arms. The Syracuse student ID in my back pocket felt six sizes larger. I aborted an impulse to reach back and verify it hadn't slipped out.

Swanson the football coach frowned. Maybe he wanted me to take a lap. "Tell us how you got this job, Mr. Langston."

Halfway through my recounting of my hiring experience, Stan Caputo popped into existence. He appeared at Czerniak's shoulder and vultured over him, ostensibly reading the brown-haired cop's notes. "What a dope," Caputo said. "He's spelling Craig's list as all one word."

"And I, uh... and, and they hired me." I tried making eye contact with Caputo, who ignored me. "I haven't decided if I should stay or, um, *leave right now.*"

"Oh yeah," said Swanson, "you in a hurry to get outta here?"

Caputo snorted. "He's writing that you're acting nervous, kid. Watch out they don't try'n frame you for this."

"Maybe he's got something to hide," Czerniak said to his partner without looking up from his notebook.

"Izzat right, Langston?" Swanson said. "We run your background, you gonna come back dirty? Drifter like you takes a dead-end job like this? Gotta be something wrong wit'cha, I bet."

"Dead-end job!" Caputo fake laughed, slapping his thighs in mock hysteria. He stuck his nose right up against the cop's cheek and squinted into Swanson's earhole. "Hey, look! I can see out the other side!"

A grin threatened to pull at my cheeks, but I fought it off. "I'm, yeah, no..."

"Yes or no, which is it?"

"Lookit me, I'm a cop! Ook-ook-ook!" The dapper gangster danced in a circle, his arms hanging out loose like an organ grinder's monkey. I struggled to keep my face frozen in an expression of polite concern. *Don't look at Caputo, don't look at Caputo.*

"Nothing. I'm clean, I mean. Not even a traffic ticket."

"Ever kill anybody, Langston?" Czerniak tossed in, like it was nothing.

"I... wait. What?" *Don't think about the fire. That was an accident.* "No! Of course not."

"What was your relationship with the deceased?" asked Swanson.

"With the..."

"With the dead girl," Czerniak supplied. He consulted his notebook. "Maria dello Consuelo... Spanishola."

"Her name is not—"

"Whoa, stop, kid! Don't correct him," Caputo warned. "It's a trap!"

I pulled on my best confused expression midsentence and ended with "Ah, her name was Spanishola? For real?"

Czerniak and Swanson traded a look. It was not one I could interpret, but Caputo seemed annoyed.

"I've had about enough of these flatfoot clowns." The ghost vented a long breath, closed his eyes, and held his palms out as though seeking benediction. The air condensed around him, and light seemed to leach out of the sky as though the sun had dropped behind a low cloud even though I could see the big orange ball just over the top of the western horizon, unblocked by any obstruction. My skin prickled, and my breath fogged. It felt as though a freezer door had opened, and all the cold air poured out to surround us. I had once stood near an electrical transformer carrying enough voltage to light a dozen city blocks, and that sensation of humming power felt much the same as that coming off the ghost of Stan Caputo.

When his eyes opened, they glowed.

Caputo focused his attention on the detectives, and I felt—*the push?*—the desire to leave, to get away, the strong need to be somewhere *else*, that flowed off the ex-gangster and rolled over Swanson and Czerniak.

Swanson shivered. "Man, this graveyard's givin' me the creeps."

"You got that right," Czerniak said. He crossed his arms and buffed his biceps. "Brr. It's freezing out here. Let's roll."

"You." Swanson pointed a finger at me. "We're not done with you yet, ya hear me? Don't go leavin' town."

"No," I said. "I won't." *I won't as long as Pippah doesn't threaten to slice off my kielbasa again.*

The detectives tromped away, yelling at the crime scene people to hurry and wrap it up. Caputo watched them go, a smirk plastered on his face. "Yeah, take that, ya bums." He offered an Italian salute as a parting gesture. "And don't let the door hit your ass on the way out."

I waited until I was sure everyone was out of earshot. "All right, Stan. Thanks for that, but hey, listen. We gotta talk."

"Oh yeah?"

"Oh yeah. Enough of this mysterious ghost bullshit. It's time to fess up, Caputo."

"Ha! If I had nickel for every time I heard that."

I walked away from Pvt. Verbeek's grave, and Caputo followed me. I ambled around the edge of the thicket, putting as many trees between me and the detectives as I could. No way did I want them to see me talking to the air. As soon as we were out of earshot, I said, "What the hell is going on here, Stan?"

"Which part, Ace?"

I whirled on him, hands poised like I wanted to strangle him. Which I did. But he was dead. So I didn't.

"Let's start with the dead girl in the woods, huh?" I demanded. "How did she get here? Where did she come from? Who killed her?"

"We got more pressing business, my friend."

"More pressing... what? That girl was murdered—"

"Which don't mean squat right now." Caputo patted his pockets and came up empty. He frowned. "I hear you met Pippah last night."

I pulled up short. We had reached the perimeter wall, near the broken-down section. I clamped my hands atop the gritty, crumbly brick and squeezed like I wanted to crush the concrete with my bare hands. Which I did. But I couldn't.

"Yeah. Let's talk about Pippah. What the actual fuhhh—"

The words stopped in my throat as Consuelo popped into existence, just on the other side of the wall. The two previous times I had seen her, Consuelo appeared as solid as a real woman, fully fleshed out, so to speak. This time, her form was more opaque, like cloudy glass, and her faint, sad smile was gone, replaced with a twisted expression of terror, or maybe she was distraught with panic. She flapped her hands to get my attention, hopping on her toes.

"Holy Moley with a side of bacon," Caputo said in awe. "I've died and gone to heaven. Look at those things bounce up and down. How do they do that with no gravity?"

"Shut up, Stan." I concentrated on the ghost of the dead girl. "What is it, Consuelo? What's wrong?"

She jabbed a finger at the thicket, held her arms in a carrying gesture, then pointed at herself and waggled her fingers as though they were birds fluttering away. My mind made an intuitive leap.

"The crime scene guys, they're taking your body away?"

Her head bobbed emphatically. She pointed at her wrist and then pinched two fingers together until they met. Then mimed an explosion with both hands.

"There's a bomb about to go off?" Stan asked.

Consuelo shot him a dirty look. She jabbed her sternum in a way that said, *No, dummy. Me!* Then she repeated the explosive gesture, only softer this time, more like a poof than a bang.

"When they take her body away..." Dread crept into my chest and gripped my heart with hands of ice. "She won't be able to manifest here anymore. She'll be... gone."

Consuelo clapped and pointed at me like I'd just won at charades.

"Are you kidding me?" Caputo griped. "The first naked dame I see in over eighty years, and the cops are taking her away? What have they got against me? Yeah, I robbed a bank here and there, maybe shot a guy once, but sheesh! Come on!"

"Wait, she's trying to show me something."

"She's showing me plenty," Caputo said. "Haut-chee-mamma."

Consuelo was gesturing, waving me to come closer with cupped hands. I looked at her, at the wall separating us, then at the farmhouse, whose lights were barely visible in the darkness across the field. She wanted me to come with her, to see something on the other side of the wall. To do so, I would have to trespass on Vic Tarwater's land again, a guy with a history of violence and a shotgun. Consuelo gestured again, more emphatically. *Come on!* I suspected I didn't have long, only until the forensics people finished loading the black bag with Consuelo's remains and she made her final journey through the cemetery gates to a waiting ambulance. From there, they would take her to the morgue and no doubt release her body to her loved ones for burial, probably somewhere in Kansas. My remaining moments with Consuelo were short.

"If I don't come back," I told Caputo, "then show the cops where I went."

"You're asking *me*? To talk to the *cops*?"

He said something else, but I had already jumped the wall and was hurrying after Consuelo's diminishing form, so I missed it.

Consuelo cut a diagonal path across Tarwater's field. Brittle stalks of mowed hay crackled under my feet, and the heavy soil clung to my shoes. The sun was a memory, leaving nothing but a purple glow on the horizon to mark its passage. The air had turned chilly. I tugged my hoodie over my head and zipped it up the front. Something whipped past my nose, and I jerked to a stop, only to belatedly recognize the shape of an owl swooping away on silent wings.

"Was that an omen?" I asked aloud, mainly for the comfort of hearing a voice.

I rushed to catch up to Consuelo, who had grown not only more distant but also more translucent. She had faded to the shape of a glass figurine, filled with only a trace of smoke. I kept my voice pitched low, ever aware of the hulking shape of Tarwater's farmhouse to my right. "What is it, Consuelo? What do you want to show me?"

The girl glanced over her shoulder and motioned me onward without pausing. After about two hundred yards of labored effort—on my part, at least—we came to a barbed wire fence, the border of Tarwater's field. Beyond the fence was Orchard Road, which bordered the eastern side of Shady Terraces and continued almost due north into the farmlands of Pennsylvania.

Consuelo passed through the wire without stopping. I, on the other hand, learned why the wire was called "barbed."

"Ow, ow, ow," I said. "Wait up! Oh shit."

That last one was because I'd hung my crotch on a barb, pulled instead of lifted it free, and heard a nice, loud rip. The sharp bit of steel passed way too close to my testicle for comfort, so I panicked and tried leaping free.

"Oof!"

For the second time today, Consuelo stood over me as I lay face-down in the mud, although this time, I had one leg hung in the air, snagged on a bit of barbed wire. Her smile was exasperated, indulgent, and not a little impatient, as though she were my mother and I'd dripped ice cream on my Sunday clothes. She twirled her hand in a hurry-up gesture.

"Yeah, yeah, I'm coming." I fought the snag in my pants until I could pull my leg free. More fabric ripped in the process. "Damn, this was my last good pair."

I scrambled up and ran after Consuelo, who had drifted north on Orchard Road. I say "drifted" because her shape faded as she moved farther from the cemetery, becoming more of a suggestion of an outline rather than something fully formed. I splashed through the drainage ditch and climbed the verge of the two-lane blacktop. A vague memory of looking at a Google map a few days ago came to mind... something about Orchard Road becoming a rural highway as it cut north. I couldn't remember the highway's number or even the next town up the road, nor did it really matter. Consuelo wasn't going to make it a hundred feet, let alone to the next town.

A glistening, gossamer shape, outlined by starlight, Consuelo turned to me, and I knew by her expression this would be the last I ever saw of her. She ghost-cupped my cheek with one hand. Maybe I dreamed it, but her eyes seemed to suggest such infinite sadness, a recognition of what might have been, had we met in a different time and a different place. Her sly smile hinted that we could have been great friends and possibly more. Maybe it was nothing but a projection of my own needs and desires, but I thought I read in the tilt of her head, the curl of her lip, and the simple beauty of her supple body that she wished nothing more than to stay with me, to be alive, and to experience all the hopes and dreams, triumphs and failures, that life had to offer. And that she wished she could do so with me by her side.

A lot to read into a look, I know.

With her last gesture, Consuelo Hinojosa Espinoza pointed north, along Orchard Road, toward nothing I could see, and with a simple quirk of her eyebrow, asked me to seek what she needed me to find. I almost heard her voice in my head—that was how in tune with her expression I was. *"Why, Brad? Why did I have to die? Find out who killed me and ask them that. Why me?"*

"I will," I said.

And she was gone.

Chapter 15

I took the long way around to get back home: south along Orchard Road until the barbed wire gave way to the Shady Terraces perimeter wall then farther south still. I reached the junction of Orchard and Shady Elm Road, turned left, and followed the wall until I reached the cemetery gates.

The last batch of paramedics, police, and Pottsville firefighters was wrapping up, loading up, and driving away as I made it to the gates. I saw no sign of Swanson or Czerniak, for which I was grateful. One more stupid question from either of the detectives would likely send me over the edge and land my butt in jail. A cop stood by his open trunk, stripping out of his shiny yellow slicker.

"Am I good to lock up?" I asked him.

"Yeah, sure. Everyone's out."

I locked the cemetery gates, waved to the cop, and entered the office building through the front door. George met me at the door and danced around my feet. I switched on lights as I went down the hall to the apartment. *Lights.* I needed light, something bright enough to dispel the darkness staining my mood and draining my soul.

Melodramatic much?

I toyed with the notion of hiking back up Orchard Road and trying to find whatever Consuelo wanted me to see. I rooted around the kitchen drawers until I found a plastic flashlight. The batteries were dead. I tossed it back in the drawer and flopped into a chair at the table, too tired to even find my notepad and add batteries to my to-do list. George came over and settled his chin on my thigh. I scratched the scruff around his neck and absorbed the dog love radiating from his blue eyes.

"Yeah, buddy," I said. "You guessed it. It's been a rough night."

George huffed.

"True. Not as bad as last night. Damn, I almost forgot. Caputo! Stan!" I said to the empty air. "I need to talk about Pippah! You around? Delmont? Anybody?" No spectral beings appeared at my summons. "So much for ghosts. Never one around when you need it."

My prepaid smartphone didn't have much in the way of a data plan, and my provider had been sending me helpful texts reminding me about topping off my balance for the past three days. I could do very little internet searching or social media dabbling. About one quick search for a sale on batteries would suck away my remaining minutes. Using the office computer was a nonstarter, at least until I upgraded it. The old beast would take an hour to load a page.

I held my breath, sent up a prayer to the God of Data, and fired up my phone's Facebook app. I typed Consuelo Espinoza in the search bar.

Half a dozen accounts appeared, some with pictures, some without. My breath caught when I recognized my Consuelo in the fourth thumbnail. I clicked on her profile.

A big fat nothing burger came back. Her profile was set to private. I would have to send her a friend request to see what was on her page, which of course would go nowhere because she was gone. *How do I friend a ghost? Do ghosts have social media?* Face-boo! maybe? Insta-ghost?

What've I got to lose?

I clicked the friend request.

For a while, I just sat there, idly scritching George's ears and studying Consuelo's profile picture. It was a different shot than all the others I'd seen, which had been institutional photos on ID cards. Here she was caught in some moment of complete delight, her eyes sparkling, mouth wide open with gusty laughter. She looked so happy.

A little red dot appeared over the Friend icon. My scalp prickled. I thumbed it, and a message appeared: *Your friend request has been accepted. Say "Hi" to your new friend, Consuelo.*

I dropped the phone.

By the time I'd scrambled under the table and retrieved it, my screen displayed the helpful tiered plan of rates to reload my minutes.

OCTOBER 19TH, DAY 4

Morning found me hiking north along Orchard Road. George quested along ahead of me, blazing a trail of dog pee along the verge in case I got lost. Tabitha had gotten a snootful of cold air when I opened the door and elected to remain behind. I didn't blame her. A cold front had moved in overnight, bringing with it a quilt of low gray clouds and a blustery wind that cut to the bone. Scattered snowflakes danced on the gusty breeze.

I passed the point where I had fought and lost the battle with the barbed wire fence—it had claimed a patch of blue denim as its trophy—and continued toward Tarwater's farmhouse, the roof of which I could just make out through the trees lining the road. On my right lay the field where the old man had confronted me with his shotgun. To my left, the ground had been cleared for farming at some time in the distant past but had since been allowed to go feral. Saplings, briars, and junk growth filled the space where fields had once been harvested. Birds and squirrels darted away as I approached, and they filled the air with chattered scolding. George side-eyed the small critters and kept his distance.

My brain continued sifting through the mystery of Consuelo Espinoza. *What had she been doing, stopping in Pottsville, of all places? Was she meeting someone? Did she run out of gas?* I found it ominous that her last act as a spirit had been to point to the Tarwater place. Had she been trying to tell me Vic Tarwater was the one who killed her? If so, exactly how was I, Brad Langston, loser extraordinaire, going to obtain the evidence that would convince a jury the old man was her murderer? It wasn't like I was going to march up and demand a confession from that shotgun-wielding maniac.

A swinging metal gate set into the barbed wire fence appeared between the weeds on the left-hand side of the road. Overgrown tracks ran from a cutout off the main road, across a metal culvert, and through the gate before disappearing into a tunnel between the trees. A hefty padlock secured the gate to the post. I crossed over for a closer look.

The remnants of an abandoned house and outbuildings hid back amongst the overgrown forest. All I could see of the house was a portion of a moldering side wall, including one gaping window with a dry-rotted frame. Above it drooped a section of debris-caked roof. Beyond the house hulked the vaguely rectangular shape of a barn being reclaimed by nature. It was like one of those Can You Find the Hidden Object pictures. I had to turn my head just right to make out the outline of the timber-and-tin structure.

I tugged at the padlock, which appeared new and rust free. *Good lock. Very solid. Very secure.*

"C'mon, George." The place gave me the willies, with its rot and greenish mold. Climbing the gate to go exploring did not even rate a spot on the very bottom of my to-do list. "No, we're not going back there, so quit whining, and let's keep moving."

George howled a bit, no doubt disappointed at not getting to pee in new and interesting places. He remained behind, sniffing and snuffling around the gate, as I continued north along the side of Or-chard Road. He ran to catch up when I whistled.

The moment I had been dreading approached. The Tarwater farm came into sight on my right. I stayed on the far side of the road, tramping along the gravel shoulder, and George remained close to my heels, either picking up on my mood or catching a whiff of the man who had recently scared him. The main building was a two-story home of no particular style. If I had to place it, I would say Generic American. The place was not in pristine condition, but neither was it a deteriorated mess. Its squarish construction was covered in white clapboard and topped by a gabled roof with greenish shingles. The front porch was screened. Tinfoil covered the windows.

"Huh," I said. Even though I had seen people do it elsewhere—cover their windows with tinfoil to trap or block radiant heat, depending on the season—I couldn't help but wonder if the application here served a more sinister purpose. What secrets was Tarwater trying to hide? Did he have a house full of trophies from his kills? A wall-mounted display of severed heads, perhaps? Or were his rooms filled with cages, each holding captive an innocent college girl, caught by some skillful trap concocted by the crazy old man and his inbred sons?

Overactive imagination, engage!

When I came abreast of the turnout to Tarwater's place, I flinched. A woman of middle years stood in the yard, wearing a thick coat over a cotton dress, with mukluks on her feet and a bucket of feed suspended from one hand. Her eyes narrowed as I passed, yet her free hand continued dipping into the bucket and scattering feed to a platoon of squawking hens. Now that I focused on the sound, I realized I had been hearing their clucking for some time.

I raised a hand in greeting. She did not return the gesture.

Of old man Tarwater, there was no sign.

A smattering of icy flakes hit me in the face, driven by a stiff north wind. I looked at George, and he looked at me.

"Come on, buddy. Let's get back and get to work on that to-do list. Whaddya say?"

The husky needed no urging. He bolted toward home without looking back. I followed at a slower pace, feeling the old woman's gaze bore into my back until the trees blocked her from view.

WHEN I REACHED THE front door, I found a Jeep Wrangler parked in the lot and Saiera Khosani teaching my dog how to avoid giving the stick back. In fairness, he already knew that trick, so Saiera had an easy time reinforcing the lesson. George would come close with the stick in his mouth, wait for her to reach for it, then bound away, happy as an otter in a bathtub.

"Hey," I said, articulate wonder that I am. "You're early today."

"Hey, yourself. It's Sunday. No mail." Saiera gestured at her attire—jeans and Uggs along with a thick, full-sleeve coat in deference to the biting wind. "Yeah, when I came by yesterday, there were cops and ambulances all over the place. I was worried about you. Then somebody said they found a body?"

"Yeah, go figure. Body in a graveyard." My light tone sounded hollow and felt disrespectful. Consuelo deserved better. More seriously, I added, "A college girl. I think she was murdered."

"Murdered! Seriously? Oh, that's awful."

"Yeah, probably sometime around August of last year. A couple of months before Arlo was shot."

Concern pricked Saiera's eyebrows. "August of last year? The cops found that out already?"

"Ahh... I'm not sure what the cops know. I may have... umm..."

"What?"

"I looked through her purse," I blurted. I told Saiera how I had pieced together the trail of receipts and the college ID to create a narrative that seemed to fit. Of course, I left out being visited by the naked spirit of the victim herself and the connection I felt I had made with her. *Hey, look! Brad learns discretion!*

"Wow, you're quite the detective. What else have you discovered, Sherlock?"

I shrugged. "That's pretty much it."

"Two deaths, so close together," Saiera mused, "both in proximity and time. Do you think there's a connection?"

"It's possible. Maybe Arlo saw something he wasn't supposed to see. Or," I said, thinking of Pippah, "there's an evil spirit on the loose in the graveyard, killing people like in a bad horror movie."

"I don't think evil spirits use shotguns."

"Have you met Tarwater?"

"Fair point."

"Hey, it's pretty chilly. You want to come in for a cup of tea?"

Saiera winced. "I can't. I have to go see my mom, and I'm late as it is."

"I'm sorry, I—"

"No, no, it's okay. I wanted to make sure you were all right. But I have to run." Saiera leaned in and delivered a buddy hug. "See you tomorrow!"

"I—uh, okay."

She jogged to her car after giving George a final pat. The husky looked between me and the retreating woman. His expression seemed to say, *What the heck, dude? I'm doing my part. Why did you run her off?*

"Being my wingman is a thankless task," I told the dog. "Try harder."

⸺ ⁙ ⸺

AFTER FORTIFYING MYSELF with fresh and nasty coffee, I tried again to find Pippah's mausoleum. I started out at the gates, just as I had the night she appeared, and followed my nose along path after path after path. For two hours, I crisscrossed the front half of the cemetery, scouting for hills and brick-faced crypts. The snowfall grew thicker but never so much that it blurred visibility. On my third attempt, which ended as had the first two—right back at the front gate—I gave up. Either I had dreamt the whole thing, or Pippah and her tomb had been dragged back down to hell. Wandering in circles would accomplish nothing but carving tracks in the snow.

"Fine," I said. "I've got enough to keep me busy without hunting ghosts."

Namely, I had a to-do list that was stretching to three pages, Tabitha's tuna supply was dangerously low, and I had no data on my phone and one pair of jeans to my name. I would have to do laundry in my Fruit of the Looms if I couldn't find a thrift shop and supplement my wardrobe with some suitable pants. Plus, the mysterious friend request acceptance from Consuelo's Facebook account nagged at me. Who was monitoring her account? Or had she done it herself, somehow, from beyond the grave?

Yes, I had a Wishful Thinking merit badge to go along with my Overactive Imagination belt buckle.

In the parking lot, a middle-aged man was getting out of a Toyota SUV. He lifted a flower arrangement out of the passenger seat, closed the door, and locked it with a key fob. We exchanged nods of greeting as he passed me on his way into the cemetery. I made a mental note to lock the gate after he left.

By the time I finished dithering around the apartment—cleaning up, throwing some stuff in the washer, and taking care of the furballs—true night had fallen. Darkness came early that time of year, and with low winter clouds spitting ice, it felt like deep night though my watch read 7:20 p.m. when I headed out.

The Toyota was still there, so I left the gates unlocked.

I hopped in the Mazda and buzzed a few blocks into town, where Orchard Road became Martingale Avenue and crossed Winchester, to an independent phone dealer that sold my brand of wireless carrier. Called GetConnected, the store was detached from the strip mall that occupied most of the corner lot, a small, square box of a place with a glass front and signage advertising all the major phone makers.

A chime rang when I opened the door to the place, and a goth girl with curly black hair and pale skin popped up from behind a counter. Gutted shipping boxes with packing material strewn about suggested she had been stocking the cases before I entered. The girl gave off a serious nerd vibe at five four and as lean as a lightsaber with heavy eye shadow and the pale complexion of a Dungeons & Dragons addict. She wore over-wide glasses with thin black frames.

I held up my dead phone. "I need to reload my plan."

"Sure," she said, moving to the register area. "Do you have a card?"

"A credit card?"

"No, sorry..." The woman's bouncy curls fell over her glasses when she ducked her head. A tiny collar pin fashioned in the shape of a horse's head, like a knight from a chess game, was affixed to her collar.

Have nerd, will travel?

"I meant a reload card."

"Oh, sorry. Of course. I'm an idiot. Hold on." I fished out my wallet and found my reloadable cellular card. When I handed it to her, I read the girl's name tag. "You're Addy? Hi, I'm Brad."

"You're the new cemetery guy."

"Wow, how'd you know?"

Her eyes grew big and round behind her glasses. "You smell of the grave," she intoned. "The aura of death surrounds youuuu."

My jaw dropped. "Waah?"

Then her lips curled in a smile. "Sorry, I'm just kidding. I have a weird sense of humor, I know. My dad calls me 'tetched' in the head. Seriously, though, I walk by the graveyard on my way to work, and I saw you. You were there, in the cemetery. Last night. So I figured. You know."

"Oh good." I made a production of sniffing my armpits. "Because death... It's hard to get out of your clothes. Bleach just won't do it."

"I hear Dead Tide works. Ectoplasmic stain fighter."

"Do they sell it at the grocery store?"

"Nah, it's more of a Ghostco thing."

"Or maybe Specter Supply?"

"Now, that's a spooky store. How much do you want on this?"

"I—huh? Sorry, what?"

"The card." Addy held up my minutes card. "How much do you want to load?"

"Oh. Uh, twenty-five, please."

"Twenty-five, it is."

Addy took my cash and performed the sleight of hand that brought my phone back from the dead. It chirped happily when I switched it on, and my new message alerts started chiming. I had a voice mail, which surprised me, a few dozen new emails and texts, and of course, the little red ball on my Facebook messenger app appeared, reminding me I needed to say hi to my new "friend," Consuelo Espinoza. As if I needed reminding.

"You're a popular guy," Addy said, bringing me out of my phone-induced coma. Her black-rimmed eyes held mine for a long moment before she dropped her gaze.

"Hmm?" I snapped out of my trance. "Me? No, not really." I grinned. "Except, I have to say, people are dying to meet me."

Addy rolled her eyes. "Ouch."

"Yeah, lame, I know." I held up my phone and added, "Thanks for getting me back in touch with the rest of the world."

"Yeah, sure. No problem. Have a nice night."

I recognized my exit cue, but for some reason, I lingered, stretching my brain cells to find something to say. Addy seemed to have retreated into her shy nerd persona, fiddling with stuff around the register, her head down and dark curls falling around her face. Where had the funny, playful woman with a quipster attitude gone?

"So you walk by the graveyard," I said.

"Every day. Well, every night, I mean. I work nights. I walk to work, which isn't *every* night, but... you know... like almost every night." Addy shrugged without looking up. "I like the graveyard," she blurted after a pause. "I used to play there... when I was a kid."

The words *That's weird* leapt to mind, but I held them back. "I hope you weren't playing archaeologist."

"No." Addy glanced up at me with her shy smile. Her hands were busy straightening a hanging rack of earbuds. "I liked it there. It was... peaceful."

Not so much anymore. "How do you feel about trimming rosebushes?"

"Oh. My. God. Those rosebushes so need—"

The door chime sounded, and the voice of God bellowed from the front of the store. "You again! What are you doing here, you little shit!"

I spun around, and my blood turned to ice. Standing in the door was none other than Vic Tarwater in dirty jeans, a rough shirt, and a plaid CPO jacket. He did not have his trusty shotgun, but his granite jaw could split firewood, and both bony-knuckled hands were clenched into fists.

"First," Tarwater said like he was spitting gravel, "you sneak around my back field, then just this morning, you come around and make eyes at my wife. And now, here you are, sniffing around Adamantine like a bluetick hound."

"Daddy!" Addy said. "Stop being a jerk."

Daddy? Daddy?

What the actual hell is this?

Chapter 16

I spared Addy an incredulous glance. "This guy is your *father*?"

Tarwater stalked across the floor and invaded my personal space like a malignant cancer. He smelled faintly of bacon grease and chewing tobacco. "As if you didn't know. What the hell are you up to, gravedigger? Why are you poking around my place so?"

"I'm not—"

"You best keep your hands away from my daughter!" Tarwater punctuated that with a finger poke to my chest, which lit a small kernel of anger down deep in my back brain. I felt it catch fire, an almost audible crackle in my ears. My face heated, and the blood thumped in my chest. I recognized the signs of my anger, which I had thought was well under control after years of therapy and much practice with various coping techniques, but when it happened like this, it could blow up like a grass fire and burn everything in its path—including me.

I swelled up and bit out through clenched teeth, "Listen to me, you sorry motherf—"

Tarwater shoved me back a step. "Don't you bare your teeth at me, puppy!"

"Daddy!" Addy jammed herself between us, her back to me, and pushed her father with both hands on his chest. "Stop it! This man is a customer, and you're being an asshole. Now leave him be and get out of here."

"Adamantine Tarwater—"

"Don't you 'Adamantine' me!" The shy nerd girl had transformed again, this time to a cold-rolled steel avatar of gothic vengeance. Much like her name, Adamantine, she confronted her father as an immovable object. Frigid anger drew the heat from the air around her such that I imagined ice crystals frosting her garments. "I've told you before not to come in here and terrorize my customers."

"But he's—"

"I know who he is," Addy said. "And he's harmless as a flea."

"Hey!" That stung. *A flea? Really?*

Tarwater and I glared at each other over Addy's curly hair. His glittering eyes promised me a slow death and a shallow grave—like Consuelo's, my mind supplied—whereas my own subconscious assured the old man I would welcome his attempt and raise him a potful of misery if he tried. *I'm all in, Mr. Charm. All in.*

"I was leaving anyway," I said once I was sure the message had been received. "Thanks for your help, Addy." With that, I gave the father and daughter a wide berth and pushed through the exit, hearing the chime ring its cheerful farewell.

The cold outside quenched my face like a hot rock dropped in a snowbank. The precipitation had turned to sleet, which fell in needle-sharp droplets and dotted my windshield with ice bumps. I dug my scraper out of the glove box and attacked the thin coating of ice. When I glanced back into the store, Tarwater and his daughter were going at it, nose to nose in a red-faced, hand-gesturing full-on family squall. Even as I watched, they seemed to run out of steam, wind down, and ended up in an awkward but conciliatory hug.

I felt the last heat of my anger coal burn out. I sighed. Twin plumes of breath fogged from my nose, like a sad dragon losing steam.

"And there goes another woman I'll probably never see," I told myself. *A flea? Jesus wept.* But seriously, who could ever date the poor girl with a potential father-in-law like that. No wonder she looked so nerdy and pale. The only amazing thing was Tarwater allowing her out of his Doom Castle of a house to go work on her own in a Pottsville wireless phone store. "Good for you, Adamantine."

I got in my car and left.

IT TURNED OUT THE VOICE mail was from Chesterfield, the attorney. I sat in the car while the windshield defrosted and listened to the message. "*Hello, Mr. Langston. It occurred to me that I failed to get your email address, so instead of sending your employment documents electronically, I have sent them via overnight courier. They should arrive today, so please be on the lookout for them. Additionally, I am pleased to inform you that I have secured some funding for improvements and upgrades to the property. Please send me your budget so that we may prioritize your needs and get started as soon as it is convenient. Thank you again, Mr. Langston. Take care and Godspeed.*"

"Prioritize my needs, huh?" I said aloud. "How about an exorcist? Or a pair of proton packs? Sam and Dean Winchester? How much do they cost?"

I found a late-closing thrift store and stocked up on some clothing, bought some cheap batteries from the grocery store, then hustled back to the cemetery just as the sleet turned to snow. The Little Mazda That Could fishtailed up the slope of Shady Elms Drive, wipers bravely batting the falling flakes away from the windshield. Dots of white floated in my headlight beams.

I rushed over to lock the cemetery gates.

And paused.

The Toyota SUV was still there, parked in the same place as when the man with the flowers had left it. I peered through the ice-encrusted windows and saw nothing. The man had entered the cemetery more than three hours ago. *Is he still here? This late? After dark?*

Maybe he had car trouble and rode away with someone else. But why leave the car? Wouldn't he have towed it? Should I go look for the guy? Maybe he fell. Broke an ankle or something.

One of my thrift store purchases included a winter coat, but I wanted to wash it before I wore it, as I did with all things bought from thrift stores. *I mean, uck, really? Put that thing on with some stranger's sweat, skin cells, and assorted cooties all over it?*

No coat meant I was shivering as I stood there, bits of ice mixed with fat, granular snow accumulating on my head and shoulders, like frozen dandruff. My hoodie wouldn't hold up for an extended search. I'd be a Bradsicle before I made it halfway through the grave-yard.

But if the guy was hurt, having broken an ankle or gotten lost—

Dammit. There's a reason I hate responsibility.

"This job sucks."

I sighed, put on my thrift store coat, then went to put new batteries in the flashlight.

I SEARCHED THE CEMETERY for an hour before giving up. My "new" coat was nice, but even so, I was chilled and shivering by the time I called it quits and reached the gates. I left them unlocked in case the man with the flowers was still somewhere inside the cemetery grounds, playing hide-and-seek with the spirits of his loved ones. I ducked inside the office and flipped the dead bolt behind me.

The lights in the reception area were still on, so it was easy to see that Stan Caputo had manifested himself onto a comfy seat on the sofa.

"Heya, kiddo," he said. "Good to see you're not in the pokey."

"Stan! Man, am I glad to see you." I flopped into one of the over-stuffed chairs across from the sofa. "What in the hell is going on here?"

"Can youse be more specific?"

"Jesus, where do I start? First of all, what happened to the dead girl back in the... back in the thicket?"

"I would call it more like a copse."

"And Arlo, the old caretaker, who shot him? No, wait, put a pin in that. Let's talk about the elephant in the graveyard. Who the hell is Pippah, and what is it she wants?"

"Ah. Yeah." The dapper gangster picked at the perfect hem of his trousers. "About that. First, lemme say, I don't know nothing about nobody getting offed, okay? I wasn't, ah, I wasn't in my material form, so to say, when that happened. Either one. All I know is, one day, a new gal... dropped in, as it were."

"Dropped in?"

"Look, kid, this'll go a lot faster if I put you in the picture, okay?"

"Sure."

George trotted in from the back room and proceeded to sniff and snuffle all around Stan Caputo's immaterial body.

"Nice pooch." Stan patted his pockets and twisted his lips in a half frown when he came up empty. "Okay, so let me draws you a picture. You know these things they're putting in houses these days? Boilers to heat the water so's you can take a hot bath, wash your clothes, all that stuff?"

"Hot water heaters, sure. But how does—"

Stan held up a palm. "Hold your horses, doc. Yeah, a water heater. Dangerous as hell, you ask me. Tommy Spigone had one installed in his place—Tommy always had to have the latest gadget—and the damn thing blew up. Took out one side of Tommy's house. Good thing for him and the missus, they was both out at the Boyd when it happened, watching a flick. Killed the housekeeper though, sorry to say."

"Stan, focus. About Pippah?"

"Yeah, as I was saying, you take a water heater, it can only hold so much hot water at one time, right? When it runs out, it runs out, and you gotta wait for it to get hot again to run a tub. It's kind of like that for us"—Stan gestured vaguely, rolling his hands in circles—"people of the nonliving variety. We sort of have this energy, you know? Like a battery, only not contained-like. We can tap the juice and, ah, you know, appear as real bodies here on Eart' and, like... make stuff happen. Blow out a candle, bang a pot. And so on and so on."

"Like you used on the detectives last night."

Stan grinned. "Yeah, that was something, huh? The look on their faces."

"Something. Right."

"It takes a lot of practice and... call it willpower... to do stuff like that. I've had a lot of practice, so I'm pretty good at it. Had you fooled at first, didn't I? Old lady Fairweather and the Rose Queen, Madame Perry, are pretty good, too, and Delmont—sheesh, Delmont's a natural spook." Stan winked like he was telling a joke. I didn't get it.

"What about Pippah?"

"Ah," Stan said. He stood up and crossed the room to stand in front of the brightly colored painting—Pottsville East Shady Terraces, 1959—and put his hands on his hips. "Now, that's a spade of another color, you wanna know the truth." He threw me a wink over his shoulder. "Ha. Get it? Spade of another color?"

"No, what—Oh. No, that's not funny. You don't have to use racial epithets—I don't care how scary she is. And wait, were you calling Delmont a spook earlier? Jesus, Stan, not cool."

"Simmer down, kiddo." Stan tamped down the air with his palms, as though trying to calm an unruly child. "Jeez, nobody can take a joke these days."

"A joke, yeah, but racial slurs aren't jokes."

"Okay, okay. So you wanna know about Pippah, right? So, Pippah, the *colored woman*—"

"No. Stop. Don't call her that."

"What? Colored?"

"Correct. It's more appropriate to say person of color."

Stan's face twisted in confusion. "What? That's the same thing."

"No, it's not."

"It is. It's saying colored person, only backward."

"Okay, fine. 'African American' is also appropriate."

"But..." Stan clamped his head in both hands. "She's not *from* Africa. She came from Haiti, I think."

"I—look, skip it." I stood and paced the room. "Just get to the part about how dangerous she is."

"Oh. Okay. Sure. Remember that thing I said was coming, and you should know about it? That thing was Pippah." Stan "leaned" against the wall, legs and arms crossed in a gangster pose. "She's as dangerous as they come, kid."

"What does she want?"

"Revenge, babe. She wants to get back at everyone in Pottsville who ever done her wrong."

"And who would that be?" I huddled in my sweatshirt, fighting to keep from shivering. The reception area suffered from the same lack of adequate heating as the rest of the building, and even with the old furnace working overtime, the cold outside seeped through the walls and stole through the crevices.

"I don't know the details," Stan said, "but I get the sense she's really hot under the collar about something that happened here. How she died, prob'ly. She's building up her... ah, abilities, shall we say. Gaining control over the juice, learning how to come back to the world of the living. I got a notion Pippah wants to come back—full-time, like—and do some serious damage. Already she's really, really strong, you know. Motivated. She can drain the energy like... Well, you ever see the lights dim when they throw the switch on Old Sparky? It's like that. That witch can suck the juice out of the other side faster than a mick can down a bottle of rye. It's like... I can feel it when she starts powering up. It's as if—I don't know—I can feel the life draining right outta me."

"What happens when she gains control? When she learns to... come back full-time, here on this side?"

"Nothing good, kid. That I can tell you."

"Well... can you ask her? On the other side, I mean."

"Ha! It's not like we're hanging out down at Ralph's on Ninth Street, having a glass of chianti and dancing the tarantella." Stan stared off into space for a moment, a wistful smile on his face. "Man, I miss them days. Anywho, it's more—shoot, I can't describe it. We're like blobs of electricity or something. Kinda floatin' around a big bathtub, bumping into things and each other. The only thing keeping us from drifting into the nothing is our... call it willpower. We don't *talk* like I'm talking to you, but sometimes when we bump into each other, we can, you know... share information if we want. Pippah's not the sharing type, shall we say. All I get from her is a hate bomb, filled with high-explosive anger, with the fuse lit."

"How do I stop her?"

Stan shrugged. "Hell if I know, kid. Hell if I know. Hey, look, I can feel the juice running out. I'll be seeing—" The gangster blipped out of existence without finishing his sentence.

George barked and ran in circles, sniffing at the spot Stan had occupied. My stomach rumbled, and I thought of the deluxe-size box of mac 'n' cheese I had picked up at the store. Comfort food. Exactly what I needed right now was some good, old-fashioned, carb-heavy comfort food. At least that way, if Pippah came back for real tonight, I would die on a full stomach.

IT WAS LATE. I WAS full. The mac 'n' cheese residue in my bowl was slowly becoming yellow cement. The sludge of once-hot cocoa in my cup had gone tepid. Empty boxes, open packets, saucepans, spoons, and debris littered the stovetop, the table, and the counters. I would have to clean up soon, but it could wait a few minutes.

While I had been cooking the macaroni, a dry noodle had escaped to bounce across the floor. Tabitha was busy batting the bit of pasta around the kitchen, and George watched her like he wanted to join the game, but he wasn't quite sure how. The rattle of the noodle, followed by the clitter-clatter of tiny claws, was the only sound in the kitchen.

I powered up my freshly charged and reloaded phone. When the screen came to life, I found a red ball atop the icon for Facebook Messenger, indicating I had three messages.

All three were from my new "friend," Consuelo Espinoza. While my phone had been down, someone had been trying to communicate with me via Consuelo's account. Silly as it sounds, my heartbeat trilled in my chest as I tapped the icon to read the messages. I couldn't kill the tiny, weird little thought that Consuelo was trying to communicate with me from beyond the grave.

"Who is this?"

"Are you there?"

"Please, do you know my daughter?"

My blood ran cold. *Oh no. Not Consuelo at all.*

One of her parents.

All the messages were dated and time-stamped from the day before, roughly at eight p.m., my time. Nothing since that last, plaintive query.

Had the police reached out to Consuelo's next of kin already, or were these poor people still in the dark about their daughter's fate? And how should I respond? Now, that would truly suck, getting an instant message from a stranger: *"Hi, this is Brad. In case you didn't know, Consuelo is dead. I found her bones in a graveyard in a thicket. Hit me back if you want to talk."*

"Did you know my daughter?"

The new message appeared, as if by magic, a near-repeat of the last one, except now in past tense. *Did* instead of *do* you know my daughter.

My mouth was suddenly dry. *How did she know I was online? Oh. Of course.* There was an icon next to my avatar, showing I was active on the site. No magic was involved, unless you counted the mystery of online communication. *"Did you know..."* Past tense. It sounded like Consuelo's parents had gotten word of the discovery.

With shaky fingers, I typed out, "This is Brad Langston. I found a skeleton..." Backspace, backspace, backspace... "I found your daughter's body..." Backspace, backspace... "your daughter's purse..." Backspace, backspace, backspace... "This is Brad Langston. I work at Shady Terraces. In Pottsville."

I hit enter and waited.

"Oh, are you the one who found her? In the graveyard?"

I read the message with a sense of both relief and anxiety—relief that I didn't have to be the one to tell Consuelo's parents she was dead and anxiety because I had no ready excuse for why I was friending a dead woman, whose body I had discovered, on social media. Besides that, talking to people who had suffered great loss was not a skill I possessed. Enter into evidence Tim's parents, who always said they harbored no grudge but whose protestations always came a beat too late or without conviction. I had moved far away from my hometown as soon as I could, partly to escape having to see them ever again.

I typed a response slowly and with deliberation:

"I am the one who found your daughter. I am so sorry for your loss. I discovered Consuelo's purse, too, and I read her name off the ID there. She seemed such a nice young lady. I looked her up on Facebook out of curiosity, and I apologize if I've disturbed you." *Enter.* I realized I was rocking in my seat and made myself stop. A new message appeared.

"No. Please don't apologize. I'm Consuelo's mother, and I've been watching this account from the computer in her room. Hoping, you know. I happened to be here last night just"

The message ended abruptly, then a new one appeared after a pause.

"Just going through her old posts."

I nodded in understanding. I could picture Consuelo's mom as clearly as if she were my own, sitting by the computer. Waiting. Hoping.

"Can you tell me what happened to her? The police haven't told us anything."

"No," I responded. *How do I say "Your daughter appeared before me in the nude and has, quite literally, haunted me ever since." *Instead, I typed, "Do you know what she was doing in Pottsville?"

"No. I had to look it up on a map. When she left for college, Chelita said something about seeing a friend. Near Pittsburgh. I didn't pay attention to where. Or who."

Chelita? That must have been their pet name for Consuelo. I liked it.

There came a long pause. I pictured Consuelo's mom, wracked by grief, tormented by all the missed opportunities, tearing herself up over not having paid attention to an offhand comment that would have meant nothing had Consuelo made it to school, safe and sound, but now meant missing a vital clue in her daughter's disappearance. If only she had paid better attention. If only she had listened, asked more questions.

If only's could drive a person insane.

I knew that better than anyone.

I stared at the blinking cursor. It was testing me by saying Type a Message...

"What message? What the hell do I say now?"

George looked up at the sound of my voice. His tail slapped the floor, inciting Tabitha into stalker mode. I watched her eyes zoom in on the waving tail, her butt wiggling for traction, the pitch, elevation, and distance-to-target calculus of an F-22 Attack Cat flowing through her targeting computer.

Another message popped up: *"We're driving up. Tomorrow. Chelita's father and I. Would it be okay—"*

"No," I said to the screen. "Don't say it."

"if we saw where you found her?"

"Ah hell."

Tabitha made her leap. She grappled George's tail, wrapping herself around it and savaging it with her fangs. The thick fur defeated her efforts to inflict any harm, and George regarded her with an expression of *What the hell is this thing attached to my butt?*

I contemplated my phone screen as if it had shown me a sick joke. What the hell possessed me to start a conversation with a dead girl's mother? And now she wanted to see the place where I found her daughter's body? Like I was some kind of personal tour guide to the most tragic moment in their lives? *Step right this way, folks. Through the thicket, you'll see where Chelita's skeletal hand poked from a tangle of brush!*

It would mean meeting Consuelo's parents face-to-face. Answering their questions. Looking them in the eyes.

Dealing with their grief.

"Jesus, George," I said. "I don't know if I can do that."

"The place is restricted by police tape," I typed. Backspaced it off. I tried another half dozen responses and cleared them all.

Okay, I keyed in finally, *I'll be here when you're ready. Let me send you the address.*

George whuffed at me, his expression curious.

"I know, man," I told him. "But what else could I say?"

Chapter 17

Delmont appeared as I was stacking the last of the dishes in the drainer. George bounced up and started baying at the ghost, and Tabitha shot from the room. I jumped a little myself, startled by Delmont suddenly materializing at the kitchen table.

"Boo," he said.

"Sweet love of Jesus, Delmont." I rested my fingers on my damp bowl to stop its clattering. "Can you ring a bell or something?"

"Sorry, man, it don't work like that."

"George! Stop it." I scrubbed the dog's ruff then held him under the chin and looked him in the eye. "It's just Delmont, okay?" The husky lapped at my face and danced in a circle. I recognized the signs. To Delmont, I said, "I need to let the dog out, okay? But stick around. I want to ask you something."

"Sure, man. Turn the TV on first."

George had forgotten about snow, it having been more than two minutes since the last time he experienced it, so he took longer than normal to take care of his business. The husky frisked in the drifting flakes, jumping and snapping at the delicate white crystals as they fluttered down. He brought me a stick to throw then chased it into the darkness, blowing up small mounds of snow in a frenzy as he claimed his prize. I wasn't as into the game as the dog was. Instead, I kept an eye on the surrounding darkness, half dreading the appearance of a sickly-green glow emanating from the tombstones. The third time he brought me the stick, I decided I'd had all the night games in the graveyard that my nerves could stand. "Come on, George. Let's get inside before the witch shows up."

Delmont hovered cross-legged in the middle of the living room, six inches off the ground, watching a syndicated rerun of *Babylon 5*. "Man, I'm still trying to catch the last episode of season one of this show. I kicked it a few days before it came on, and it's like an itch I can't scratch."

"I can probably find it on Amazon or Hulu, maybe," I said.

Delmont shot me a suspicious look. "Say what?"

"Ah. On the internet, you can stream TV shows, movies, things like that. If Chesterfield lets me buy a decent computer, I can hook it up to the TV—well, maybe not this TV. I'll have to check out the connections—but even so, I can stream any episode you want. If I can't make the TV connection work, you can watch it right on the computer."

"No shit? Watchin' TV on the *computer*? You know what, Agent Mulder? You are living in the best of times. Mm-mm-mm. The best of times." The last bit, he said almost to himself, his attention back on the screen.

"What other shows did you like? Back when... you know..."

"I watched *The Cosby Show* a lot," Delmont said without taking his eyes off the TV. "It was funny, and that Keshia Pulliam... Man, she was something else. So was the mom on that show."

"Yeah, too bad about Bill Cosby, though."

Delmont's head swiveled to give me a fishy stare. Just his head, nothing else. Like an owl. "What about Bill Cosby?"

"He, ah... he was indicted. Convicted, I think. Something about sexual assault? A lot of women came forward and made allegations."

"*Day-am.* That sucks." Delmont's head rotated back around. "I liked that *Cosby* was about Black folk, you know? Too many white people on TV back then—not like it is today. *Friends, Frasier...*

Roseanne... Ugh. And that thing with the cutesy twins, what was it called? Ahhh... *Full House.*"

"Lori Loughlin played the mom in that show. She was indicted too."

Delmont's head spun around like it was on a turntable. "Rebecca's going to jail! What is wrong with you people?"

During the commercial breaks, I peppered Delmont with questions. Who was Pippah, and why was she angry? Who killed Consuelo? Who killed Arlo? Delmont's answers were even less helpful than Stan's.

"Look, Jethro," he said at one point, "time is different over there. I dropped out one time, thought I was gone for a couple of nights, but found I missed a whole season of *Buffy* by the time I popped back. This Pippah chick... she might show up tonight. She might not be back until you're down here with us."

"Do you know why she's pissed?"

"Never met the woman, so I can't say."

My eyes were drooping, and I had turned into a perpetual yawn machine. I left Delmont in the middle of an *X-Files* marathon and crawled between the sheets. I marveled at how readily I'd accepted Delmont Riggins's presence in my living room as nothing more unique than, say, a college roommate. Somehow, I had gotten so blasé about the supernatural that I could tune out the reality of a ghost watching my TV the way I'd once tuned out Conner Bostwick's late-night study sessions, my fellow sophomore hunched over the glow of his laptop while I slept in a nearby bunk.

The sheets were cold at first. With the help of my furry pals, the chill didn't last long. Tabitha seemed willing to concede the foot of the bed to George as long as she could have everything from the waist up. She accepted a long stroking, accompanied by much twisting and turning, then finally settled under my chin, her tiny motor set on vibrate.

I lay awake, listening to the silence of the snowfall outside, hearing the muted mumble of the TV from the other room. But not for long. Within minutes, I was asleep.

OCTOBER 20TH, DAY 5

Lines of fire burned my neck. I spasmed awake from the pain of my little tabby furball scrambling across my bare flesh in full-out panic mode. She leaped from the bed and disappeared. George jumped up and started baying as if the world was ending. I sat up, bleary-eyed and confused.

"What the hell?" Over the husky's racket, I barely made out the sound of the front-door buzzer droning. Someone was punching the thing like they wanted to wake the dead. Or me, I supposed.

I fumbled my phone off the nightstand and read the time: six twenty. "Are you kidding me? Who comes to a cemetery at six in the freaking morning?" I scrubbed my eyes with my palms. "Pants. I need pants. George, hush!"

Wearing nothing but jeans and a T-shirt, I shuffled barefoot down the hall to the front door, the floor cold on my feet. The doorbell never ceased buzzing. George stayed well behind me, barking like the valiant protector he was. I thumbed the dead bolt and opened the door to find a uniformed police officer and Detectives Czerniak and Swanson standing on the porch. Czerniak was the one wearing out the doorbell.

The detective had a half-moon shadow on the bottom of his face, like he'd missed his morning shave, and he glared at me with blood-shot eyes. He resembled a short-order cook in a greasy spoon except he wore a black padded coat with a Steelers logo. The fair-haired Swanson seemed more awake but equally unhappy with me.

"Langston," Swanson barked. "What the hell took you so long?"

"I was in bed."

"In bed," Czerniak said with a sneer. "Yeah, right. What happened to your neck? You been in a fight?"

I touched the sore spots where Tabitha had plowed new furrows in my skin. My fingertips came away spotted with blood. "My cat—"

"Yeah, bullshit, your *cat*. Mind if we look around?" Czerniak didn't wait for permission, pushing past me and—accidentally?—stepping on my bare toes in the process.

"Ow! Yeah, sure. No problem."

Swanson and the uniformed cop trooped past me, both fixing me with looks that suggested I was a dead mouse they'd found in their cereal. They tracked wet, muddy snow across the linoleum floor, and a chill breeze blew in with them. I shut the door to block the cold.

"You mind telling me what this is about?" I asked.

"Where were you last night?" Swanson asked. The uniformed cop assumed a parade rest stance near the door, looking vaguely bored with the whole procedure. Czerniak continued down the hall, poking his nose into the office before heading for the kitchen. George slunk away from the detective, his tail between his legs. The poor dog wasn't afraid of ghosts, but the chunky cop in the padded Steelers coat gave him the willies.

I don't blame you, buddy.

"Where were you last night?" Swanson repeated.

I blinked at Swanson's question. "Last night? What time?"

"Why'd'ya wanna know what time?"

"I was at different places." I shrugged. "Around seven p.m., I was at the cell phone store, GetConnected, off Winchester. Then I went to the Safeway over on Parker Road. And the thrift store in the same strip mall. After that, I was here."

"Here all night?"

"Yeah, all night."

"Didya see or speak to anyone?"

I almost said, "Delmont," but caught it in time. "No. I mean, yeah, at the stores. Not here."

"And how'd ya get those scratches?"

"I told you. My cat. She freaked out when you rang the bell."

Swanson leaned closer, his fluffy mustache bristling. "You sure it wasn't when you were wrestling with your latest victim?"

"I—what? No! What are you talking about?"

Czerniak tromped back into the reception area. He traded a look with Swanson and shook his head in a minimal negative gesture. To me, he said, "Why is the TV on? I thought you said you was asleep."

"Huh? Oh... the TV? I forgot to turn it off last night."

Swanson pointed a finger at me. "What'd ya do wit' him? Huh?"

"What? Who?"

"What he's asking," Czerniak said, "is if you know the current whereabouts of Mr. Donald K. Glatfelter, whose brand-new Toyota Sequoia is sitting in your parking lot, where we have tracked it via the vehicle's locating system and found that it's been sitting there all night. Given the accumulated snowfall and whatnot, we have ascertained that said vehicle has been undisturbed since it arrived here sometime around four thirty yesterday afternoon."

Swanson chimed in, "And what I'm furt'er asking is are we gonna find Mr. Glatfelter in your graveyard somewheres, like maybe-kinda stuffed under a brush pile? Like Maria del... del..."

"Del Consuelo Hinajosa Espinoza," supplied his partner.

I gaped from one to the other. My feet were blocks of ice, and my heart was thumping. I wondered if they could see the cold sweat breaking out all over my body. "You mean flower guy?"

"Huh?" said Czerniak.

"What?" said Swanson.

The cop shifted and said nothing.

"The guy with the flowers? When I came back from the—No, let me back up. Before I went to the store. GetConnected? I saw this guy get out of the SUV with a flower arrangement. He went into the cemetery, and I left to go to the store. When I came back, the car was still here, so I looked around the graveyard for him because I didn't want to lock him inside. I thought maybe he was hurt or something—"

"Why'd ya think that?" Swanson stepped in closer, invading my personal space. "That he was hurt?"

"It-it was late. He, uh, he'd been in there, like, four hours. I was worried he'd, you know, tripped, broken an ankle. Or something." Jeez, I sounded like a criminal even to myself. *Pull it together, Brad. You did nothing wrong!*

"And did you find anything?" Czerniak asked. "When you went... searching?" He finger-waggled air quotes around the word *searching.*

"No, nothing." I crossed my arms and chafed my bare biceps. "I wandered around out there for an hour, freezing my balls off."

"Freezing his balls off," Swanson said to Czerniak, the sneer evident in his voice. "As if this guy has balls."

"He had balls," Czerniak said, "he'd take 'em out and play with 'em."

The cop by the door covered his mouth and coughed.

"Get dressed, Langston," Czerniak said while his face flushed pink. "We're gonna take a look around this graveyard of yours, and I want you out where I can see you."

We searched Shady Terraces for most of the morning. Or more correctly stated, the Pottsville Police Department searched while I stood and shivered, sandwiched between the two detectives, who sipped mugs of coffee supplied by cops who made regular runs to the diner for refills.

They even brought a tracker dog, which George found highly entertaining. He kept trying to make friends.

"Get that mutt back inside, Langston," Swanson ordered. "He's distracting the search dog. Or is that what you want, huh?"

A woman whom I presumed to be Mrs. Glatfelter showed up with the spare keys to the Sequoia. She opened the door for the dog to sniff then stepped back and took up a position not far away from the front gate, glaring at me with red-rimmed eyes the entire time.

About midmorning or a little later—my stomach was saying much later—a cop with sergeant's stripes on his sleeve reported to the detectives.

"Nothing. No hits on the dog though the snow could be damping the scent. And..." The sergeant toed a furrow with his boot, like digging through white frosting to show the chocolate cake underneath. "The snow cover's not that thick. Less than a half inch, maybe. But it's possible it's hiding the body, like maybe in a deep drift."

"Or under a brush pile, maybe," Czerniak said, side-eyeing me with a dark look.

"Oh, give it a rest," I said. Frankly, I was more than a little tired of the Czerniak-Swanson Comedy Hour. If they were the best that Pennsylvania law enforcement had to offer, somebody needed to stiffen up the admission guidelines. "I was working at an auto parts store in Jersey last August, so I couldn't have done anything to Consuelo."

Czerniak squinted. "How'd you know something happened in August? To Consuelo? You sound awfully familiar with someone you never met."

"Someone you *say* you never met," added Swanson.

Shit, Brad. Learn to shut up, would you? "I... spoke to her mom. On Facebook."

Swanson looked at Czerniak. Czerniak looked at Swanson. Both looked at me.

"Let's go downtown," Czerniak said.

"This'll take a while," Swanson said. "You might want to feed the dog."

A DIRTY, WRUNG-OUT wet mop had more pep than I did by the time I made it back to Shady Terraces. A four-hour grilling by Pottsville's finest had burned out my will to live. The squad car dropped me off in the middle of the Shady Terraces parking lot, and the first thing I noticed was that Glatfelter's SUV was gone. It had been replaced by a Ford Fiesta, which had a distinct list to the driver's side, as though heavily weighted.

Andy Gluck, three hundred pounds of ace reporter, squeezed himself out of the car, which bounced upright in metal-squealing relief. "There you are!"

"Here I am," I said without enthusiasm.

He thrust a package at me. "I signed for your FedEx. You're welcome very much. It's from some lawyers down in Pittsburgh. You in legal trouble there, too, Langston?"

"What?" It took my sluggish brain a moment to engage. "No. No! These are my hiring documents. Although I must be nuts to want this job. Five days here, and all I've done is talk to cops."

"So what's with the missing dude? Glatfelter? The cops have any clues?"

"Ask them, Andy." I rubbed my tired eyes. "Look, man, I'm beat. I don't have any idea what happened to the guy, okay? I only saw him that once, when he got out of his car and went into the cemetery."

"What time was that?"

"Close to five." I yawned and started edging around the big man. It was like orbiting Jupiter. "Go talk to Scully and Mulder."

"Oh yeah?" Gluck smirked. "What'd you think of Czerniak? A real prize, that one, huh?"

"Don't answer that!"

I blinked in surprise. Saiera Khosani was marching up, decked out in full postal overcoat and sturdy boots, with an earflap hat clamped over her free-flowing mass of hair.

"Stop trying to trap him, Andy Gluck!" To me, she said, "Anything you say to this guy goes in the paper. You talk smack about the cops, and the next thing you know, it's all"—she blocked out her hands like setting type in the air—"The Cops Are Idiots, Says Langston in big, bold type."

"Heyyy!"

"You know it's true, Gluck," Saiera said. "I'm onto your game. C'mon, Brad. Don't say another word to this clown."

The mail carrier took me by the arm and led me to the office door, where I fumbled out my key and let us inside. Saiera closed the door and twisted the dead bolt. George nearly bowled me over he was so excited, and even Tabitha appeared, stretching and yawning her way toward a greeting.

I slipped a casual glance at Saiera. "Hey, I bought some fresh tea yesterday. Feel like a cup?"

"Smooth, kiddo," said Stan Caputo, who popped into existence at my elbow. I was so tired I didn't even flinch. "'Feel like a cup?' I bet you'd like to feel a cup. About a C-cup, I'd say."

"Sure, that'd be great," Saiera said. "You look beat. Why don't you lie on the sofa? I know where the stuff is. I'll make the tea. Go on, sit, sit, sit."

I let Saiera take charge, all the while ignoring Stan's off-color running commentary. She led me to the sofa, pushed me gently back on it, plumped a throw pillow, and pulled off my shoes. I stretched out, still in my thrift store coat, which smelled faintly of mothballs and mildew. Once I was settled, Saiera bustled off to the kitchen. The furry people followed her, leaving me alone with Stan.

"I'm telling you, kid," Stan said, "play your cards right, you got a good chance of making sweet music with that dame."

"Go away, Stan," I mumbled, one hand tented over my eyes.

"Listen, we gotta problem."

"I don't care."

"There's a new guy. You know. Over there with us."

I popped one eye open and peered at him from under my hand. "Do I need to draw a picture? I. Don't. Care. This place has been nothing but a nightmare since I arrived. Delmont wants the TV on, Mrs. Perry wants the roses trimmed, Mrs. Fairweather wants the weeds cut, Pippah wants to skin me alive, the cops want to put me in jail, my next-door neighbor wants to shoot me on sight... Oh, and that's not even counting the overgrown, ugly mess of work that needs doing to get the grounds—and the finances, by the way—back in shape!" By the end of my tirade, my voice had risen to a near shout.

"What's that?" Saiera called from the kitchen. "Did you say something?"

"Sorry, no," I called back. "Talking to myself!"

"Hey," Stan chirped, "at least you didn't throw me in with all the pests."

I glared at him, my jaw clenched. "No," I hissed, "you only pop in when there's a woman in my place, someone who I might like to get to know a little better, and make snide comments, drop sleazy one-liners, and... and... generally be a pain in the ass!"

"I'm gonna let that pass for now," Stan said stiffly. "You got bigger fish in the pond besides this broad. Listen, this new guy, I don't know who he is, but he didn't end well, y'know?"

I flopped back onto the pillow, covering my eyes with my elbow. "I don't care."

"I bumped into his... ah, call it his energy blob... and all I can make out is screaming. Screaming, screaming, screaming."

"Sounds awful," I commented with an utter lack of interest.

"I can't say for sure, but I think Pippah did him in. I can get the taste of her... call it essence."

"So. What."

"So what? So you need to do something. Go find the guy's re-mains. Give him some peace."

"No."

"No?"

"I'm done playing detective, Stan. Or ghostbuster or spectral cop or anything else but a simple, mild-mannered groundskeeper."

"But what about..."

I sat up and pinned Stan with a pointed finger. "You don't get it, do you? What I want is for you *to just go away!*"

"Oh." Saiera stood in the archway, carrying a pair of steaming mugs. She stood very rigid. "I see. I didn't realize I was such an impo-sition."

Stan had the grace to look embarrassed. He popped out of exis-tence.

"Saiera," I said. "Hell, I'm sorry. Not you. I wasn't talking to you."

She cocked one dark eyebrow and made a point of surveying the room—the *empty* room. "O-o-okay, Brad." Saiera brought the mugs over and set them on the coffee table. "Clearly, you're overtired. You should rest. I need to go anyway and get on with my rounds."

"Saiera, wait. I'm not... I didn't... Do you..." The words slammed to a stop, checked by a sanity cop in the back of my brain, holding up a cautionary hand. *Wait! Don't say it!* The words rushed the barricade and burst out. "Do-you-believe-in-ghosts?"

Saiera stepped back from the table. She crossed her arms, her lips pinched in a frown. "I'm a gypsy. I believe in all kinds of weirdness. Why do you ask?"

It came tumbling out, one long monologue of the past five days, starting with the television turning itself on and covering everything from Stan Caputo, ex-Philly mobster, to Mrs. Perry and her roses. I told her about Pippah and Stan's belief that she was charging up her power to come back to the world and "take revenge." Somewhere during my tale, Saiera settled into the chair across from me. She watched me with veiled eyes from over the rim of her steaming mug. When I got to the part about Consuelo, her inscrutable expression slipped to something else... Sadness? Sympathy? It was hard to say. I finished up my story by relating what Stan had told me.

"Supposedly there's a new, ah, soul hanging out in Shady Terraces. I'm guessing it's Glatfelter's. Stan said the guy was screaming in the afterlife, and he thinks Pippah might have had something to do with it."

"Well," Saiera said after a long moment. "That's... interesting."

"That's what they always say right before they strap you into the straitjacket."

Tabitha was curling around my ankles. I picked her up and set her on my lap and treated her to an ear scratch. She squinted her eyes closed and purred.

"And Consuelo," Saiera said. "She didn't speak at all? Didn't mention who killed her?"

"No." I sighed. "Not a word."

"Oh." Saiera cut her eyes at me from under her brows. "You sound like you might be a little... infatuated. This naked woman shows up, and you say you felt a, ah, connection? I bet I know what kind of connection you felt."

"No, it wasn't like that." The protest sounded lame, even to me. "She just seemed so... I don't know... sad."

"Maybe this Pippah killed her."

I blinked and sat back. "I... never thought of that."

"If she's as dangerous as you think..."

"Yeah."

"And if she did in this other guy, Goldblatt or whatever."

"Glatfelter."

Saiera shrugged with her eyebrows. "It could be this Pippah is more dangerous than you know. She might even have killed Arlo, come to think of it."

"With a shotgun?"

"Hmph. Okay, you have a point. Maybe not Arlo."

Tabitha flopped in my lap and squirmed under my hand, sticking her chin out for a scratch. George had found a spot by Saiera's feet and watched us both with his startling blue eyes. The lamps cast a warm glow on the room, our empty cups rested on the table, and I suddenly got the impression we were sharing a homey, domestic scene from an idealized version of one of my fantasies of a normal life. Just a couple, sharing a moment together, discussing dead people instead of the mortgage.

Perfectly normal.

"We need to find Glatfelter," Saiera said, breaking into my daydream.

"What? We do?"

"We need to know what happened to him. Maybe your guy Stan is full of crap. Maybe nothing happened to the man except he got lost and fell in an open grave, and the snow covered him up."

It occurred to me that Saiera was buying into my tale. She didn't say, *"We need to find a good place where they take care of people with your problem and feed them oatmeal from a plastic spoon."* She was talking about taking action based on my unsupported claims regarding talking ghosts and evil spirits coming back to life.

Her liquid brown eyes met mine. Her brown-sugar skin practically glowed with inner heat. A tumbled mass of midnight hair fell around her shoulders. A strange feeling flushed through my nervous system, and I was seized by an overwhelming desire to lean across the table and kiss Saiera on her full, ripe lips.

That was, of course, when Tabitha dug her claws in and started milk-treading my crotch.

"Ow, you beast. Stop that."

Saiera jumped up, patted her uniform, and straightened her slacks. "I-I have a flashlight in my bag. Do you have one? A light, I mean."

"What? You want to go look now? It's full-on dark outside."

"C'mon," she said with an impish grin. "Let's take a stroll in the cemetery."

"In the freezing cold."

"Under the moonlight."

"Looking for a dead body."

"It'll be romantic."

Well. Okay, then. "Let's do it."

Chapter 18

"If this is your idea of romantic..." I didn't have a good ending to the sentence, so I let it trail off. Besides, it was hard enough to keep my teeth from chattering, and talking only made it harder. Saiera and I had been prowling the graveyard for over an hour and had turned up no sign of Donald Glatfelter. On the other hand, Mrs. Perry had shown up about halfway through our search and started berating me about the roses. She paused in her tirade long enough to appraise both Saiera and I as we clomped along yet another snowy trail deep in the Shady Terraces grounds.

"I think it's very romantic," Mrs. Perry said. "Both of you together, investigating a mystery. You make a very handsome couple, if I say so myself."

"Thank you, Mrs. Perry."

"What did she say?" Saiera asked me. I had given up trying to hide my conversation with Mrs. Perry's ghost and had been playing interpreter between Saiera and the much older, and much more dead, woman.

"She says we should go inside and get warm," I said. "Before we catch our death of cold. And snuggling under a blanket would help."

Mrs. Perry narrowed her eyes and shook a finger at me. "Don't be dishonest, young man. It doesn't become you."

"Sorry, ma'am."

Saiera huddled in her post office coat, and her breath plumed silver under the nickel-bright half-moon hanging overhead. Snow camouflaged the black earth with white patches and drifted into ramps against the headstones. My hiking boots had long since lost any claim to water-repellent properties and were soaked from toe to ankle. My toes were stuck together like a tray of ice cubes.

"She's right about one thing," Saiera admitted. "I'm about done graveyarding for one night."

I turned in a circle to get my bearings. "Uh, Mrs. Perry? Which way is the office from here?"

"Follow this footpath," she said, "then take the next two rights, and you will reach a walkway. Turn left there."

"Thank you, Mrs. Perry," I said. "When the weather turns a bit better, I promise you I'll get on the roses. I checked out some books on rose maintenance, so I'll study up on how to do it right."

"Books," the old lady said with a sniff. "You'll never learn rose care from books, Mr. Langston."

"Well, I hope you'll show me what you know as well."

Mrs. Perry straightened and seemed happy for the first time since I'd met her. "Count on it, young man. Count on it." Her face took on an impish expression, and she leaned in to confide, "You bring this young lady of yours around again, and I'll teach you a few tricks about how to stroke her petals as well!" With that, Mrs. Perry disappeared, leaving a hint of a happy giggle lingering in the air.

"What did she say?" Saiera asked.

"This way." I led off at a fast walk, happy the darkness concealed the heat flushing my face. *Now I'm getting sex advice from grandmas? Does everybody think I need help with my love life?*

We walked for a time in companionable silence, our flashlights crisscrossing beams of silver dancing along the path. I noticed the top of Saiera's head was almost at eye level. She walked close by my side, close enough our shoulders brushed at times. It would be very easy to slip an arm around her. Is that what she wanted? Was I missing a hint? Was she giving off one of those social cues women believed so obvious yet remained so indecipherable for guys—in particular, guys like me, to whom social cues were a mystery written in hieroglyphics using invisible ink? Or would I get slapped across the face if I tried it?

Better not risk it.

My hands stayed firmly in my coat pockets, fingering bits of lint.

I cleared my throat and asked a question that had been bugging me all evening. "So how come you haven't called the loony bin to have me admitted? You seem to be accepting my ghost stories at face value."

Saiera made a *brrr* noise and linked her arm with mine. She leaned into me, and I swear I felt the swell of her breast through my coat, her coat, and numerous layers of clothing. I forgot to breathe for a moment.

"Hmm." She grimaced a tiny bit. "Honest question deserves an honest answer. Remember I mentioned that I was a Roma, right? A gypsy. What I did not tell you is that I come from a long line of *chovihani...* witches. I know from experience there is more mystery on this Earth than there is understanding. Science is a process, not an end product, and though you *Gorgio* have practiced science for many centuries, the Roma have practiced witchcraft for far longer."

We were on the main path back to the office. I noted several familiar landmarks that placed us a few minutes away from shelter, tea, and a roaring space heater. I needed all three to get the chill out of my bones. First, ghosts. Now, a witch. What would I get tomorrow? A werewolf? A vampire?

Saiera's head snapped up. She stopped, focused on something to her right, on her side of the trail. She asked, "Did you see that?"

"See what?" I paused and peered into the dimness.

"I thought I saw a flash from over there." She pointed approximately northward, more or less in the direction of the parking lot, as the crow flies. "A green flash of light."

"That can't be good. I saw green light when Pippah appeared."

"Let's go take a look."

"Let's not."

She tugged me with the arm hooked through mine, and I could either let go that connection or come with her.

I went with her.

We crossed row after row of grave markers and traipsed over the brow of a small hill. A pair of twisted oaks grew on the far side of the hill, one farther away than the other. Our flashlights' beams fluttered around, revealing patches of illumination like scenes from a wobbly movie camera. Dead, bare branches laced with ice. White granite markers poking from crystalline snow. Black soil and sprays of unruly brush. A pair of human feet, dangling in midair...

Saiera shrieked.

I choked out a horrified sound of my own.

Our beams of light swung together, focusing on where the brief glimpse of suspended feet had appeared.

I had seen dead bodies before. One, in particular, haunted my days and nights with regularity—a charred and brittle corpse that retained only a small resemblance to something once human. But beyond that instance, I had seen others who had passed, including a woman dead in a car crash that happened right in front of me when I was twenty. And I had walked into the laundry room of a college dormitory and found a student—unknown to me—who had overdosed on a bad cocktail of cocaine and crystal meth. In all, I had seen more dead people than I ever cared to. Though come to think on it, maybe that was what gave me the ability to see and speak with the spectral remains of the denizens of Shady Terraces. Like the characters in the Harry Potter series, maybe my special heritage allowed me to see things others couldn't. Sure, and pigs can fly to Mars if you give 'em rocket ships. Whatever.

I had seen dead bodies. That was the point.

But never one like this.

Donald K. Glatfelter hung from the lowest bough of a winter-black oak, the one closest to us. He was nude. Things... had been done to him. The rope used to hang him—

"Is that his..." Saiera whispered.

"Intestines, yeah." My voice croaked as if it was clogged with barbed wire.

Saiera gulped convulsively. A moment later, she had turned away, retching. That triggered my own bout of nausea. When we were done, Saiera and I exchanged a look, both of us bent over, hands on knees.

"Who..." she started then grimaced and spat some gunk out and tried again. "Who could have done this?"

"We searched this area earlier today. With the cops. I remember seeing that." I pointed at a grave marker featuring a lamb with a missing head resting atop the double-wide stone—a family plot. Simpkins, if I recalled correctly. "There was nobody hanging around then. Ouch. Sorry."

"So how did he get here?"

Pippah.

The damage done to the body was... horrific. Stan had mentioned a new soul in the afterlife, one who wouldn't quit screaming. Saiera had seen a green light flare, which led us to the corpse.

"It's Pippah," I said. "She wants us to see this. She's making some kind of statement."

"Brad..." Saiera drew out my name. Her tone conveyed a lot, such as *Believing in your imaginary ghosts was cute when they were just part of your quirky personality disorder, but this is a whole new level of crazy shit right here.*

At least, that was what I thought she was saying.

"I know. But Stan said she's getting stronger. Learning control."

"You also mentioned something about not hurting the living. You said that. I remember you saying that."

"I took the word of a guy who's been dead for eighty years," I said. "May not be the most reliable source."

"What're we going to do?"

"Ah hell. I guess I'm going to have to call the cops."

"Oh no."

"Oh yeah."

"They won't be happy with you."

"Probably not." I winced, picturing another long session with Czerniak and Swanson. They had covered every detail of my life, from conception through the last bowel movement. They had called my old bosses, verifying my whereabouts for the last six years. Adding a new corpse to their workload would make them dive ten times deeper.

"But that's not what I meant," Saiera said. "I meant, what are we going to do about Pippah? If she's really getting stronger, strong enough to... to do this..." She gestured vaguely toward the body. Neither one of us had looked directly at it since that first, horrified inspection. Glatfelter remained an object half-observed in our peripheral vision. "We have to do something about her. What if she... I don't know... *manifests*... and you're the next one she snaps up?"

"That would be bad."

"You *think*?"

"Know any good exorcists?"

Saiera compressed her lips and shook her head, then her eyes popped open wide. "Hey! What if she was the one who killed your girlfriend? Consuelo? And maybe Arlo?"

"You said it yourself: evil spirits don't use shotguns."

"Oh. Right."

"And she wasn't my girlfriend."

"You sure?" Saiera's pale, drawn expression brightened a little. "You got pretty dreamy-eyed when you were describing her, bucko. Made me jealous."

I pulled out my cell phone and checked the signal. "I have bars," I said. "I'll make the call—Wait, what? Jealous?"

"Focus, Brad. Focus."

CZERNIAK AND SWANSON were two very angry detectives. They separated Saiera from me, and Czerniak escorted me to an interrogation room. Before he could draw breath to start hammering me with questions, I spoke up.

"I want to call my lawyer."

"You?" His face twisted in disbelief. "You have a lawyer?"

"Yes." At least, I hoped I did. Maurice Chesterfield might decide his new employee was more trouble than he was worth and wash his hands of me without thinking twice. Then it would be a Pottsville public defender between me and the noose. "And I want to call him. I, uh, invoke my right to counsel."

Czerniak waved at me like I was a bad stink and left the room. I pulled up Chesterfield's contact info on my phone and selected his cell number. It was after nine p.m. *Please don't be asleep already.*

"Hello." The deep voice sounded loud in my ear. "Mr. Langston? How can I help you?"

I poured out my version of the events from past two days, starting with the discovery of Consuelo's remains. I carefully censored all mention of ghosts, demons, and spectral appearances. Bringing the supernatural into the conversation seemed the least likely way to convince my new boss I was Employee of the Month material. Chesterfield listened as I babbled, jarring me back on track with an astute question when I wandered too far down a rabbit hole.

"I see," he said when I finished bringing him up to speed with current events. "Please call the detective back into the room and put me on speaker phone."

Czerniak answered my pounding on the door so fast I suspected he may have been listening all along. I sat back at the interview table, placed my phone on the middle of the scarred surface, and performed introductions. Chesterfield's voice rolled out, deep and confident and sure.

"Detective Czerniak, has the coroner ruled on cause of death in Ms. Espinoza's case?"

"Uh... no, not yet. But we're betting on murder."

"Please tell me the Pottsville Police doesn't arrest suspects on the basis of a gamble."

"No, but—"

"Have you confirmed my client was employed at the Snack'n'Shack in Mount Laurel, New Jersey, from May through December of last year, during the time in which it is presumed Ms. Espinoza lost her life."

"I have, but—"

"Have you any evidence linking my client with Ms. Espinoza, except that he discovered the poor girl's remains?"

"His prints are all over her handbag." Czerniak glared at me when he said this.

"Which would be because he found the bag and picked it up then examined the contents to determine ownership, correct?"

"Yes, but—"

"Did you substantiate my client's whereabouts during the time Mr. Glatfelter attended the graveyard?"

Czerniak pounced on that opening. "He could have done it. Langston here doesn't show up at the GetConnected store until 5:06, according to the security cameras. Glatfelter's wife says her old man went to the cemetery around 4:30."

"How long is the drive? Between Glatfelter's home and Shady Terraces?"

"Excuse me?"

Chesterfield sighed gently. I could picture his expression as one where a kindly but disappointed father speaks to a child having difficulty understanding simple math. "How long would it have taken Mr. Glatfelter to have driven his motor vehicle"—he actually said *motor vehicle*—"from his home to the cemetery? I assume you've driven the route and clocked the time yourself."

"Oh... uh... sure. About ten minutes, give or take."

"And what was the condition of Mr. Glatfelter's body when discovered?"

"I see where you're going with this," Czerniak said. His face had grown steadily redder, as though he was an empty pot left on the stove to overheat. "And Langston could have knocked our victim out cold then come back and finished him off later that night. He had all kinds of time between when he left the last place he was seen and we came looking for Glatfelter."

"And where was the body when you and your vigilant and well-trained officers searched the cemetery?"

Czerniak shot me a dirty look. "He must have hid it somewhere."

"And at what point did he remove the body from its hiding place, drag it to a tree, and hoist the poor man up by his own entrails? And I presume you found the drag marks from where the deceased was brought from his hiding spot to the tree?"

"Well—"

"I understand my client was in police custody from the end of the search until four p.m. then was in the company of a member of the US Postal Service from then until the body was discovered."

"They could've done it together."

"Excuse me?"

Czerniak's face was as red as a boiled lobster, and sweat beaded on his forehead. "They could've been in on it together. Him and the gypsy."

Chesterfield allowed the silence to grow. I kept perfectly still and didn't say a word, for once mastering my tendency to blurt out the first stupid thing that came into my head.

"What was the condition of their clothes?" Chesterfield asked at last.

"Their what?"

"Their clothes, detective." Chesterfield leaned on the word, strongly suggesting Czerniak's detecting ability lacked an ability to detect his own ass with both hands and a full-length mirror. "One would presume that after eviscerating a man and stringing him up in a tree, one would be covered with blood and other tissue from such grisly work."

Czerniak gave me a once-over, clearly wishing he could shoot me in the face and call it attempted escape. "They... they could've cleaned up."

"So my client and Ms. Khosani, who met less than a week ago, have embarked on a murder plan together, whereby they manage to render Mr. Glatfelter unconscious, torture him, murder him, hang him in a very public location, wash up, do their laundry, and then report the discovery of the body to the police. Is that your working theory?" A pause. "Detective?"

"All I have right now," Czerniak admitted, "is a bunch of questions. And your client is in the middle of lot of dead bodies all of a sudden."

Because I work in a graveyard, I wanted to say. I rubbed my cheeks to cover the inappropriate grin that threatened to stoke Czerniak's suspicion. Flippant humor would be the death of me yet.

Chesterfield and Czerniak went back and forth for a while longer. I tuned out because it was apparent to everyone in the room that the detective had lost the initiative. He was outmatched, out-gunned, and outmaneuvered at every turn. At that moment, I wanted nothing more than to grow up and be Maurice Chesterfield. *Should I ask him to adopt me now or wait for a better time?*

I relaxed for the first time since the cops had pounded on my door and woken me from a sound sleep. Assuming I could get back to bed soon, maybe I could pack in a few hours of steady z's, get up, and have a solid breakfast before getting back to work.

After all, I had a cemetery to take care of, and those roses wouldn't trim themselves.

Something Czerniak said tripped me out of my caretaker daydreams.

"Wait," I said. "What did you just say? About Saiera? She went to Syracuse?"

The detective narrowed his eyes at me, inspecting me like a bug he wanted to squash. "What? Are you saying you didn't know that your little post office cutie went to Syracuse University at the same time as Maria del Whosis Espinoza?"

"Are you serious?"

Czerniak chuckled. "Yeah, buddy, I'm dead serious. Which makes me wonder how far back this little conspiracy of yours goes. Tell me, you ever take any classes in Albany, Langston?"

"Me? No," I muttered. My mind circled this new revelation like a dog snarling at a snake in the grass. I spoke aloud from habit more than intention. "Two years at Virginia Tech, two years at Norfolk State, and about five semesters at UV Wise."

"So you're saying you never been to Syracuse University," Czerniak said. "Or Albany neither."

"No, never," I answered on remote control, thinking about something Consuelo's mother had said in her instant message. *"When she left for college, Chelita said something about seeing a friend. Near Pittsburgh. I didn't pay attention to where. Or who."*

Saiera Khosani? Was that the friend Consuelo had stopped off to see? Saiera Khosani, who happened to be very interested in all the police activity around the discovery of Consuelo's body. And, come to think of it, who happened to lead me by the arm right to the corpse of Donald Glatfelter.

I was lost in my own thoughts for a bit, vaguely aware of the droning discussion between Chesterfield and Czerniak. I only came back to reality when Czerniak pushed back in his chair and said, "Okay, Langston. You can go. If you want to wait a bit, I'll have an officer drive you and your girlfriend back to the cemetery."

I swallowed something dry and fuzzy that wanted to stick in my throat. "Um, no. That's okay. I think I'll take a Lyft if it's all the same to you."

Chapter 19

October 21st. Day Six.

I made it home without incident, slept without interruption, and woke feeling human again. Daylight brightened the windows, and a quick check of the weather forecast gave me hope that the rest of the day would be warmer and full of sunshine. I showered, stuffed myself full of oatmeal and coffee, and took care of the fur people. I packed a lunch for later and carried it outside.

When I opened the shed's double doors, musty, weedy smells puffed out. I hauled the riding mower into the sunlight by brute force. I drained the old gas and replaced it with fresh then checked the oil, which needed changing. The blade needed sharpening, too, but as I only wanted the little tractor to haul myself and my gear to the back forty, I could ignore the oil change and dull blade for the time being. Arlo had attached the battery to a trickle charger. It took a few minutes to get it hooked back into place.

The engine fired up on first crank. I hitched the small trailer to the back of the mini tractor and loaded it with tools, including an eighteen-inch Stihl chain saw. Fortunately, the saw teeth of the chain seemed damned sharp, based on my fingertip test. I sucked the blood drop off and carried on gathering bits and bobs. I filled two sprayer jugs with water and added those to the trailer.

In my digging around for tools, I stumbled over a stack of charcoal briquettes in ten-pound bags. Next to those, I found an old coal bin, full to the top with dusty chunks of black anthracite, probably left over from the days when heaters were fueled by the stuff. The black gunk coated me the second I picked up a chunk. I threw it back and closed the bin.

When I had a load ready, I whistled for George. The black-and-white husky wanted nothing to do with the chugging mower and elected to range along behind me, barking his opinion about Brad riding on a smelly, loud, strange roar monster.

I puttered my way to the thicket.

A low, early-morning sun shot through the wet snarl of underbrush. Snowmelt dripped from the overhanging canopy of bare limbs. The police tape was gone. Nothing remained of Consuelo except my memory of her ghost. The enigmatic curl of her lips haunted me even though I knew she was gone—and gone for real this time.

The tangle of twisted trees, fallen branches, and choking brush offended me. Consuelo had been left in there to rot, just another discarded piece of trash in a world full of cast-off containers, disposable packaging, and single-use plastics. She had been a person—a living, breathing, vital young woman going to college and breaking out into the world at the dawn of her life. Then somebody killed her and threw her away, leaving her to the elements like a windblown plastic bag. The thicket where her undiscovered body had laid for so long angered me. I couldn't define why, exactly, I wanted to clean it out, but I knew I was going to do it. Maybe I would erect a shrine in amongst the trees once I'd converted the twisted mess into more of a glade-like setting, one of those crosses with flowers like people put up beside the road where someone died.

I fired up the chain saw and got to work on building a brush pile.

The trick to a controlled brush burn was to find an open area, surrounded by bare earth or mowed grass, and build a long, low pile of material. Don't build a bonfire, in other words. With the ground saturated by melted snow, I wasn't too worried about the fire spreading. Just the same, I chose a spot well away from the trees and downwind of the mild breeze to prevent any possible sparks from spreading my fire. I didn't want to burn down the thicket, just clear it out.

I managed to avoid dropping trees on any obvious graves. Double bonus points for Brad. Chain saw skills.

By noon, I had the first pile of brush aflame. Wet wood not only kept the fire danger down, it created a hell of a lot of smoke. I took a break, sitting on my riding mower and eating my lunch while George roamed around the burning brush in a wide circle, snapping at the smoke.

I was a bit surprised no one from the ghostly community showed up to offer advice, kibbutz, or otherwise tell me what to do. Maybe they didn't like chain saws and fire. *Huh. Make a note of that. Next time Pippah shows up, I'll go all* Texas Chainsaw Massacre *on her. Show her who's the baddest creep in the valley.*

I got back to work. At one point, I motored back to the shed and retrieved a length of chain, which I hauled back and used to drag out fallen logs that were too big to carry. With some fancy driving, I managed to pull the limbs onto the smoldering coals of my fire. Each chunk burned filled me with satisfaction.

It was late afternoon by the time I cleared enough ground to tackle the limb that had fallen across the back wall. The temperature had stayed mild, melting all but the most stubborn patches of snow. I was stripped down to my shirt and jeans, which worked fine except when the breeze kicked up and chilled the dampness soaking my clothes.

I backed the mower into the thicket and brought the tail up close to the monster limb that lay across the broken section of wall. I fired up the chain saw and began lopping off secondary branches that might snag as I towed the behemoth out to my brush pile.

A figure caught my eye as I clambered around the big limb. I paused and shaded my eyes for a better look. Vic Tarwater stood in his field, a good hundred yards away, still as a scarecrow. An armed scarecrow, at that. He held his trusty shotgun over his shoulder, as if he were a Queen's Guard standing duty at Buckingham Palace.

"You should be happy, you old coot," I said under my breath. "I'm getting this mess off your property." I tossed him a jaunty salute and went about my business.

When the limb was as trim as I could reasonably make it, I looped my chain three turns around the ragged butt and hooked it up to the mower's hitch. The base of the tree that had dropped the limb was going to be a problem, as it partially blocked the path I would need to drag the broken limb. There was a good chance it would hang up on the mothership as I tried to drag it from the breech in the brick wall. I fired up the little tractor and engaged low gear. The chain tightened, and the limb shifted half a foot, crackling and groaning in protest. A foot. Two feet... and stopped. The mower bucked and clawed for traction, digging ruts in the soft earth, but the monster refused to budge. I killed the engine before I bogged my rear wheels so deep I'd be stuck.

"Okay, then," I said in resignation. "Looks like I'll have to cut you up into small bites."

I climbed off the tractor and hefted the chain saw with tired, protesting muscles. I would pay for this much exertion tomorrow when I tried getting out of bed. This was more exercise than I had done in many months. But I had to say it—the hard work made me feel good. I was accomplishing something, seeing the result of my labor, and pride infused my aching muscles with a powerful dose of painkiller.

The limb had shifted, scraping across the debris from the fallen wall, like a kid's toe scuffing up loose gravel in a playground. A bit of bright orange, so unlike a natural color of the surrounding detritus, caught my eye. I bent to pick it up.

It was a cell phone.

My heart double pumped when I read a logo on the phone's protective shell cover: Syracuse, in stylized font. Go Orange, in smaller text below.

I shivered as if I'd touched a live wire.

Of course the battery would have long run out. The screen was wet, beaded with moisture. I wiped it off, and some cloudiness remained though I saw that it had a screen protector covering it, so maybe the moisture hadn't penetrated to the electronics. It was a different make than mine, so I would have to buy a charger to power it up.

A passing thought of turning it in to the police crossed my mind. *Here, Czerniak, look what else I found.*

Oh, you just happened to find that, did ya? And how'd you know where to look, huh?

"Screw that," I said aloud.

No. I was keeping this piece of Consuelo Espinoza to myself. There could be tons of evidence on it. Contacts, text messages, photos. A thousand things might point toward her killer. I had a queasy moment when the thought crossed my mind the killer's fingerprints may have been ruined by my handling the phone. But no. Fingerprints wouldn't have lasted through fifteen months of exposure to the elements. There was a strong chance the phone would be dead and gone forever, its only value being a possession once held by my ghost girlfriend.

Does it count as a date if you meet them as a spectral being?

Regardless, I was keeping the phone.

I pocketed the device and looked up. Across the field, Vic Tarwater remained vigilant, watching me with his hooded eyes.

OCTOBER 22ND, DAY SEVEN

I slept like the dead, woke up late, and felt like a hanging side of raw beef. I pushed through the muscle soreness with a hot shower, ate some toast, and was out the door by nine forty-five. A fluttering note stuck in the mail slot caught my eye on the way out, and I had a bad moment, thinking Saiera might have written a "Screw you, jerk" message. I unfolded it and read, "Brad, Sorry we missed you. We'll come back tomorrow at 1:00 p.m. Anna and Sal Espinoza. (Chelita's parents)"

Ah hell. I had forgotten all about the Espinozas coming yesterday and Consuelo's mother asking to see the place where her daughter had been found.

I touched the phone in my pocket and felt guilt seeping out of the hard plastic and soaking into my heart. The phone belonged to the Espinozas. I had no right to keep it and less justification to try to break into it. It was selfish of me to hang on to this piece of Consuelo's memory. I pulled the phone from my pocket and looked at it again. I had removed the cover and screen protector and left the phone buried in a box of rice overnight, which I'd read was a way to dehumidify electronics when inadvertently soaked. The screen was still cloudy though maybe a little less than when I found it. Or was that just wishful thinking? Would it power up when charged? Could I break through the password even if it did power up? The answers to those questions were *unlikely* and *probably not* and *are you a complete moron?*

I slid the phone back in my pocket.

SINCE ADDY HAD MENTIONED she worked nights at the GetConnected store, I waited until after dark to make my appearance there. The doorbell chimed, and the pale girl looked up from a magazine spread open on the counter.

"Oh. Hey," she said.

"Hey back." A feather tickled my heart. Something about the tiny emo girl drew me the way a bug light attracted moths. Okay, bad analogy, but still... "I need a charger. To fit this."

Addy glanced up then did a double take when she saw the phone. "That's not yours!" She flinched and changed her tone from accusing to apologetic. "I mean, you had a prepaid last time I saw you."

"Yeah, I found this in the graveyard. It's been out there a while. I'm going to charge it up, see if I can figure out who it belongs to."

"Oh. Okay."

"Say, do you know a way around the password?"

Addy flashed me an inscrutable look from under her bangs. "You mean the secret factory default technique they teach us in training so we can crack lost phones and find their owners?"

"Uhh... there is no such thing, right?"

"Are you kidding me?" Addy snorted. "Even the FBI can't break the encryption on these things. Although... I could..." She tapped her chin with a finger, one arm propped by the other.

"What?" I prompted.

"I could call my hacker friend at the NSA," she told me. "The guy I just happen to know who's an expert at breaking smartphone encryption and who's willing to violate all kinds of federal statutes to help me out because I'm so irresistibly sexy and he's had a secret crush on me since we grew up in the creche together back in Romania."

I looked at her. She looked at me.

"You're totally making that up, right?" I said.

"Totes."

"For someone so irresistibly sexy," I told her, my face set to neutral to keep the innuendo out of it, "you're very cruel, you know that?"

Addy ducked her head again, treating me to a view of her curly, brown hair. "You still want that charger?"

"Sure," I said. "It may not even come on, so..."

"Yeah. Over here." Addy pointed to a four-way rack in the corner of the store, pegged out with all kinds of accessories. She picked one off and handed it to me without meeting my eyes. "These are the best for the money. We have some cheaper ones, but I don't trust them. Although if the phone doesn't work anyway..."

"No, this is fine." I smiled at the top of her head. "I trust your judgment."

"You could leave it here," she said. "If you want."

"Excuse me?"

"We have a service." Addy motioned to a sign hanging on the back wall. "For phone repair. I can take it, dry it out, change the battery... things like that."

"Call your hacker buddy? Crack the password?"

The hint of a smile flashed from under her bangs. "Sure. No extra charge for that."

I rubbed the smooth surface of the phone, which was once again safely tucked in my pocket. Addy's offer had merit, I had to admit. A professional restoration job might make the difference between a working phone and a paperweight. Change the battery? Dry out the insides properly? I could do neither of those things. And yet... in a way I couldn't articulate, even to myself, I felt uneasy about entrusting Consuelo's phone to someone else.

"Nah," I said after an awkward pause. "Let me give it a try. If I can't make it work, I can bring it back in and pay you to do it."

"No worries." Addy shrugged, her face hidden behind her bangs. She rang me up, took my money, and handed me my change. "And I'm sorry. About the other day. My dad."

"Oh. Yeah. He's... intense."

Addy rolled her eyes. "Intense. That's one way to describe it. I would say, 'wrapped so tight bacteria can't even get in.'"

"You know, he fired off a shot at me the other day. Scared my dog... which, I have to admit, is no great trick. But still... what's his deal, anyway?"

"The paranoia runs deep in this one." Addy intoned in a deep voice then continued normally, "He and Arlo never got along, and he's always been, ah, overprotective of me. I have xeroderma pigmentosum, which means any UV light can burn me instantly. I haven't been able to go out in the sun for... a long time." She held up a hand as I opened my mouth for a quip about vampires. "Please. Spare me the vampire jokes, okay?"

"Never crossed my mind."

"My father... He is crazy overprotective of me because of it. Of course he knows..." Her eyes lost focus for a second, and I could tell her thoughts had strayed far afield.

"Knows what?" I prompted, but Addy shook me off.

"Huh? Oh. Nothing, sorry. Don't mind me. Here's your charger." She handed me a yellow plastic sack emblazoned with the store's logo—a stylized phone outlined by a power plug. "Good luck with the dead. Phone, I mean."

"Ha. Maybe I can use it to talk to the dearly departed."

"If you do, find out if they have sunlight. There on the other side."

I smiled my thanks and left.

A jangling ringtone warbled, and I froze in the doorway, thinking somehow Consuelo's phone had come back to life. It took me a second to realize the sound and vibration emanated from a different pocket, and it was my phone ringing, not hers.

"Hello?"

"Good news, Mr. Langston," said Maurice Chesterfield. "I have secured agreement from the board to fund some capital improvements. The amount is not yet specified, but I should be able to lock down a sufficient amount to cover many of the repairs we discussed."

"Ahh, that's great news."

"I do, however, need your estimates... You were going to draw me up a list?"

"Oh." *As in, Oh look, Brad screwed up again.* "Yeah, sorry about that. I've been a little... preoccupied."

"Indeed," Chesterfield said, though, miracle of miracles, he didn't sound pissed. "Please endeavor to avoid any more free-range cadavers on the premises. Nonpaying guests are not allowed."

"Riiight." *Next time I find a murder victim, I should charge them rent?*

"That was a joke, Mr. Langston."

I chuckled dutifully. "Good one, Mr. C. I'll do the list tonight and tomorrow. Call a couple of contractors about the wall and get some estimates."

"Excellent. Thank you, Mr. Langston," Chesterfield said and ended the call.

Well, that's some good news for a change.

Things might be turning around for me. Finally, I might get to make a real difference somewhere. Make some improvements rather than just working for a time and moving on, leaving nothing to show for it but some hard-earned experience. All I had to do was stay out of jail and avoid being sliced to hamburger by a vengeful spirit.

I touched Consuelo's phone in my pocket.

Oh yeah, and hopefully solve a murder somewhere along the way.

Chapter 20

October 26th. Day Eleven

The next three days passed in a blur of activity. Brad in hyperdrive. I made up a sign for the front door that said "On the grounds. If you need help, please call my cell phone" and listed the number in big block print. Nobody called, and nobody bothered me. If the Espinozas came by, they didn't call or leave any kind of message. Hopefully, they'd given up the idea of seeing where I'd found their daughter's remains, especially considering how I had transformed the thicket into something much less... thickety.

The fourth day after my trip to GetConnected for a new charger was a Sunday. A brilliant bright-blue sky capped the world from horizon to horizon, and the weather app promised a high near sixty. Visitors trooped through the gates in dribbles and spurts, dressed in their church clothes and carrying everything from flower arrangements to small American flags. More people arrived in one hour that Sunday afternoon than I had seen in my previous eleven days at Shady Terraces. I wanted to believe the uptick in attendance had to do with my miraculous transformation of the grounds, but that transformation had barely begun.

On Wednesday afternoon, I left Consuelo's phone on the desk, plugged into the new charger, then tackled the list of capital improvements Chesterfield had requested. The rest of that day saw me looking up contractors, arranging for estimates, and jumping into the office organization. Delmont showed up that night, but I was too tired to do more than wave on my way to the bedroom.

Thursday and Friday found me out on the grounds. I started new burn piles, mowed down weeds, sawed up and dragged off dead tree limbs, clipped rose canes—under the supervision of Mrs. Perry—and treated my thorn injuries with antibiotic ointment and Band-Aids.

Thursday morning, I tried powering up Consuelo's phone. Nothing. No go. I left it on the charger.

Late Friday, Chesterfield released some funds, so Saturday, I drove to the office store at the edge of town and splurged on a new laptop computer with a docking station, monitor, printer, and other peripherals. I toured the aisles and loaded my cart with everything from highlighters to a dry-erase board.

Paper clips and thumbtacks and Post-it Notes, oh my.

Saturday afternoon was devoted to installing my new gear and transforming the office. Tabitha helped. She chased down errant bits of paper and slapped them to the ground, explored empty boxes and made them her own, then discovered the new computer's keyboard and walked on it, her tail brushing my nose and making me sneeze.

Stan Caputo offered advice from the corner.

Mrs. Fairweather appeared, wanting to know when I would stop fooling around and get back to trimming the weeds.

Delmont showed up and wanted the channel changed.

George barked and ran in circles, adding to the fun.

Saiera did not stop by for a visit. For three days, I found the mail pushed through the slot, and I didn't know how I felt about that. Was she avoiding me because the last time we were together, the experience verged on the traumatic? Or was it more likely she was mad that I left her at the police station without explanation?

And how did I feel about her? I was decidedly nervous that she had a connection to Syracuse University and possibly knew Consuelo and possibly had been the "friend" Consuelo was intent on seeing north of Pittsburgh. As the days passed and Saiera made herself scarce, I was by turns relieved and disappointed.

At breakfast, I declared Sunday a day of rest. Tabitha yawned and stretched, much as if saying, "So? What's new?"

The three of us spent the morning at leisure, me catching up on my personal email—the new laptop rocked!—and the furry people finding new ways to knock things over.

George and I went for a predinner walk. I nodded to a family of four who were the last to leave the grounds. I paused while George absorbed a serious amount of kid-love from the two children while the parents added in a few pats of their own.

George and I ventured a long stretch southward on Orchard as darkness crept in from the corners and swallowed the sky. An early moon, three-quarters full, painted diamonds on glistening black pavement.

I U-turned and headed back north, unconsciously following the path I had taken the last Sunday. I had no intention of walking as far as Tarwater's place and in fact was about to whistle George back to turn around when I noticed a solitary figure standing at the gate to the abandoned property. It took me a moment to recognize Addy Tarwater as she was wearing a "church" dress under a waist-length, sheepskin-lined jacket and not her GetConnected yellow shirt. Low-heeled pumps had replaced her running shoes.

When I said, "Hey," she jumped like a startled deer.

"Oh, wow," she said, "I didn't hear you come up. Oh, who's this?"

"George, meet Addy. Addy, George."

The dog lost no time throwing himself at her feet and groveling for love. I wondered if that would work for me. If I flopped on my back, would she rub my tummy? I managed to hold on to my dignity. Addy scratched his ruff and made a fuss over him.

I leaned against the gate and frowned at the twin tracks leading toward the house and outbuildings, all of which had disappeared into a black hole of vegetation.

"Who does this belong to?"

"It used to be the Hixtons," Addy said while fending off forty pounds of husky trying to climb into her arms. "I don't know now. The bank owns it, I suppose."

"What happened to the Hixtons?"

"Moved away a long time ago. When I was a kid. I sorta remember playing with their kids. They had a trampoline."

I tugged at the lock securing the gate. The ironwork and fittings on the swinging metal gate showed signs of heavy rust and neglect, but the lock—

"Huh," I muttered.

"What?"

"This lock is nearly new."

"Hm." Addy barely glanced at it. "The bank probably put a new one on. Maybe they changed property managers or whatever. Or maybe they lost the key and had to replace it."

George gave up on his quest to become Addy's best friend forever. He nosed the ground in a widening circle and sniffed things at random then peed on a fencepost.

Addy laughed. "You should be glad that fence is not electric, George."

"Ow." I winced.

"Any luck with that phone?"

"What phone? Oh! No, dead as a doorknob."

"Bring it into the shop," Addy suggested. "Maybe I can breathe life back into it."

We talked as George wandered. I learned Addy was a *World of Warcraft* player and liked strawberry ice cream on pancakes. She had lived under her father's thumb in the same house they currently occupied until she went away to college, then for reasons she couldn't explain, she came back to Pottsville after earning a degree in comp sci. She had worked in the GetConnected store for two years.

"Where'd you go to school?"

"Pitt." She lifted a fist and deadpanned a fake cheer. "Go Panthers. Yay."

Something I hadn't realized was tight in my chest relaxed a notch. *Not Syracuse. Okay, good to know.* "A BS in comp sci and you're working in a phone store?" Not the most tactful thing in the world to say, so I tried to amend it with, "I mean, it seems like a waste of your skills, you know?"

"I know." Addy examined her shoe tops. Softly, she said, "That's what..."

"What what?" I prompted after a pause.

"Nothing." Addy held back the mass of curly hair hiding her face and squinted up at me. A smile tugged at her lips. "What about you? Cemetery caretaker? What, the guidance counselor couldn't find you a job in as a sheepherder? Or milking cows?"

"Umm."

"Checkmate." Addy smiled then looked away. "Sometimes, we all settle for what's convenient instead of what's right. Hey, you might want to call your dog back. It's not safe over there."

George had ducked under the fence and was roaming the Hixton property, visible only by rare flashes of his black-and-white tail as he crossed under moonbeams. He seemed fine though I suspected he had managed to cover himself in mud and leaves and burrs and Brad-killing ticks. George was a muck magnet and could get dirty faster than a four-year-old in Sunday clothes.

"What's not safe about it?" I asked.

"It's just... Ah, there's all kinds of farm equipment and things out there. Hidden by the tall grass. I'm worried he'll get hurt. Best to call him back. Please?"

I shrugged. "Sure, no problem. Just don't mention the word *bath* where he can hear you."

George ignored my whistle and disappeared into the brush near the run-down buildings. My cheeks heated a bit. Nobody liked having their dog ignore them in front of others though I'm not sure why.

"He must have his nose into something interesting. George! C'mon!" I whistled again. "Oh hell. I'd better go get him."

"No, wait," Addy said when I made to climb over the fence. She put two fingers in her mouth and shrilled a whistle that pierced my skull. George's head popped up above the grass, ears perked high. He bounded toward us, tongue lolling from the side of his mouth.

"As I suspected," I said when he wriggled under the fence. "Covered in gunk. You're going home to get a B-A-T-H."

Addy laughed at the expression on George's face. "I think he knows what you're saying."

"Maybe so," I said. "What about it, George? Have you learned to spell as well as just smell?"

When Addy laughed again, it lit up her shy expression, and something prompted me to ask, "Hey, are you doing anything later?"

She froze, her eyes wide.

Way to go, Brad. Smooth operator you are.

I valiantly stumbled forward anyway, feeling the beginnings of panic nibble at my confidence. "I mean, I thought maybe... you know... if you wanted to. We could, um, grab some dinner or something. Nothing too heavy, you know. Just. Like pals." I winced internally, hearing the babble leak into my voice.

"I'm sorry, Brad." Addy looked pained. I almost felt sorry for her having to turn me down. "I don't date... um. My father..."

"No, sure. That's okay."

"I mean..."

"No, no worries. It's all good. I just thought... you know."

"Yeah. But thanks."

"Sure. No problem." I fluttered a weak wave. "Hey, take care of yourself, okay? I'll see you around."

I gathered the tiny particles of my dignity into my palm and led George back down Orchard Road. When we were far enough away, I turned to my dog and said, "We need to up our game, big guy. We're oh for two so far here in Pottsville."

George barked and danced in a circle. *"How is it my fault you can't close the deal?"* he seemed to say.

"Yeah, fair point," I told him. "Let's go home and get you in the tub."

George ducked his head and looked at me with, literally, a hang-dog expression.

SUNDAY NIGHT DINNER consisted of panfried hamburgers, baked beans, and oven-toasted fries. George forgave me for his bath when I tossed him a cooled burger patty, and Tabitha forgot about her normal tuna when I crumbled a bit of beef into her bowl. Dishes washed, I stepped outside with a cup of coffee to take in the glitter of stars washing the night sky and the clatter of branches stirring in the light breeze. According to the weather report, a winter storm was brewing up in Canada, threatening invasion by early next week. It promised to dump a few inches of snow by Halloween. But for now, the air was clear and crisp and cold, with the temperature dropping fast from its daytime high.

A dab of green light flashed from deep in the graveyard.

Cold, prickly spiders crawled over my skin.

I tossed my coffee and set the cup on the ground, never taking my eyes from the spot where the green light had flared. Tombstones rose between here and there, limned with starlight and sparkling with dew. The trees had grown still, the breeze absent.

From the trailer parked by the shed, I retrieved a double-bit ax, four feet of hickory shaft and twin blades of American steel. Say what you will about Arlo, he maintained his tools. The blades of the ax were honed sharp. They gleamed with a perilous edge. The weight of the thing felt good in my hands.

The light flared again. As though that was a starter's signal, I stepped off at a measured pace, winding between graves with an almost unconscious placement of my feet. I had been avoiding stepping on graves for days now, and the path I navigated was nearly instinctive.

I did not hesitate.

I did not waver.

Despite the frigid chill in my stomach and the ball of ice blocking my throat, I meant to confront this evil spirit and have done with her. How I planned to make that happen with a double-bit ax over my shoulder, I had no clue.

Give her forty whacks, maybe?

The greenish glow appeared again, ahead of me and slightly to my left. I angled my approach to compensate. The light bulged brighter, as ugly as oozing pus. My skin prickled, and I tasted copper. Like the headlights of a possessed car rising from a swampy grave, the glimmer blared between the trees, backlighting them in emerald radiance. One particular monster of a tree blocked most of the light. I paused long enough to chop a divot in the tree with my ax, leaving a tell-tale gash in the black bark—a marker, should I again have a need to hunt for the entrance to Pippah's crypt.

Right at this moment, a blind man could find the witch's lair by sense of smell alone. Along with the sickly malachite fluorescence came a choking, cloying vomit-inducing stench akin to walking upon a lakeshore covered with the discarded remains of bloated, sun-baked, decaying fish. The strong smell of compost underlay the primary stink of the place.

I rounded the freshly marked tree and found Pippah with no trouble at all. She squatted by the entrance to her crypt like some malevolent toad, stirring and poking at the earth with a crooked twig.

No. Not a crooked twig but the skeletal remains of twinned arm bones, connected to a wrist, with the tapering, bony fingers flopping loosely as the crone jiggled it about.

I stopped at dartboard distance, hefted the ax, and slapped the haft into my palm. I inhaled a deep breath of frigid, reeking air and said, "Okay, lady. Time to get the fuck out of my graveyard."

Pippah afforded me a fishwife stare as though I was a bug crawling across her freshly mopped floor. "Lookie the big man," she crowed. "Come to scare off de po' witchy-woman with his doughty hatchet. Or you t'ink I'm a tree need'a choppin?"

"I think you're a dead woman in need of staying dead." The steady timbre of my own voice surprised me. By the way my insides were shaking, I half expected my words to come rattling out like ice cubes from a tray.

"You t'ink Pippah's dead!" And *zip!*, just like that, she was in my face, the grave stink of her filling my sinuses strong enough to blow off the top of my head. Her fishy, toad-like face leered inches from mine, and I met her soulless eyes with an effort of will that was as physical as it was psychic. "If I'm dead, then you a killah. I smells it on you, clear and sharp as moldy cheese."

"I've never killed anybody—"

Pippah cackled and leaned close. She sniffed me as though inhaling the scent of a fine bouquet of flowers, eyes dreamy and half closed. "I know my killahs, boy. And youse one a' dem. How many you done in, my puppy? One? Two?"

"You're insane. I—"

"I smell... smoke," she crooned. "Youse burned someone alive, din't ya? Burnt him alive like a pig at a barbecue."

"I... I... That was an accident!"

"You shore 'bout that?" Pippah's eyes glittered, two slits in her moon face. "You doan gotta lie to old Pippah. Judgment ain't mine to give, boy. But a killah knows a killah, make no mishap about that."

My heart thudded hard as though I was running uphill against a strong wind. It took all my effort to not step back, to hold my ground as memories pulled free of the muck where I'd buried them.

Tony stayed over at my house after school. Latchkey kids, they called us. A Wednesday afternoon, much like any other. Monopoly game suspended. I had used my two-year age advantage to claim the race car token. Tony used the top hat. He was mad because I snagged the Boardwalk and Park Place on back-to-back rolls. Stomped upstairs to do his homework. *Cinnamon toast sounds good. Why don't I make some?* Johnny Bravo on the Cartoon Network. The smell of smoke, strong and acrid and bitter.

"It was an accident," I whispered.

"Sho' it was, puppy," the crone's voice whispered back. After a pause, she added, "There's a thing I can do, with them what's killed."

"Huh?" My head snapped up, but it was too late.

Pippah was gone.

But not gone.

She had vanished.

Inside me.

Chapter 21

Ah, this is nice.

Such a strong, healthy body.

A different feeling, a man's body. Weight all hanging different. Balance strange, with no teats flopping in the way. And strong! Oh my word, but I could chop a cord of wood in a couple of whacks, the ax feeling light as a feather in my hands. A young man in his prime, long and lean and tall as a tree.

"And with a nice-sized root, too, now that I taken notice of it." Pippah giggled like a schoolgirl.

What to do, what to do? Mm-mm. I gots me an ax and a strong young body to sling it. Could be some fun to be had, huh now, cher. Oh, you hush up, boy. I gots you fair 'n' square, and you gonna stay got until I say otherwise. Yap too much, and I'll chop this here dangly part right offa you.

Pippah walked the graveyard for a time, just a-wandering, hoping for easy prey. She swung the ax in lazy circles, feeling the oily wood slide under her palms. 'Twould be hard finding a play-pretty this late at night with the graveyard closed for the day. Got lucky last time, what with the man staying until after dark. Pippah shivered with the memory. His screams had fed her with such power, like drinking straight corn likker, fresh from the jar. She'd made him last and last and last.

"You shoulda heard him, boy," Pippah told the graveyard man whose body she'd taken as her own. He was there, buried way down there in the back of their mind. "When I commenced to peeling on him... Whoo, you shoulda heard him squeal."

The squeals and the blood and the pain, they were a crank charging a battery for Pippah. She felt her power grow with every death, big or small. The first murder woke her from her restless slumber, as would the insistent crowing of their old banty rooster, Mr. Peckers, wake her from her iron-framed bed in the old house, down in Bienville Parish. She suckled at the taste of spilled blood as it seeped into the summer-warmed earth, past the ants and beetles, worms and grubs, and down to where it tingled her soul like an electric current. Innocent blood saturated the hallowed grounds of the cemetery and nourished Pippah, yes it did. And she grew stronger.

After that first time, Pippah had taken matters into her own hands, so to speak.

Not long now. All I need is a little bitty taste, and I'll have enough juice to come back full-time. Mayhap even leave the graveyard. Wouldn't that be nice? Go to town and find them what needed killing the most, take my time about doing that business.

Something needed to die tonight. It didn't have to be a lot. If not a man or even a woman, then maybe she could snare up a rabbit and make do. And if not a rabbit, maybe a...

A memory bubbled up from the graveyard man, one he tried to catch and bring back before Pippah saw it, but it was too late.

"A dog will do," Pippah said. "Yes, sir, thankee kindly, but I believe I know just where to find one, now. Oh, and a kitty too. My, my, you are so thoughtful, boy. Jes' too kind."

Pippah reversed course and set off for the graveyard man's house. Her lips smacked in anticipation.

THIS IS HORRIBLE.

I had no control of my body. Pippah had the wheel, and she was taking me on a test drive, hitting the gas, turning me this way and that, checking the mirrors. I tried pumping the brakes, but nothing happened. Her spirit rode on top of mine, as if I had slipped into her dead skin suit and become Pippah... Phillipa Fontenot—*Jesus, how did I know that?*—and she disconnected me from the nerves that controlled my own body. In an ill-advised attempt to fit in with a high school clique, I had once smoked way too much pot through a bong filled with creme de menthe. The resulting high had left me near comatose, on a couch, watching reruns of *Bonanza* on a big-screen TV without motor control or the capacity for speech. I hated the loss of control, the helplessness. The experience had cured me of the desire to smoke pot, hang out with heads, or ever set foot on the Ponderosa.

This was worse.

I watched from a distance, as through binoculars held backward, as Pippah piloted me through the graveyard, whacking my ax—*Oh, why did I bring an ax?*—at random targets. I listened to her thoughts as she muttered about murder. I cringed at the images creeping and crawling across the horror show of her mind as she contemplated dismemberment, butchery, and bloody death.

Who next? she murmured. *Don't have to be a man. No, rabbits and squirrels is hard to ketch. Mebbe a dog. A dog would do, fo' sho.*

George...

The thought escaped my brain before I could snatch it back. I felt Pippah's attention focus on me. She pried my mind open and peered inside. I was powerless to stop her.

"A dog will do," Pippah said in my voice. "Yes, sir, thankee kindly, but I believe I know just where to find one, now. Oh, and a kitty too. My, my, you are so thoughtful, boy. Jes' too kind."

No!

I fought back, but it was like trying to fight a cloud while suspended in zero gravity. I could find no purchase, no leverage, nothing that I could grasp with my hands to tear loose the monster invading my body. I was being hijacked, and there was nothing I could do about it.

The scenery passed by as if observed from a train window—headstones, crypts, trees, overgrown rosebushes. Places I recognized even in darkness, the graveyard having become familiar to me over the past week and a half. The glowing back windows of my small apartment waited ahead. I could see them through my eyes now that Pippah had her attention focused in that direction. Coming closer. And when she got there?

She would slaughter my dog and my cat and use their innocent blood to power her engine of evil. She would grow in strength. Who knew where she would go from there? Would it be enough to power her outside the cemetery walls? To ride my body into town, bloody ax dripping, and find everyone—*every peckerwood ofay*—she could reach and chop them into pieces?

"Gonna whip 'em to da red," Pippah mumbled in a sing-song voice. "Gonna kill dem Mister Charlies dead. Tee-hee, I done made up a song."

We reached the back door. I saw my hand, long and extended, reach for the knob. I watched it turn and felt the cool metal under my palm. Heard the click of the latch. Bright light from the kitchen flooded my eyes. I stepped inside.

"Whoo-ee," Pippah said. "Ain't this fancy now?"

George trotted into the kitchen then skidded to a startled halt when he saw me. His lips curled back, and he growled. I'd never seen him do that before. *Go on, George! Get your game on!*

"Hey, little doggy," my voice crooned. "Come to Momma, now."

My foot took a step closer. My hands slid along the ax handle. Sour sweat oozed from my pores, vinegary and stale. We were close but not close enough for a sure strike. George kept his distance. His hackles were up, and he bayed his unhappiness to the world.

"Shush, now, fuzzy one. Pippah loves her some doggy, yes she does." It sickened me, hearing my voice doling out syrupy words intended to lure my dog to his death. "I be quick, li'l puppy, yes I will. Quick like a bunny."

"Who the hell are you," someone snarled, "and what have you done with Brad?" Delmont Riggins materialized at my side, a flash in my peripheral vision.

Pippah slashed with the ax, the double-bit head swishing through Delmont's spectral body. The ax raked the stovetop, cleaving the kettle with a *whang*. Pippah's return swing whipped through Delmont with the same lack of resistance, and we staggered. The kettle remained embedded upon the ax head, stuck there and sloshing water all over the floor. Some splashed on George, who retreated to the hall, barking to wake the dead. *Bad metaphor, Brad.*

"Well, you ain't nothin' but a haint, boy," she crowed. "No more than a nappy-haired ghost, is you?"

"She got in you," Delmont said. "Didn't she?"

No shit, Delmont!

"Dis ofay cracker's a killer," Pippah said. "He as easy as climbing t'rough a window."

"Hold on," Delmont said and closed his eyes.

Delmont! This is no time to take a nap!

Pippah cackled and turned away. "Now, where'd dat mutt go?" She made smooching noises and sang out, "Here, Georgie, Georgie, Georgie. Here, boy!"

George scrambled farther back, howling and snapping. Normally, the husky would race for safety under the bed if I dropped a pan, but now he acted like he was actually trying to hold his ground. *Run, George! Get around me! Get outside!*

"Uh-uh, none o' dat, boy." Pippah closed the back door, sealing off the only exit. She tried shaking the kettle free of the ax, but it rattled and sloshed. Water pattered like rain. "Well, for the love of... If it ain't one thing, it's another." She tucked the ax handle under my arm and started picking at the stainless steel kettle to free it from the head.

Stan Caputo popped into existence next to Delmont. "What in the ever-lovin' hell is going on here?"

"The hag got him," Delmont said. "Took over his body."

"Ah no," Stan moaned and looked at me. "Can you throw her off, kid? No, of course you can't. I need to get in there. Sorry about this kid, but you gotta give me permission. Open yourself up and just, you know, *will* it to happen."

Say what?

"Whachoo up to?" Pippah snarled. She flung the damaged kettle across the room. It banged and clattered until it spun in a lazy circle and came to rest.

George broke and ran, trailing barks down the hall.

We took a step toward Caputo. "Another haint? Good Lawd, they's a lot of you, ain't they?"

"Open up, Brad," Caputo urged. "Come on, kiddo."

I closed my eyes—figuratively speaking—and tried to clear my mind. I blocked out George's barking, Pippah's oily presence, and the grainy feel of the ax handle sliding through my hands and... opened up...

And then we were three.

THIS IS COZY.

Stan?

Yeah, it's me.

"Won't make no difference. Soon as I kill me that dog, y'all be gone." Pippah grimaced at the wet ax handle. "Too slick."

Okay, kid, listen up, Stan said. *One thing I meant to tell you about blocking ghosts out of your life, okay? One thing you gotta have, more'n anything. Confidence and willpower.*

That's two things.

Stop being a wisenheimer and pay attention.

My body, with Pippah in control, shook with silent laughter. "Ooh, I'm a-scared of y'all, yes I am."

Two things, yeah, Stan continued, *but all twisted together, right? Inner-twined, like. Confidence comes from willpower, and willpower builds confidence. You don't believe in yourself, you got no chutzpah, read me? No chutzpah, you can't find the* testicolis *to kick this bitch out.*

Testicolis?

Balls, capisce?

"The dangly bits, honey." Pippah finished drying the ax handle and tossed the dish towel in the sink. "Down under yo' pecker. You pop 'em out dey sack, they slide around yo' hand like wet grapes. Pippah know dat, fo' shore. I show you, soon as not. Now, let's go find yo' puppy, be done wit' all dis mess."

There must've been a weakness, Caputo said. *Something this nasty old broad used to get in your head. Something holding you back from finding your ground and standing on it. What is it, kid? C'mon, tell Uncle Stan. Better yet, let me see. All you hafta do is open that door and let me peek in.*

There could only be one thing, the single event that had defined my life from the age of twelve and stamped my character as defective from that moment on. I had never told anyone the full story—not my parents, not the cops, and certainly not the kindly but useless shrink I saw Tuesdays at four p.m. for every single week until my sophomore year of high school. Pippah had called me a killer. Well, I was that, all right—a disgusting, cowardly useless excuse for a human who had murdered his friend on a chilly day in February in a moment of cowardice so profound my own memory wouldn't go near it. I buried that bloody wounded moment under piles and piles of scar tissue, where it refused to heal and instead leaked pus into my bloodstream forevermore.

I wasn't dumb. I knew the reason I was a world-class screwup. Deep down, I knew I didn't deserve success. How could I when Tony Denby would never see another sunrise? Would never eat another Pop Tart or race Hot Wheels or blow out candles at a birthday party or kiss a girl or drive a car...

All because of me.

Pippah navigated the kitchen, tracking wet footprints into the hall. The next door on the left led to the living room. Straight ahead was the bedroom door. Both were ajar, but I knew—and consequently so did Pippah—that George would be in the bedroom. Probably under the bed. Trapped in a dead end. No escape.

Another death to lay at my feet.

And with George gone, would Tabby be far behind? And then how many dead would feed this deranged bitch's insanity?

"No need for name-calling, now," Pippah muttered, as if talking to herself. Which I supposed she was, in a way. "Sticks and stones, and all, but still... t'aint nice."

Is that the way you want it to play out, kid? Just give up? I pictured Stan leaning against a corner of a building, one leg cocked back against the bricks. He wore a slim-waisted double breast in gray wool, a fedora tipped low, and an unfiltered Chesterfield dangling from the corner of his mouth. Smoke trailed up and curled around the brim of his hat. He was the very image of Humphrey Bogart or George Raft in a black-and-white gangster flick. *It don't hafta be that way, Brad. I know you, man, and you ain't like that. Not deep down.*

You're wrong. That's exactly how I am. A prize-winning coward. The guy never counted on to stand up and do the right thing.

Stan shook his head and thumbed a fleck of tobacco off his lip. *Nah. Peddle it to the Irish, kid. I'm not buyin' it.*

You don't understand—you weren't there!

So show me. Show me what makes Brad Langston a killer.

Pippah passed by the open living room door. She glanced inside, just to be sure. Delmont flowed out, his face a mask of anger and frustration. Teeth bared, he snarled at Pippah to stop. She neither flinched nor altered course. We were steps from the bedroom. Six long strides away from where George waited. Poor, innocent, cowardly George. Maybe a coward but not nearly as cowardly as his human companion.

Fine, I said. *Fine. You want to see? No problem. What difference could it make at this point?* With that, I ripped the scab off a memory I hadn't exposed to the light of day in fourteen years. *Here. Take a look at the time I killed my best friend.*

Chapter 22

The memory starts where the memory always starts: that first acrid scent of smoke drifting to my nostrils followed by the piercing wail of the fire alarm.

Tony stayed at our house from after school until his mom came home around six. I think she paid my mom something for day care though I never had the impression it was much. Not as much as a real day care place, for sure. Which I guessed made the old adage true—you get what you pay for.

I was twelve. He was nine. Despite our age difference, we got along well enough. To me, Tony was kind of like the kid brother I never had. He looked up to me, followed my lead, never whined or complained. He had a crow's wing of black hair that fell across his forehead, and he would keep flipping it back out of his eyes. Used to drive me crazy, that hank of hair. I wanted to take a pair of scissors and cut the thing off.

My mother was out that day—at the store or running errands—so Tony was my responsibility. I was old enough to be on my own at home. Old enough to know the rules: stay inside, don't open the door to strangers, call the police if somebody tries to break in...

If there's a fire, leave the house, then call 911.

The living room was off-limits unless we had special company, so Tony and I hung out in the basement/rec room. Our ongoing Monopoly game crowded the ping-pong table we used for board games. The board was old. Well used. Tony had lined up rows and rows of houses and hotels in make-believe neighborhoods, waiting for deployment to our improved properties. It was hour two of match three in the best-of-seven, winner-take-all conflict, and truth be told, I was getting sick of it. We both were, I think. Tony had quit an hour earlier and stomped off in anger because I had hit Boardwalk and Park Place on back-to-back rolls, snagging both properties for a monopoly.

Well, to hell with him. Stupid brat.

I had Cartoon Network on. *Johnny Bravo,* thankyouverymuch. Way more entertaining than Monopoly.

Our house was a two-story walk-up in a quiet neighborhood of Trenton, New Jersey. Two bedrooms on the second floor. On the first, a tiny parlor with a bay window faced the street. From there, a hall connected a living room—reserved for company—and beyond that, a dining room. At the back of house was our kitchen, and in the kitchen were the stairs down to the basement.

Tony had gone upstairs. I let him go. When he got sulky, Tony would head for the parlor, where he would play with his ever-expanding collection of Hot Wheels or sit in the window seat and read. Leave him alone long enough, and he'd get over his moody self. We would declare detente and pack away the Monopoly board in exchange for Life or Stratego.

It was cold as hell that day. I lay under an old quilt. The basement was all but soundproofed with insulation, and I had the TV on loud enough to be heard in China. I don't know how long the smoke detector had been wailing before I connected the sound to an alarm. An acrid coil of smoke burned my nostrils the instant I twigged to the sound.

Oh shit, the toast.

I had started a snack ages ago, covering six slices of white bread with thick, rough-cut slabs of Velveeta cheese. Oven-baked cheese toast, a specialty of mine. I must have left it in the oven. Forgot about it. *Cheese is probably all over the oven. Mom will kill me.*

I vaulted off the couch and pounded up the basement stairs.

They teach kids in fire safety to always check the heat of a door before opening it. If it's hot to the touch, don't open it. Had I ever heard that lesson? I don't know. I sure as hell didn't remember it right then. I flung open the door, and flames reached for me with eager arms. I staggered back. Tripped. Fell.

Or I must have, for the next thing I knew, I was on my face at the bottom of the stairs. I had two broken arms. Greenstick fractures, they called them, where the bone is cracked but not split apart or sticking through the skin like a compound fracture or anything, but still... it hurt like crazy. A sprained left ankle. A twisted right knee. Smoke swirled and eddied overhead. It was filling the basement from top to bottom.

I had to get out and get out now.

I could move, but the stairs were out of the question. The fire was leaping and crackling around the doorway at the top. I could sense the flames' hunger. Hear its eagerness. It sounded almost... happy. Gleeful.

There was another way out of the basement. Another staircase led up to the backyard. The men who delivered our fuel oil used it when they came to fill the tank.

The tank.

Of highly flammable oil.

In our basement.

I raced up the stairs and slammed into the door, but it was locked with a padlock, which dangled in my face. The key was in the kitchen. Mom hung it on a peg by the back door, where she kept all her spare keys. The one for the garden shed, the two-key set for Granny's house, the keys we had no idea what they fit, and the cars and the chain for the back gate. Now all were probably being melted to slag. I slammed my shoulder into the door again and again, ignoring the pain shooting down my forearms. If I couldn't break out, I would die in this basement, burned to a crisp and found among the charred remains of Monopoly money and stale potato chips. The door bucked and banged at every wallop but refused to break open. I bounced off it like a rubber dodgeball.

I'm gonna die.

I paused for a moment at the top of the steps, pressed into the door panel. Rough splinters pricked my shoulder. *This is it. My time is over.*

"Help!" I howled that word, over and over. Big, fat sobs wracked my body. The stink of smoke clawed at my throat, irritated my sinuses. It wasn't bad, not yet. I could still breathe. But it wouldn't be long unless—

The windows.

A pair of thin, elongated ground-level windows allowed daylight into the basement. They were higher than I could reach, and I had never seen them opened. No idea if they even *could* be opened. I scrambled back down the steps. The ping-pong table was closest. I grabbed it, dragged it across the room. Green Monopoly houses rattled and bounced like they were undergoing an earthquake. Entire neighborhoods were destroyed.

I shoved the table under the window on the right side. Access to the one on the left was blocked by an upright freezer. The window frame looked awfully small. Narrow and thin. Too thin? Have to try it and see.

I clambered up onto the rickety table. It shivered under me, and I had to shift suddenly to catch my balance. I stood on wobbly legs and examined the latch, which was crusted thick with rust and old paint. I pressed it hard, digging an imprint into the pad of my thumb. It refused to turn. I needed something... a tool...

Dad kept half a dozen softball trophies from one of the various leagues he'd played in, back in his pre-fatherhood days. I used the base of one of those as a hammer. The latch gave, reluctantly, fighting me all the way. When it popped loose, the window lifted with a squeal. I shoved myself into the gap, squeezing through into a hedge of boxwoods that lined the back of our house. As I fought my way clear of the clinging branches, the kitchen windows overhead blew out, and superheated bits of glass rained down around me, hissing as they buried themselves in the snow. Flames rolled out, and the air was thick with smoke. There were no sirens. In fact, everything was eerily calm.

The memory stuttered here, like an old movie, badly spliced.

In a mixed, muddled sequence of events, I ran next door to Mrs. O'Neil's house and banged and banged on the door until the old lady appeared. I screamed at her to call 911, then I ran around to the front of our house and tried going in the front door. Locked. I staggered through the front hedge and banged on the bay window, ignored the pain in my forearms, and cupped my hands around my eyes to peer through it. I kept screaming, "Tony, Tony, Tony!" Mrs. O'Neil came and dragged me away or tried to. I think I bopped the old lady on the nose. I circled the house, searching for a way back inside that wasn't certain death.

"Tony, Tony, Tony!"

Tony never came out.

My house burned to a shell, and Tony burned with it.

And it was my fault.

"ALL YO' FAULT," COOED Pippah. "Now, where'd that dog go?"

We pushed back the bedroom door. A glimmer of moonlight through the high window—vaguely reminiscent of the basement window through which I had crawled so many years ago—painted the unmade bed in silvery light. Shadows crawled up the walls. A tiny shape moved atop the twisted sheets—Tabitha, bowed up and hissing.

"Pippah see to you in a bit, little kitty," Pippah said. "Right now, we lookin' fo' your big brother."

Wait a sec, Stan said. *Let's back up here. You say you killed this kid because you left some stuff in the oven, and it set fire to the house?*

Cheese toast, I said. *Cheese toast was his favorite.*

Let's see how that happened.

Why does it matter? I did it.

Humor me. A sensation followed... it felt like someone rooting around a drawer for a pair of socks, only inside my head. *Oh, here it is.*

Memories skipped by, like an old VHS tape played in high speed and paused at random moments. I hadn't revisited these moments in time in many years... if ever. The playback came through crystal clear, as though I was watching a hi-def replay from a camera mounted behind my eyeballs.

There I was, getting out a baking sheet and covering it in foil, buttering bread, going back to the fridge, having to detour around the electric space heater, slicing thick chunks of squared, squishy cheese, arranging the slices on the bread, setting the pan in the oven—Tony calling me from the basement—me going downstairs—

Wait a sec, I said. *That can't be right.*

What?

The oven's not on. See? No, go back a bit. There. The dial lights up when the oven's on, and it's not on. I must have turned it on later. Go forward.

The replay picked up again, skipping faster: Tony and I arguing about trading St. Charles Place right after I collected Boardwalk—there, me getting mad at him for being a jerk—him stomping upstairs—me switching on the TV—watching—watching—watching...

The smell of smoke and the wail of the fire alarm.

I never turned it on.

Nope, Stan said. *No, you didn't.*

Then how did—

The fire start? I felt Stan shrug. *Maybe the kid did it. Turned the oven on. Or maybe the fire started some other way. You ever hear anybody talking about it?*

I... don't know.

Let's see. I think I'm getting the hang of this now. Hold on.

Memories fluttered past, like the fanned pages of a comic book, or a researcher, scrolling for a key image. In real time, I was aware of my hand reaching out, flipping the bedroom light switch on, and Pippah closing the bedroom door behind me. No escape for George. The ax weighed heavy in my hand. She was speaking in a sing-song voice... calling to George to come out from under the bed. Tabitha squalled and zipped away under the dresser, gone in the blink of an eye. Smart cat.

Wait, Stan said. *What's this?*

A memory plays out. I'm in a car, riding in the passenger seat. My mother is driving. She smells of spearmint chewing gum, which she chewed to try to cover the burnt-paper reek of the cigarette habit she thought no one knew about. I am in a light jacket, and it is bright outside. A sunny, early spring day in Trenton. We are driving home from one of my therapy sessions.

"Bradley, honey," Mom says, "you have to stop blaming yourself."

I mumble something that isn't even a complete sentence or real words, even.

"You didn't start the fire."

I come back with "Sure I did," in a voice that sounds very thin and whiny.

"No, sweetie, listen. It was the space heater. It was old and worn out. I told your father a million times to throw it out and get a new—"

Suddenly I'm screaming, my face blowtorch hot. "It was my job! I was supposed to watch him! Tony was my friend, and I left him there. It was my fault. Not yours, not Dad's. Mine!"

So it was the space heater! Stan said. *Not the toast.*

It doesn't matter, I whispered, a ghost in my own body. *It was my responsibility.*

I watched as Pippah hooked a toe under the bed and kicked it up. The bed flipped back and crashed against the wall. George shot away, a fur missile blurring between my feet. He bumbled into the closed door.

"Damn you, dog," Pippah squawked. "Hold still, now."

That's not... You didn't murder your friend any more than the captain of the Titanic *murdered those passengers.* The dismay in Stan's voice came through, loud and clear. *You're not a killer, and trust me, I should know. It was an accident, and you did all you could.*

It doesn't matter. I—

It does matter! You want this bitch to kill your dog? Would Tony want that? You gotta forgive yourself, kid.

I... I can't.

Look at your dog, Brad. Look at him, fer chrissakes.

George huddled in a miserable ball by the door. He cowered as I approach, afraid to meet my eyes. He had made a puddle on the floor. Pippah crooned to him in my voice, and the ax handle slid through my hand as she cocked it back to swing, like a batter at the plate, getting ready for the pitch. It was heartbreaking.

Brad, listen, Stan said. *Do you love your dog?*

Yes. Yes, of course.

Do you feel that love? Deep down inside you?

I... yes. And I did feel it—everything George meant to me. Companionship. Trust. Unconditional love. All of it solidified into a rock to which I clung like a shipwrecked soul as the storm of Pippah's hate raged around me. He was my cowardly lion, and I loved him with all my heart.

Use it, Brad, Stan urged. *Stand on it. Take a good grip and tear this bitch out!*

Delmont appeared next to me. "Go small, Icabod Crane. Concentrate on a finger. C'mon, dude, you can do it."

Pippah was at the apogee of her stance. The next moment would see her slicing downward.

George whimpered. He looked away.

Concentrate on a finger. Okay. I focused my attention on my right hand where it gripped the ax haft. Sensed the muscles there. Tensed. Tightly wrapped. *Let go,* I willed. *Let. Go.*

My thumb came free.

Pippah squawked. "Watchoo doin', boy?"

The rock of my love for George gave me purchase. I found I could trust it not to let me down, so I pushed harder against it.

My right hand released the ax.

"Too late!" Pippah cried. "I can use one hand, do this job."

The ax swung down, controlled only by my left hand. Even one-handed, the ax would bury itself in my dog's skull. The momentum would be enough.

No. You. Don't.

Now that I knew how, I poured all of my will into the muscles of my left arm. Twisted. Turned.

The ax thunked into the floor, inches from George's tail. In fact, it may have shaved off a few black-and-white hairs. The husky yelped and sidled away, pressed so tightly against the wall that he scooted along it.

Now, I said to Pippah. *Get. Out.*

I stood my ground. Having found it, I would not be budged. I gathered all of the vile essence of the vicious little harpy inside me, and I heaved. It felt like pulling a tree stump out of the ground by hand.

Pippah shrieked and dug her tendrils into my soul. "Oh no, boy. I gotchu now. Ain't never gonna let go."

I sucked in a deep breath and shifted my grip. I was panting like a blown racehorse, and my sweat pattered the floor in a steady rain shower. I felt like I had done three days of heavy landscaping, all rolled into one moment.

Stan Caputo's spirit slipped into position beside me.

Here, lemme give you a hand with the trash.

Delmont's ghost stepped in on the other side. *Let's get it done, bro.*

On three, Stan said. *One, two, threeeeeeeee!*

We pulled together. With the sensation of ripping, popping roots torn from the ground, we broke Pippah loose. One second, she was in my body, and the next, she was standing in front of me, glaring her hatred from froggy eyes.

"You ain't seen the last of me, boy," she hissed. "Not by a sight."

And she disappeared.

The next thing I knew, I was on the floor.

Everything went black.

Chapter 23

My dream: A fairy princess who resembled Taylor Swift kissed me.

The reality: George licked at my nose until my eyes popped open. I guessed he had forgiven me for trying to kill him, or maybe his doggy senses had been able to perceive I had been possessed but was now returned to normal. He wiggled around and lapped at my face while his tail kicked up a breeze.

Tabitha remained skeptical. A pair of green eyes regarded me from the darkness under the dresser. I smooched at her, but she was having none of it and refused to budge.

The ghosts were gone. No Pippah, no Delmont, no Stan. By the quality of the silence, I suspected I had the apartment to myself. The overhead light was on—I vaguely remembered Pippah using my hand to flip the switch. I squinted, holding up my Brad-controlled hand to block the brightness.

"What time is it?" I checked the bedside clock: 12:09 a.m.

I had been out close to six hours.

My muscles ached with that hard-workout kind of misery, as though I had done a thousand squat thrusts followed by a million sit-ups. I groaned and covered George's ears before saying some bad words then crawled from the floor to the bed. I straightened it out and collapsed on my back with an arm tented over my eyes. The light dazzled me—too bright, too intense. Too bad. I would have to lift the world off my chest before I could get up to turn it off.

Far beyond the physical pain, a deeper, duller ache settled in my stomach and refused to budge. Dredging up the memories of that day in February when the house burned and Tony... died... had torn off a scab and opened the doors to a hell I had kept locked tightly shut. Odd that I had forgotten about the space heater, though. My first reaction on that day—that I had forgotten the toast in the oven—was the one that stuck with me, and I had somehow blocked out the subsequent conversations about the space heater.

Through the lens of age and a little experience, I played back those dormant memories of that day and the days that followed. I gritted my teeth against the pain and reviewed the sequence of events, looking for a way to recast myself as the villain, which was how I remembered it. On high alert for anything that smacked of an excuse, I scrutinized every moment, every action, every decision I had made on that day fourteen years ago and...

Found nothing I could use to continue blaming myself.

Yes, I had let Tony go upstairs by himself. So what? I had done that a thousand times. Yes, I was distracted by my own teenage nonsense, mesmerized by a silly cartoon show, cocooned in my basement, and didn't realize the kitchen was on fire until it was too late. Was it reasonable to assume I could I have done anything differently? Well, yeah, probably. Maybe. I could have gotten up sooner to check on Tony, who was my responsibility, but he was a mature nine-year-old, not a baby, and didn't need constant supervision.

But still...

That day would haunt me forever. The expressions on the faces of Tony's parents when they would look at me... his mother glaring at me across the tiny casket at the funeral... his father pointedly looking away. The endless *what if*s and *coulda-woulda-shoulda*s... I would never lose the guilt, not completely. Of that, I was sure.

But maybe... maybe I didn't have to carry the full weight of Tony's death on my shoulders. Maybe, if I allowed it, I might be able to forgive myself, just a little, for being a stupid kid without the experience to know that space heaters were dangerous, one who had done everything reasonably possible to save his friend from a freak accident.

I hugged my dog and cried for Tony, a sweet kid with a flap of raven hair that used to drive me crazy, who had hidden in my closet for safety as the smoke gathered and the fire threatened. Who liked Hot Wheels and *Star Wars* action figures, and who could quote Aragorn, son of Arathorn, chapter and verse from his favorite book. Who ate my cheese toast like it was a gourmet meal and followed me around like a lost puppy.

"I'm sorry, man," I said through the tears. "I should have just given you the damn Boardwalk."

OCTOBER 27TH, DAY TWELVE

Monday morning found me at the computer early, after a short and fitful night's sleep. A cup of coffee steamed at my elbow, and George curled at my ankles. He hadn't moved six inches away from me since I'd thrown Pippah out of my body, as if by maintaining his vigilance, he could prevent a recurrence. Or maybe he wanted to prove how much he loved me so I wouldn't want to chop him up with an ax anymore. Tabitha, by contrast, remained under the dresser, suspicious even when I tried coaxing her out with a bit of tuna.

Some of Pippah's memories had leaked through while we shared a body, seeping into my subconscious the way sludgy oil soaked into concrete. Her name: Phillipa Fontenot. Images as well, such as a street scene highlighted by *Happy Days* storefronts and patrolled by bulky, rounded, shark-finned cars of the 1950s. Women swished by in calf-length skirts, and the men had slicked-back hair or wore snappy little hats and two-piece suits.

So I had a name and a time frame in which to do a little searching. I took a sip of coffee and got started, typing "Phillipa Fontenot" into the search bar. An hour turned into two as I chased internet rabbits down website holes, reading, reading, reading, skimming, skimming, skimming.

Phillipa "Pippah" Fontenot was a ghost. Pun intended. At least, the person I knew as Pippah existed nowhere on the internet. Seeing as how she'd lived and, presumably, died in the fifties, this wasn't tremendously surprising—disappointing but not surprising. I had hoped some archived news article would have made it onto a server somewhere, or a reference to an event bearing her name would have been of sufficient merit to warrant a snippet in a local history blog. But no. Pippah and the internet did not intersect, at least anywhere that I could find.

"Fine," I told George. "We do this the hard way."

But I wasn't exactly sure what the hard way was. Did I call up Andy Gluck, ace reporter of the *Pottsville Post*, and see if he could dig up anything from the graveyard? That was, ironically, the nickname given to a newspaper's archives, so pun fully intended. Or did I dare venture into Thelma Entwistle's domain, risking an overdose of sexual innuendo and/or a nasty bite from her dog, and see if the library retained any old records using the technology of the ancients known as a microfiche reader? Maybe I should ask the ever-helpful detectives, Czerniak and Swanson, if the cops had any reports from the 1950s related to Pippah Fontenot, and would they be kind enough to share them?

My list of choices triggered an acid burn in my stomach.

I jumped in my seat when the front door buzzed and Saiera Khosani's voice sang out, "Hello? Anyone home?"

"In here," I called.

Then I winced. I had been avoiding the gypsy woman on purpose because of her potential connection to Consuelo Espinoza. Had they known each other at college? What was the enrollment at Syracuse? Fifty thousand? Sixty thousand? What were the odds that two women from far different backgrounds had met during the brief intersection of their college lives?

Could I chalk it up to simple coincidence that one of them had lived in tiny, little Pottsville, Pennsylvania, and the other one had died there during a pit stop?

Anything was possible, I supposed. In a town the size of Pottsville, there had to be at least some Syracuse alumni, right?

Saiera appeared in the doorway while I was busy struggling with the math on those equations. She wore her USPS uniform, and her mailbag hung off one shoulder. "Hey there," she said.

"Hey."

"Haven't seen you in a while."

"No. Sorry."

She leaned against the doorframe. "You're looking a little pale. Everything okay?"

"Sure."

"Uh-huh."

"And you?"

"Fine."

Truth be told, Saiera did look fine. She reminded me a little of a lioness: golden skin over well-toned muscles, hawkish eyes, and a sleek figure. But was she a predator lion or a protector lion? I searched her eyes for the telltale signs that would reveal her as a murderer.

"Um," I said after the pause ticked on for a beat too long. "Tea?"

She hesitated, and I saw the no forming on her lips.

"Look," I said, "I'm sorry I abandoned you at the cops. That was really uncool. I was freaked out. Finding the body and all. I didn't know. What to do." Jesus, I was speaking in Captain Kirk commas.

C'mon, Brad. String together a whole sentence. "And Pippah. I have to tell you about Pippah. She came back, and she... possessed my body."

"She *what?*"

I told Saiera the whole story over a cup of tea. Well, her tea, my coffee. I edited out the backstory about Tony and the fire and the years of guilt poisoning my soul. The scab had recently been torn off that wound, and it was still sensitive to touch.

"Oh, poor George," she said when I got to the part about chasing my dog around with an ax. George leaned against her shin and regarded Saiera with adoration. She scratched his ruff, and the husky melted into a puddle.

Tabitha strolled into the kitchen about that time. She oiled away from my hand in the way cats do when they don't want to be touched and proceeded to her food bowl. Which was empty. The look she gave me left me with no doubt about whom she believed responsible for the failures of household management. I opened a can of tuna for her, which meant I had to open a can of stinky dog food for George. Both animals set to work demolishing lunch while I continued my story.

I wrapped up with "So with Stan and Delmont's help, I finally shoved her out. If felt like yanking out a tooth. With pliers."

"What does she want?"

"Huh?"

"I mean, what's her motive? Why's she doing this? What does she want?"

"Blood," I said. "Blood and death. It seems to feed her. Make her stronger."

"That gives her power, sure. But why?"

I shook my head. "Sorry. Not following."

"Why have power if you don't do anything with it? Once she gains control of a body, what's the endgame?"

"Oh. Sorry. Yeah, got it." Part of sharing a physical body with another soul was the added bonus of getting a sense of their goals and desires. I had absorbed those needs at the cellular level, so much so that I failed to realize others didn't see how obvious it all was. "Revenge. She feels wronged by people... uh, more specifically, by white men living in Pottsville. Pippah wants to come back to this world and kill every white man she can get her hands on. And then destroy the entire town if she can."

Saiera covered her mouth with one hand. "We have to stop her."

I liked that Saiera said "we" as if Pippah was a shared problem. A load shared is a load lightened, and all that. But I still wasn't quite ready to leap on the Saiera Khosani bandwagon or sign her on as my ghost-busting partner. Her affiliation with Syracuse nagged at me. Her continued interest in hanging around a graveyard seemed suspicious as well. Were her visits driven by a burgeoning attraction to the suave and debonair Brad Langston, or did she merely wish to keep tabs on the progress of the investigation into Consuelo's death by sticking close to the one who'd discovered her body? And had she guided me to the scene of her latest kill, or was the discovery of Glatfelter's body merely a coincidence?

"Where'd you go to school?" I blurted. "College, I mean."

Saiera's lower lip pooched out, and her eyebrows crinkled together. "What? Uh, I spent two years at Syracuse before I dropped out to get a job. My dad died, and my mom doesn't work. She's blind. Why? Do I need a degree to hunt ghosts?"

I could tell she was a little miffed at my question. But was she upset because she thought I was questioning her education or because she was revealing a connection she wanted to keep secret? Lay it out there, Brad. Just ask her: *Did you know Consuelo?*

"No, no. No degree required," I heard myself saying instead. "How do we stop her?"

Saiera sat back in her chair. "Oh, that part's simple. I called my *bunica*—"

"Your what?"

"My grandmother." She waved a hand to dismiss the sidetrack. "Doesn't matter. She has some... experience in these matters. She said we have to find Pippah's bones and remove them from the cemetery. We have to take them far away and burn them in a hot, hot fire until they're nothing but ash."

"Find her bones."

"Yes."

"Remove them."

"Yes."

"And burn them."

"In a hot, hot fire. Yes."

I buried my head in my hands. "Why couldn't I have been a lawyer?"

AFTER SAIERA HAD GONE about her rounds, I sat in the office and did some more research. Saiera's solution presented two challenges. First, I had to locate and remove Pippah's remains from the crypt in which they lay. That sounded easy, but I had a strong suspicion Pippah was exerting some kind of influence to keep people away from her resting place. Every time I had gone looking for her, I wound up wandering in circles. I had not tried since last night, when I had marked the trees with my ax as I went.

Before I searched again, I needed to put some thought into it rather than traipsing off with an ax and an attitude. Maybe some rope or tape to mark the route. A hammer and chisel to open the crypt. Some brown underwear to hide the—

Stan Caputo popped into existence, and I nearly jumped out of my skin.

"We got trouble," he said by way of greeting.

"Trouble?" I slumped back in my chair. "Of course. What now?"

"I lost track o' time, kid," Stan said. "Sorry, but it's hard to keep up wit' current events from the other side, you know. It's not like we got calendars or nothing."

I squinted at him. "What the heck are you talking about?"

"The moon."

"What about the moon?"

"It's gonna be full," Stan explained, as if to a simpleton. "In four days... nights, I mean."

"Sooo... a full moon? Does that mean we get werewolves too?"

"Naw, kid, listen. Remember when I explained to you about the power on the other side? How we all use it to charge up, so we can, like, do things. Up here."

"Yeah, sure."

"Well, on the nights of the full moon, it's like we really get the juice, you know what I mean? It's like a... boost in the charge, right? So a couple-a things happen on those nights." Stan held up his index finger then ticked it off. "One, you get lots of us wandering around. And two"—another finger ticked off—"when we come back that night, we're... more real... than any other night. We come back strong is what I'm saying."

"Oookay." My brain refused to process what Stan was saying. I was counting days off in my head and coming up with a full moon on October 31st.

Halloween. Oh joy. Super-ghosts scampering around the cemetery on Halloween.

"Hey, kid? You hearing what I'm saying?"

I focused on the ghost. "Huh? No, not really."

"Pay attention. This is important." Stan ran his ghost fingers through his ghost hair, which mussed not a single strand. It was as perfect and slick as if he'd never touched it. "You know I've been telling you about the juice? The fuel, the gas, the mojo, the energy—the whatchacallit that we draw on to get us up here? Yeah? Good. Well, it's building up for the full moon, or I should say, it oughta be. Somebody's sucking it all up, and I got a good idea who. Now, on the full moon, which is in a few nights—you heard that part, right? Good. On that night, we should be getting a pretty strong dose of the energy, due to moon cycle or whatever. If this witch who's been causing all the trouble—"

"Pippah."

"Pippah, yeah, right. If this Pippah can gather all that power for herself... well, it won't be pretty. She'll come up here and tear this place apart. She gets her hooks in you, it won't be as easy last time, pulling her out."

"Ha! Easy? You called that easy?"

Stan threw up an apologetic shrug. "I'm telling you, kid. That was Pippah on about a tenth of what she'll draw, come the full moon. I can feel it now. My juice is running out even as we speak."

"Can't you do anything?"

"That's what I'm getting set to do—go down there and duke it out wit' her. I'm gonna try and pull away as much juice as I can so I can maybe slow her down a little. I wanted to give you the heads-up in case you maybe wanted to do something up here. Ah shoot. I gotta go—"

With a two-fingered salute, Stan winked out of existence.

I tried to imagine a superpowered Pippah, and my mind balked. She had damn near owned me at ten percent power. With her at full strength, I would never stand a chance. She would arise from her grave like some B-movie monster, and I would be the dumbass kid who ventured into the dark tomb to check out the scary noise, only to die in a gruesome, blood-splattering kind of way. How often had I yelled at the screen, "Don't go down the basement steps! Don't go into the abandoned amusement park! Don't have sex in a cabin by the lake!"? But instead of the smart thing, the dumbass kid would go down the steps or whatever and wind up dead. *Not me,* I would say. That ever happened to me, I'd run the hell the other way.

And so here I was. Open Pippah's tomb and remove her bones? Certain death. Load up the car and run far away? Certain life.

Really and truly, no choice at all.

Chapter 24

Assuming I had the guts to enter Pippah's crypt, there remained a second obstacle: burning her remains in a "hot, hot fire." A little more internet research proved the fire needed to be very hot indeed. (I hoped no cops were tracking my browser history. Typing in "How hot does it need to be to cremate a body" gave me the shakes.) It turned out that cremation requires a temperature between fourteen hundred and eighteen hundred degrees Fahrenheit. No outdoor barbecue or casual firepit would achieve that kind of heat. No, to get the temperature I needed, lacking a forge or a crematorium, I would need to build a fire of coal.

And since I had coal and charcoal briquettes in the shed, and since there were no crematoriums in Pottsville...

I typed, "How to build a hot, hot fire with coal," and settled in to read.

THE FRONT OFFICE BUZZER announced someone had entered the lobby. I went out to find a prosperous-looking middle-aged couple standing awkwardly near the office door. They watched me as I walked up, with the hesitant manner of people who were unsure of themselves, like strangers at a party to which they weren't sure they were invited. Based on the social media photos I had seen, I had a pretty good idea who they were.

"Mrs. Espinoza?" I said to the woman, who had taken a couple of steps closer to me as I entered the office.

"Yes. Are you Brad?"

"Yes, ma'am." I accepted her soft, birdlike hand, gave it a tiny squeeze, and released it.

"I'm Sophia Espinoza," she said, "and this is my husband, Ernesto."

Ernesto's grip wasn't much stronger than his wife's, but he had a warrior's face, chiseled and handsome, with dark eyes and a strong chin. Ernesto Espinoza stood no higher than my nose, with his wife a head shorter. She wore an elegant cream dress under a cashmere, hip-length coat and modest, taupe heels. My eyes watered a bit when I recognized Consuelo's features reflected from her mother's more mature face. Had their daughter lived, she would have grown to be a classic beauty.

"If you would be so kind," Ernesto said. "We have come to see…" His voice grew hoarse for a moment. "Come to see the place where our daughter was found."

"Sure." I hesitated, unsure of how to phrase what I wanted to say. I gestured vaguely at Sophia's nice shoes, at Ernesto's suit and black Oxfords. "It's not exactly… It's kind of rough back there. Muddy, I mean."

Sophia's lips bent in a kind, motherly smile. Tiny streaks of gray ran through her lustrous black hair. Those and the almost-imperceptible wrinkles formed at the corners of her eyes enhanced her beauty rather than detracted from it.

"These are only clothes, Brad," she said. "They mean nothing compared to our daughter."

"Ah…" I felt my face heat. "Of course. Please. Follow me."

I led the Espinozas through the back door and into the graveyard. "This part's not so bad. It's paved for a good ways back. Watch the roses, though. I have only cut back about a third of the bushes so far, a point that Mrs. Perry brings up at least twice a week."

"Mrs. Perry?"

"Ahhh... a patron of the cemetery. Anyway, there's still places where the bushes will reach out and grab... uh... grab..."

I stood, rooted in place, my eyes fixed on a tree that overhung the main trail. A divot had been chopped in the side of the tree, and beside it, a path of footprints in the bare mud revealed where I had cut across the open ground. The footprints beelined straight between a pair of rosebushes, which concealed most of what lay beyond. The hump of a hilltop showed above the tangle, and I had a pretty good idea what I would find if I followed my old footsteps—a certain crypt containing a certain evil spirit who had a proclivity for bladed tools and a will to use them.

"Brad?... Brad?"

"Brad?"

It took a moment to realize both Sophia and Ernesto had been speaking to me, trying to get my attention.

"Oh. Sorry. I just saw something that I forgot to take care of. Please. Follow me."

From there, every time I tried to speak, the words fizzled before reaching my lips. For once, I was completely out of things to say. Seeing the blaze I had chipped in the tree had frozen my tongue as effectively as if Superman had swallowed kryptonite. We walked in near silence until we reached the former thicket, now transformed into something resembling a glade.

"This..." I cleared my throat and started again. "This area was choked with brush. Lots of fallen limbs. Briar patches. It was a real mess back here. I can't really say what led me to explore back in there"—*Your daughter's ghost, actually*—"but I found her... I found her through here." I stepped between two tall elms, and the Espinozas picked their way after me, heedless of the soggy ground. "I, uh, I didn't feel it was right, you know. The place being such a mess. So once the cops... Once the cops were done, I cleared it out."

In fact, I had done more work back here than I remembered. The thicket was gone. All that remained was a winter-bare copse of trees covering an area the size of a suburban lot. We walked between the boles of elms, mixed with a rare oak and maybe some dogwood—hard to tell from the mulch carpeting the ground. I led the Espinozas to a spot under the spreading branches of an ancient, twisted live oak and stopped.

"It was about here," I said. "There was a big brush pile here... before... but I dragged it off and burned it." My throat clogged a bit when I said, "I wanted to... I don't know... I wanted to put up a marker of some kind, you know. A monument."

"Oh, Brad." Sophia touched my arm with a gentle hand. "That is so thoughtful of you. Please, let us help."

"Yes." Ernesto's reddened eyes watered, and his voice was thick. "Please. You have a great heart, Brad. We would very much like to help place a monument."

Sophia sniffed and hugged her husband. "We will be taking our Chelita back to Kansas now that the police have released her. That is what took us so long to come. But now that we have her back, we will take her back to our home and lay her to rest among her family. Having something here, though... that would mean a lot. And what you have done... it honors our daughter."

I dug a toe into the ground. "Well... it just wasn't right. The way she was treated."

"They stole her life from her." Sophia hid her face in her husband's chest, and a sob wracked her body.

"Whoever took her from us..." Ernesto's jaw flexed, and he said no more.

"Um," I said. "Would you like some coffee? It's instant, but..."

I escorted the Espinozas back to my tiny kitchen, where they took seats around my stained and chipped table. The older couple had class. They treated me like one of the family, doted on George and Tabitha with unfeigned delight, and drank their bad coffee from mismatched cups without a grimace. At no time did they show even the tiniest flicker of disdain for my circumstances or for the poor accommodations, and if they were perturbed by the traces of muck on their shoes, they gave no sign. They asked me questions about myself, my background, and my hopes and dreams and seemed genuinely interested in the answers.

Before I was finished with my coffee, I wanted them to adopt me.

"Why do you call Consuelo Chelita?" I asked.

"It is a common diminutive in Mexico," Ernesto told me. "Like Jack is for John or Bill is for William."

"We are from Mexico City, originally," Sophia told me. "We immigrated when Ernesto was transferred to the US by Dow. He is a research chemist," she added with obvious pride.

Her husband hunched over his coffee, his face dark and brooding. "I wish I were a detective."

"Do the police, um, have any leads?"

"Those clowns? Ha!"

"Ernesto, please." Sophia touched her husband's hands where they gripped the cold mug.

"They have nothing, *mi corazon*! Nothing. No leads, no ideas… no brains."

"I know," she soothed. "I know."

"They can't even find her car."

I had lost sight of the obvious. Consuelo had driven from her home to college and met her fate here in Pottsville, Pennsylvania. Whoever killed her had to have hidden her car somewhere, or it would have turned up by now.

"What kind of car?" I asked.

"A ten-year-old Camry," Ernest said. "Dark green."

Sophia blotted her eyes with a tissue. "Chelita loved that car. She drove it everywhere, all over the country. To school, to work. Chess tournaments, tennis tournaments. She was active in a lot of college clubs."

"Did Consuelo ever mention somebody named Saiera? Saiera Khosani?"

Ernesto focused his laser-dark eyes on me. Sophia frowned and said, "No. I don't think so. That name is not familiar. Why do you ask?"

"Nothing, no reason." I shrugged. "I know someone who went to Syracuse a few years back."

"Does this person live here?" Ernesto demanded. "Maybe she is the 'friend' Chelita wanted to meet."

"No, no, no. Sorry." I stuck my palms out. The last thing I wanted was to bring the wrath of grieving parents down on Saiera. At least, not until I did some digging of my own. "Another town, another place. Long way away. Just asking about mutual friends is all."

The conversation dried up, and the Espinozas made their good-byes. Much hugging was had by all. I would have enjoyed it more, but my brain was churning with a new thought:

If I was a killer, where would I hide a ten-year-old dark-green Camry?

There was plenty of daylight left once the Espinozas left. I dithered around a bit by washing cups and tidying up the kitchen. Then I pulled a string for Tabitha to chase. She acted as though bygones were bygones, and she harbored no hard feelings about my trying to chop her up with an ax. I had my doubts. She had been known to hold a grudge, and I suspected one day in the near future, I might find cat poop in my shoes.

When I could put it off no longer, I ventured outside after telling George, "No, not this time," and closing the door on his face. I cut across the cemetery on a determined bearing toward the blaze-marked tree. I left the ax in the shed.

A line of bloated, blackened clouds swallowed the northern sky, and a frigid wind whipped leaves into chattering swirls. It didn't take a meteorological degree to predict that snow was on the way. The smell of wet ash carried from the nearby remains of one of my burn piles. I had the place to myself, and the silence wrapped me in cold fingers of melancholy. I slumped inside my jacket. The visit from the Espinozas had depressed me. Their grief was palpable, their loss as obvious as a missing arm or leg. Technically, as husband and wife, they might still be a family, but without Consuelo, they were as dead and broken as a tree split by lightning, damaged beyond repair and living on momentum only.

Lost in my own black mood, I barely twitched when Mrs. Fairweather appeared beside me.

"Mr. Langston, I must say, I'm very impressed by the strides you've made in the short time you've been here. But still—"

"Thank you, ma'am. Sorry, I don't mean to be rude, but I don't have time to talk about gardening just now. I have to attend to something." I nodded at the blaze-marked tree. I had paused at the spot where I needed to leave the path. "Unless I'm mistaken, Phillipa Fontenot's crypt is over there. I have to make sure."

The old lady's lips pruned, forming a red lipstick circle. "Now that's a name I hadn't heard in a long time. Wretched woman."

I stepped back. "You know her? Sorry, knew her, I mean."

"Of course. I had no idea she was buried here, with white people."

"Ah, yes. Well..." My jaw clenched, and I wanted to lash out, but another voice inside my head urged calm.

This was an old lady, dead years before I was born, raised in a different time and long gone from the earth—since 1962 if I remembered her grave marker correctly.

"She came from the South," Mrs. Fairweather mused. Her narrowed eyes focused on the horizon or somewhere deep in the past. She made a vague shooing gesture with one hand. "Practiced that hoodoo voodoo, sacrilegious nonsense, as I recall. She lived in a shanty over in Beeville, and the sheriff said he could do nothing about her as he had no jurisdiction over there."

"Beeville?"

"The colored town," sniffed Mrs. Fairweather. "Down by the river."

I had no clue about any Beeville and didn't recall seeing any such town on the map though that was not unusual for a "colored" town in the old days. Many such places once existed—little settlements of former slaves or migrating African Americans who weren't welcome inside the boundaries of "white" towns and so formed their own communities nearby. They worked in the factories and shops or cleaned the homes in the towns they were denied residence. Often these communities were absorbed as the dominant town grew, or they sank into the soil and disappeared forever as times changed and the residents moved away.

"Why do you say she was practicing voodoo?" I asked.

"Oh, everybody knew." The old lady waved another dismissive hand. "The menfolk would go down there, over to her place, if they needed a little something to... to, ah..." Mrs. Fairweather looked away, and I could swear a bloom of red crept up her cheeks. *Whaddya know. Ghosts can blush.* "Anyway, she brewed up all kinds of potions in that shack. Who all knew what she got up to in there? The devil's work, no doubt of that."

I didn't know Mrs. Fairweather all that well, but I was beginning to dislike the woman. Her tone had the gossipy snip of an annoying old biddy, laced with prejudice and snobbery. "Any evidence of that," I asked her, "or is this all just make-believe?"

"Watch your tone, young man," she snapped. "I don't have to stand for sass. I'm dead, you know."

"I understand." I pitched my voice to sound apologetic, not because I felt sorry but because I wanted to keep the old lady talking. "Tell me why you believe Pippah was up to no good."

"Well, I don't put up with gossip, of course, but Bertie Goetz and Phyllis Steinhauer said they heard she used animal sacrifice in her rituals. Chickens and cats and dogs and such like. It's all part of that... religion, I guess you'd call it. Devil worship is more like it."

"They... heard it? They didn't see it?"

"Yes, but then some young men—white men, I mean—went down to the river to drink some beer and listen to music on their car radios—hanging out, you know? They imbibed overmuch and fell asleep—passed out, you know—and in the morning, one was gone. They found his body washed up miles and miles downriver." Mrs. Fairweather leaned in close, a conspiratorial glimmer in her eyes. "His throat had been cut. Just like how they do in those ritual sacrifices."

"Uh-huh."

"Now, there's some who said the young man had gone into Beeville for some... entertainment, if you like. But there were quite a number who believed the witch, Phillipa Fontenot, cut the boy's throat for her own business. Not long after that, two other men from Pottsville lost their lives down near her shanty, both with their throats cut and their bodies dumped in the river. Some say there were... other things... other horrors perpetrated on the bodies. The state police came to investigate, and they arrested Miss Fontenot but had to let her go for lack of evidence."

"Was anybody ever arrested?"

"No," said Mrs. Fairweather, touching a finger to her chin in thought. "No, they never did, as I recall. Soon after Fontenot was released from custody, she disappeared. No one else was murdered after that, and the case grew cold. Everybody figured Phillipa Fontenot had skipped out for parts unknown. The police ran out of leads, and the case was never closed. At least, not while I was alive."

"Hmm. When was this? Do you happen to recall?"

"Well, now, let me think. Mid-to-late fifties, I imagine. It would have been after we moved to Ford Street, because I hadn't met Bertie until I joined her bridge club, and she's the one who told me about Earl Weaver getting killed—"

"Wait. Weaver? As in Arlo Weaver?"

"Oh my." Mrs. Fairweather's eyes went round behind her spectacles. "I had forgotten that Arlo lost his brother that night. The Weaver family lived on Orchard Road, just up from the Tarwaters, and their daddy was caretaker here. Arlo took over tending the grounds after his father passed in 1962. The year before me, in fact."

A cold, wet drop of rain smacked my cheek. I barely noticed. "Are you saying... are you saying Pippah was suspected in the death of Arlo Weaver's brother and... and soon after that, she disappeared... and her bones are somewhere here, in Shady Terraces? Where Arlo's father was caretaker?"

Mrs. Fairweather flinched at my intensity. "I didn't know anything about her bones, young man. Not until you mentioned she was buried here."

I stood there a moment, like a rusty robot that had ground to a halt, letting the implications sink in. I had no problem picturing Pippah slicing the throats of three young men. After having met her face-to-face—or soul-to-soul, so to speak—it was obvious to me that Pippah was as twisted and sick as dying snake. She had been very explicit about how she liked using knives to carve people into abstract sculptures, so the "other horrors" perpetrated on the young men from Pottsville, and on Donald Glatfelter, sounded a lot like Pippah's work. And the cops having arrested and then released a Black woman suspected of the crime, in an era of "white only" drinking fountains and "colored" towns like Beeville... well, that must not have sat well with the people of Pottsville.

Had Arlo or his father, or both, sought vengeance on their own? Had they killed Phillipa Fontenot and buried her body in secret? It made sense. And now Pippah was clawing her way back from the grave, taking advantage of the special circumstances of the Shady Terrace's cemetery grounds to reanimate her evil spirit and... and what?

Resume her serial killer habits, of course.

Someone had killed Consuelo, and while bonded with Pippah, I "remembered" the trigger that had woken her from death being the innocent blood seeping into the soil of Shady Terraces. Had it been Consuelo's? And after that... what? No ghost had wielded the shotgun to kill Arlo or flensed Donald Glatfelter and strung him up in a tree. Had Pippah possessed others before me? Is that how she was gaining power, by invading the souls of living people and using them to do her dirty work?

If that was the case, no one was safe. Anyone in the cemetery could be either a vessel of her evil will, turned into a weapon, or a victim of that possessed body.

"Young man?... Young man?... Are you listening to me?" I blinked back to the present to realize that Mrs. Fairweather had been nattering on about the condition of the grounds, expounding on her favorite topic: weed control. "What will our guests think when they see—"

I spun on my heel and strode away. "Sorry, Mrs. Fairweather, but there won't be any visitors for a while. Shady Terraces is temporarily closed for business."

Chapter 25

It wasn't until I finished locking the gate that it struck me: once again, I had been deflected in my effort to locate the crypt where Pippah's bones rested. *Her murdered remains*, I amended, for I now believed that someone had taken justice into their own hands and done away with the voodoo woman who liked to play with knives.

I hesitated at the gates for a bit, twirling my key ring around one finger, my lips twisted sideways while I sorted through priorities. What I really wanted to do was head for the library and look up old news articles from the mid-to-late fifties. A series of murders in a small town like Pottsville would have generated a fair amount of press coverage, and I could get a better picture of who might have been involved in the Phillipa Fontenot case. The impulse to run for the library felt natural, like something I really should do instead of looking for the crypt.

I know where it is. I marked the tree. I can always find it tomorrow, after I know more about what I'm looking for. Or the next day.

"No, dammit." I smacked a palm with a fist. Something was pushing me away from that crypt. Either my own fear kept me from it, or Pippah was seeping into my subconscious and diverting my attention. I sort of hoped it was the latter, as weird as that sounded. One, it would mean I wasn't as big a coward as I'd always suspected, and two, it would mean Pippah felt the discovery of her remains posed a danger to her plans.

"Stay on target, Red Leader," I muttered to myself.

The bruised, ugly mass of winter weather gathering in the north darkened the entire horizon, and in the ten minutes it took me to trek back to the blaze-marked tree, the fitful gusts of wind had become a near-constant barrage of cold arctic blasts. My hair whipped around my face, and a plastic cup scudded across the ground by my feet. I huddled in my coat and considered heading home. Much better to be warm and safe inside, cuddled up with George and Tabitha over a mug of hot soup...

I was halfway back to the apartment when I pulled up short.

Are you freaking kidding me?

I turned around and forced myself to march in a straight line. I touched the scarred oak as I passed it, verifying it was real and the ax cut I had chopped into its bark was not a figment of my imagination. The path led between two overgrown roses. They looked especially thorny, and their canes thrashed around in the wind, making them appear as living multitentacled beasts guarding the entrance to a wizard's lair, which was not far from the truth, come to think on it. The branches whipped around, threatening to shred me if I dared to pass.

I should go back. Get a machete from the shed. No sense in getting cut to ribbons trying to... arrgh. No. Move, damn it.

I pulled my hood up, sucked in a deep breath, and powered through the gap like a running back hitting the line. The ground dipped, and I windmilled down a slope, skidding to a stop at a narrow path that wound along a hollow between two low hills. Trees lined the sides of the path and, during the summer, would present an idyllic stroll for the cemetery visitor to wander at their leisure—secluded, tranquil, a nice walk if they didn't mind the grave markers poking up along the path.

Now, however, with bare branches overhanging the trail and the howling of an angry wind churning the debris, the trail had turned sinister, morbid, spiteful.

Spasms of shivers wracked my body. I did not want to be here. Did not. Did not. Did not.

Daylight fled at the approach of black swollen clouds. Winter darkness stole my willpower. The next thing I expected to see was a sickly green glow lighting the path ahead. It did not come. Pippah was either recovering her strength or not aware of my presence. Stan had said time was different *over there*, and they weren't aware of events transpiring in the real world as they tapped the power and gained enough strength to manifest. Perhaps Pippah slept on, and it was only a projection of her evil nature that kept casual—or even determined—explorers away from her tomb. The other night, when she manifested, she had wanted me to find her, to draw me in so that she could possess my body. No doubt when she was on the other side, she preferred to keep people away.

Well. To hell with that.

Teeth chattering, I carried on, one foot in front of the other.

The path flared to a wider bower, a scene I had last observed by the green light of hell. A brick wall cut the back off one side of a hill. The wall arched high in the middle and tapered to near ground level on either side. Two wooden doors stood in the middle of the wall, tinged greenish with oxidized iron fittings. Rot had eaten away at the once-solid doors. As I watched, a gray worm wriggled from a hole in the wood and squirmed loose to plop into the compost below. It writhed around in a mindless, twisting ball, either sick or dying... or maybe freezing in the cold.

A loose chain was piled on the ground near the door, with a padlock as big as a salad plate next to it. The lock itself was as old as Moses's river raft and crusted with age, with one shank broken loose from the body of the lock.

Someone or something had broken the lock on the crypt doors.

I took a step closer, and it felt as if I was walking underwater. Each step required effort, and the air was as thick as soured milk.

There was a name engraved in the lintel.

It was not a name I expected or even knew.

Brecht.

That was all it said. Brecht. Did the Brecht family know they had a stowaway in their private mausoleum? Somehow, I doubted it. Arlo Weaver, or his father, had chosen the place, and I suspect they knew there were no more Brechts to be entombed here. No, whoever the Brechts were, they had not asked to have a murdered woman concealed inside their private burial chambers.

But Pippah was there. Just on the other side of those doors.

I could feel her.

Her spirit filled me with sickness as though I were drinking motor oil straight from the crankcase. I smelled her foul breath exhaling into my nostrils. The stench of her soul leached through those doors and sucked away every last ounce of decency in the world, turning it bleak and dead and corrupt.

I had to get away.

I had to.

This time, when I felt myself turning away, I didn't stop.

In fact, I ran.

ONE THING ABOUT A DOG: they have no understanding when it comes to their human not feeling like going for the Walk of Bodily Functions. George didn't care that my legs were shaky and I felt like throwing up, nor that I had just run away from a supernatural encounter with a serial killer's ghost. Not to mention, it was cold as a snowman's balls outside. No, George needed to go for a walk, and he needed to go *now*.

So be it.

George was a creature of habit, so it was no surprise when he headed east on Shady Elm toward Orchard, following the cemetery's perimeter wall as we had done several times before. I was layered up: T-shirt, flannel shirt, hoodie, thrift-store coat, and my second-best pair of jeans and hiking boots. I shivered despite all that. For George, of course, the near-freezing temperature delighted him, and the husky bounded back and forth from tree to hydrant to wall. I trailed along, mechanically using my plastic bags to clean up behind him, my Pooper Scooper routine on autopilot. My brain ran down a darker track.

I have found the wicked witch's lair. Now what?

Remove the bones. Burn the bones. Hot, hot fire. Remember?

Oh. Yeah. Good luck with that.

The amount of willpower it would take to face that hillside tomb, to open those rotted doors, venture inside...

I shuddered.

Why me? Why do I have to be the one? I'm nothing but a total screwup who needed a cushy job while I tried to write.

I sneered at myself. *Write? Huh. Who am I kidding? I haven't written a word since I got here. All this material, and I've been doing nothing but eating, sleeping, and chatting with dead people.*

Maybe that was a little harsh, but I wasn't feeling charitable toward myself at the moment. I had accomplished some things, sure. Cleaned up some brush piles. Straightened out the office and gotten the billing and filing organized. Found a couple of murder victims. Been possessed by an evil spirit and nearly chopped my dog's head off...

A busy couple of weeks, I admit. But still.

The greasy fear that had clamped around my heart when I approached the Brecht mausoleum had left me woozy and unsure of myself. No, strike that. I was already unsure of myself, and the terror seizing me earlier had confirmed my worst expectations of my own cowardice. Maybe my lack of bravery was responsible for Tony's death, or maybe not—a hung jury there. But the verdict was clear when it came to facing the horror of opening the door to Pippah's final resting place and collecting her remains for disposal. I didn't have it in me.

Heaped on top of that realization, I had to conclude I also wasn't smart enough or resourceful enough to figure out who killed Consuelo. I mean, seriously? I was no detective. No Hardy Boy or Shaggy with his faithful Scooby. In fact, the way my stomach had churned when I approached that tomb, I was closer to Nancy Spew than Nancy Drew.

Verdict: Useless as charged.

And now my dog had disappeared.

I peered into the gloom, having long since lost track of where my feet were taking me. We were somewhere along Orchard Road, shy of the Tarwater place. Hulking trees on my left. *Ah.* It was the Hixon or Mixon—*Hixton!*—place. The abandoned farmhouse was buried amongst the trees and cordoned off behind a sagging fence and a rusty gate with a new lock. George had explored the place before and was now most assuredly anointing it again with golden husky water, freshening up his marks.

"George! George!"

A happy bark answered my call. Yes, George was rambling around the Hixton property, sniffing and squirting. No, George had no interest in coming back to heel. Yes, Brad was going to have to go get him. No, Brad was not happy about it.

I sniffed and wiped my runny nose with a sleeve. The chill wind battered my coat and made my eyes water. Ice particles, the forerunners of true snowflakes, surfed the breeze. According to Addy, who should know, on the other side of the fence lurked hidden obstacles concealed by scrubby brush. Stumbling around in the gathering darkness would no doubt see me impaled on some abandoned piece of machinery, or I would tumble down a hidden well, where I would live out my last miserable hours soaking in frigid water, full of despair and weighted by regret.

I hiked one leg over the fence, careful of the barbs threatening my jewels, holding down the wire as I levered my other leg over. Of course, I hung the cuff of my jeans on a barb and wound up hopping like a stork until it tore free with a nice ripping sound. *Dammit. Third-best pair.*

"George! I'm giving you two baths when we get home. Do you hear me? Two baths!"

I cut through the weeds to the twin-rutted path of the driveway, which ran from the gate through the woods, deeper into the property. It dipped low and crossed a muddy ditch that would run with water on rainy days. To one side lay a junked-out car, shot full of target practice and slowly sinking into the earth. Other bits of abandoned equipment peeked up from the surrounding brush—a washing machine, a hot-water heater, and a hunk of farm equipment with hooks for digging the earth. *A harrow?*

Dog prints in the mud led me through the band of trees to a clearing. An old farmhouse dominated the clearing, something from *Grapes of Wrath* with a dash of *The Amityville Horror* thrown on top and left to die. Dry rot and decay. Gaping windows and boarded-over doors. A sagging porch clung to the front, its support beams leaning at random angles and threatening to drop the overhang onto anyone brave enough to step up and risk the dry-rotted floorboards. The house had once been painted white with green shutters.

A feral cat zipped into the darkness under the house as I stepped into the clearing.

To the right of the house stood a chicken coop, raised off the ground by four stout posts. Sturdy and well made, the coop seemed in better condition than the house except for the debris caught underneath it. A tangle of scrap lumber had been haphazardly piled under the coop as if somebody had planned its funeral pyre but never lit the match. Joan of Arc as played by Joan of Coop.

Beyond the coop loomed a barn. The twin-rutted drive led across the yard to the barn doors. One of the massive doors had broken loose from its upper hinge and leaned out into space at the corner. The door remained attached to the barn by the desperate grasp of three screws in the lower hinge, and its center latch pushed into its partner door. It squealed as the wind caught it, wobbling outward like a drunk holding a lamppost.

"George! Get away from there!"

The husky, of course, was busy sniffing around the base of the barn door, oblivious to the danger hanging over his head. I trotted over and grabbed him by the collar.

"C'mon, you bonehead."

When I pulled George to the side, the door wagged down in a particularly strong gust, and I did a double take. Something gleamed inside the barn. I put my nose to the gap for a better look. A hulking, metallic shape materialized as my eyes adjusted to the deep black inside the barn. Window glass. Chrome. Shaped in the familiar form of a car.

There was a car inside an abandoned barn.

My heart stuttered. I brushed aside the notion that this was Hixton's car, abandoned when they moved away. Nobody moves away and leaves a car in the garage.

How about that? Start wondering where the car went, and boom, here it is. Like maybe somebody's watching out for me. Or leading me.

George assumed I wanted to play when I pushed him back to the chicken coop, so I had to bark "Stay!" a few times... well, many times... before he got the message. I snaked out a solid two-by-four, about six feet long, from the pile of loose scrap lumber under the coop and ran back to the barn. After jamming the board into the gap atop the last hinge, I leaned into it. The last three screws never had a chance. They gave up with a dying scream as the door crashed over and hit the dirt with a solid *whump,* flopping like the lapel of the world's largest overcoat.

The husky howled and danced in a circle, upset by the big noise I was making.

Only a wan bit of daylight leaked through the winter clouds, but it was enough to push back the darkness of the barn's interior. Rodents scuttled away from the open door, disappearing into cracks and under debris, small twitches of motion barely seen. The inside was one big space without interior partitions. Benches lined both walls. Machinery and loose parts rusted in assorted piles. These impressions came to me from a distance, noted as part of my first impression and ignored. What arrested my attention was directly in front of me, taking up the bulk of the space inside the barn.

Under a coating of dust, squatting on deflated tires, rested the carcass of a foreign-made automobile. Specifically, a Toyota Camry. Kansas plates. A Syracuse Orangemen bumper sticker.

An electric sensation prickled my body, much as if I had opened a closet and found a stack of gold bars or walked into a classroom and realized the one, lone empty seat was right next to Miss Universe. This was Consuelo's car. Of that I had no doubt.

All the implications of finding the murdered girl's car in an abandoned barn behind a gate secured by a nearly new lock overwhelmed my logic circuits, and I went blank for a frozen moment in time.

George bumped my leg and broke my paralysis. I knelt beside him, put an arm around his neck, and pointed with my free hand.

"Look, Scooby-Doo. A clue."

I SWITCHED ON MY PHONE'S flashlight and picked past the barn door for a closer look. The Hixtons or some previous owner had poured a concrete slab for a barn floor, though it had not weathered well. It was cracked and buckled, with weeds growing up in patches, and grit crunched underfoot.

Grime fogged the car's windows. Dust, animal droppings, and unidentified gunk coated the once-green exterior, and the tires were well on their way to pancaking.

I sidled around the trunk and approached the driver's side door. A fine, even layer of dust covered the handle. If I touched it, I would leave a nice, clear fingerprint for Czerniak and Swanson to add to their collection of Reasons to Convict Brad of Murder. I scouted the bits and pieces of equipment and parts and junk scattered around the barn and found an anonymous angled bit of metal—some kind of bracket—about the size of my palm. It fit under the car's door handle like a cupped hand.

I pulled the latch, and the door popped open with barely a squeak. The dome light remained off. The battery would have gone dead long ago. A musty smell rolled over me from the interior. Oxidized plastic and dried leather. Stale air, underlain with the faint trace of something flowery and girlish, that faded as soon as I smelled it, as if the last Consuelo's spirit had been trapped inside the car, only to be released when I opened the door.

Consuelo was a messy traveler. Drink cups occupied both center console cupholders, one from Starbucks and one from Jack in the Box. Pink lipstick rimmed the white lid of the Starbucks coffee cup and the tip of the soft drink straw. An empty bag of Cheetos and a half-consumed package of Twizzlers lay in the passenger seat. Tissues, junk food wrappers, plastic spoons, and other trash told the story of a college girl on a road trip, more concerned with making miles than tidiness.

School supplies filled the back seat from footwell to window. Dorm stuff like lamps and desk accessories, a new-in-box HP printer, and an ironing board from Target, still in its shrink-wrap. Cases of paper. Three-ring binders. I think it was the sight of all her college stuff that hit me the hardest.

All that potential, all that future adventure—wasted.

George nosed his way in and tried to climb into the car. Lots of great smells, new places to explore. I held him back by the collar.

"No," I commanded. "We can't touch anything. Pottsville CSI will analyze your husky fur and tie us to the car. Czerniak will have a spontaneous orgasm. We don't need that hassle."

That introduced a new puzzle for me to solve. How in the hell was I supposed to notify the cops about the whereabouts of Consuelo's car? The second I called this in, Czerniak and Swanson would be all over me like a rash. They would never believe I had just stumbled upon a key piece of evidence, and even the famous barrister, Maurice Chesterfield, might have a hard time getting me off.

I could go the anonymous route, but they had equipment these days to trace calls and analyze voices, even when disguised, or so said the cop shows on TV. I would have to be very, very careful about how I reported this. And I had to report it. Pottsville's detective duo might not be the greatest pair of sleuths since Rizzoli and Isles, but they had far more resources than I, along with an entire crime lab at their disposal.

"We have to report it," I told George though I was really telling myself. "We have to."

I was leaning over the driver's seat, very carefully not touching anything while shining my light around and hip-checking George. I glanced at the dashboard as I backed away and noticed a square bit of paper near the driver's side floormat. No, it wasn't a square bit of paper. A picture. Something cut by hand from a larger picture. Head and shoulders only. A woman in the act of tucking her dark hair behind one ear, smiling, and ducking her head as if embarrassed. Someone—Consuelo, I presumed—had drawn pink hearts all around the woman's face.

"Great," I said. "I fall in love with a ghost, and it turns out she likes women. Even my supernatural relationships are doomed from the start."

I leaned in and shined my light directly on the picture. My ear was almost touching the steering wheel. There was something familiar about the expression on the woman's face...

"Oh. Shit." My voice came out in a hoarse whisper. "Oh shit, oh shit, oh shit."

The young woman in the picture had a very striking face—not exactly pretty but handsome, with dark, overshadowing eyebrows and strong cheekbones. She was younger, softer somehow, in the picture, but there was no doubt in my mind about who it was.

Chapter 26

The ramifications of finding Saiera Khosani's picture in the car of a murdered woman rattled around the inside of my head like a pachinko ball. I stood there for a long time, staring at the photo on the floorboard. Sensing my preoccupation, George tried nudging his way past me to get a better sniff of the car's interior. I held him back by reflex.

Okay, so the girl I like is a gay murder victim. And the other girl I like is a killer and gay. Time to move on, Brad. Look up the word for lifelong celibacy. Commit to it.

I used the door-opening bracket to push the trunk-release button. It popped open with a dull thunk. Pulling George by the collar, I circled around to the rear of the car then lifted the trunk lid all the way up with my bit of metal. The trunk was stuffed with suitcases and plastic bags of new dorm supplies—towels, toiletries, and wrapped bundles of clothes hangers, ten to a pack.

A rectangular leather case lay atop the pile. I flicked the brass latch with my improvised tool and levered open the lid. Twin rows of carved chess pieces greeted me, dark brown and ivory white, each nestled in its own velvet slot. A folded board was tucked into the lid, held in place with twist clips.

Something Mrs. Espinoza said came back to me. *"Chelita loved that car. She drove it everywhere, all over the country. To school, to work. Chess tournaments, tennis tournaments. She was active in a lot of college clubs."*

I squashed the impulse to dig any further into Consuelo's belongings. It felt wrong, like I was a Peeping Tom. All I needed to complete my spiral into prurient obsession would be to open a suitcase and find the poor girl's intimate apparel. Wouldn't that make a pretty picture? Creepy Guy Caught Sniffing Dead Girl's Undies. Film at ten. I closed the lid on the set and managed to seat the latch without touching anything with my bare fingers. A bit paper from an old feed sack helped me get the trunk closed.

It was time to go. I needed to get out and find a way to report the hidden Camry to the cops—maybe a postcard instead of a telephone call. Something. Anything. The barn's interior, cold though it was, had turned stuffy and oppressive, and the whisper of falling snow outside sounded like the approach of Death riding his white horse.

However, I had one more thing to do before I left.

FAT FLAKES OF SNOW blew sideways through the trees as I made my way back to the road—not blizzard conditions, by any means, but rather a wet, cold prelude to a heavy dumping to come. George raced about, snapping at the flakes as they passed his nose.

I had left everything in the Toyota as I found it, with one exception. The photo of Saiera Khosani was tucked deep in my coat pocket.

I had used a rusty nail to pick it loose from the carpet so I could take the picture without touching anything. Not one cell containing my DNA would be left in the car if I could help it. I closed the door with a push from my metal bracket then carried both the bracket and nail outside and threw them into the forest as far as I could. I buried the two-by-four that I'd used to pry loose the hinges back into the pile under the chicken coop. There was no way to be one hundred percent certain that I had prevented any forensic evidence linking me to the barn, but I believed I had done as well as any master criminal could, given the circumstances.

By the time I made it back to the fence, it might as well have been full night. I turned on my flashlight app so I could find the barbed wire before it found me. I had one leg over the top strand when the night brightened. I squinted and threw up a hand as a car's headlights appeared from the south, pinning me like a deer.

The cops! was my first thought, followed closely by *I'm going to be arrested for trespassing. They got me dead to rights. If they search the farm, they'll find the car... Maybe I should go ahead and report it now—get it over with. Which is when they match the picture in my pocket to the dust-free gap in the floorboard, and Brad goes to jail for evidence tampering.*

A blocky vehicle, like a box truck or a van, was silhouetted behind the glow of headlights. I let out the breath I was holding. It wasn't the cops, then. But the car slowed. Gravel crunched as it pulled to the shoulder.

Nope, not the cops. The USPS.

The van stopped, and Saiera Khosani leaned over to open the passenger door.

"Hey, stranger! Wanna ride?"

"OH, UH... HI."

Saiera leaned over the wheel, watching me with shadowed eyes. Her expression, lit only by the yellow glow of the dashboard lights, was unreadable. Expectant? Suspicious?

"What in the world are you doing over there?" Her tone rang a little false to my ears, as if weighted with more than simple curiosity. Did she know about the car in the barn? Had she stashed it there after she killed Consuelo? I wanted to give Saiera the benefit of the doubt. Maybe Consuelo had met her murderer before she had time to connect with Saiera. Maybe she'd stopped for gas or a flat tire—no, scratch that. All the Camry's tires were on the original rims—no space-saver spare doughnut. But maybe she'd been killed before she met the object of her affection, Saiera Khosani.

Well... it was possible...

I high-legged over the fence—no rips this time—and trudged across the verge to stand in front of the open door. Heat from the van's cab puffed out, creating an oasis of warmth.

I looked at Saiera. Saiera looked at me. The back of my hand, clenched in my coat pocket, touched the photo I'd taken from the Camry. The pause stretched into a moment then extended into a standstill.

George, of course, had no hesitancy about jumping into a car with a murderess. He bowled past my legs, tail flapping, and landed a pair of muddy paws on Saiera's leg. She laughed and scrubbed his ruff and told him what a good boy he was.

Yeah. Good boy. Can't smell a killer when he's in her lap.

"So," I said. "Late route?"

"Huh?"

"Seemed kind of late." I gestured to the mail van. "To, ah, be delivering mail."

"It's only just gone three. But I've finished my route."

"Oh." The early dark of the winter storm had me fooled. Snow swirled around me, sticking to my shoulders like big chunks of dandruff. The temperature had fallen ten degrees at least since George and I had set out for our walk. "Well. I guess we'd better get back. C'mon, George."

George indicated he had no intention of moving from the warm cab by plopping himself down in the space between the two seats, squashing what looked like a pile of junk mail fliers.

"Are you silly?" Saiera said. "Hop in; I'll give you a ride."

"I... uh..."

"Come on. I won't bite." Her teeth flashed in a sinister grin, and she waggled her eyebrows. "Unless you ask for it."

In the suspended moment before I moved, an odd collection of thoughts flashed through my mind. *If she and Consuelo were hooking up, does that mean Saiera's a lesbian? She seems to like me, so does that mean she goes both ways? Or is she just playing me to find out how much I know about the murder? It was awfully suspicious when she showed up right after I found Consuelo's remains and asked a bunch of questions. I'm bigger and stronger than she is—I should be okay. It's not like she can overpower me. But if she stabs me when my back is turned... So I don't turn my back on her. If I get in the van, she might try to kill me. If I don't get in the van, she'll know I suspect her. I'll look stupid.*

The things we do to avoid looking stupid.

"Okay," I said and climbed into the seat. The sliding door closed with a clunk that sounded much like I imagined the slamming of a prison door. Or the last nail in my coffin.

"You going to tell me?" Saiera asked.

"Tell you what?"

"What you were up to on the Hixton property?"

She knows, she knows, she knows. My face grew hot, and I shifted in the seat, putting my back closer to the door. I fumbled—casually and nonchalantly—behind me until my fingers closed around the latch.

"Oh... ah, George. Went over there. I had to... He wouldn't come back unless I went to fetch him. He was having too much fun. Exploring." *Shut up, Brad, before you babble your way onto a knife blade.*

"And did you find anything?" Saiera put the van in gear and checked her mirror before wheeling out in the start of a U-turn. Did I detect a note of false casualness in her voice? Or was I simply imagining it?

"An old house. I didn't get too close. It looked like a tetanus shot waiting to happen."

"I imagine. No one's lived there for years. Since I was in high school, at least."

"What did you do after high school? Join the Postal Service?" *Clever, Brad. The type of question worthy of a detective. Smooth as Hercule Poirot.*

"Two years of college before I decided it wasn't for me. I came back, took the civil service exam, and *voila*, here I am."

"Really? What college? I mean, where?"

She slanted a puzzled look in my direction. "Syracuse."

"When was this?"

"Couple of years ago."

Uh-huh. Then a chill broke out on my skin, despite the van's heater blowing on max. How much more coincidence did I need before it stopped being coincidence and became premeditation? The van puttered down Orchard Road, snowflakes dancing in the headlights. It was dark out. I was alone with a killer. I needed to shut the hell up before I revealed how much I knew.

"Did you know Consuelo?" The words came out of my mouth. I don't know why. They just did. So much for shutting the hell up.

"Who? Oh, the murdered girl?"

"She went to Syracuse. About the same time you did. I thought... maybe you knew her."

The van squealed to a stop at the intersection of Orchard and Shady Elm. Saiera flicked on the left turn signal but didn't move. She put both hands on the wheel and tapped a finger in time to the clicking of the signal indicator. *Tick-tick, tick-tick.*

She didn't look at me when she spoke. "What are you really asking me, Brad?"

George shuffled around between the seats and flopped into a different position. Paper crackled under him. I shifted to put more of my back against the door. My left hand was twisted behind me, cramping a bit as I gripped the latch. I mentally rehearsed my escape. Just a quick tug, and I'd be out. I took a shaky breath.

"Just curious if you'd ever met is all. While you were at school."

She turned to me with an expression of... what? Sadness? Hurt? Or remorse that now she'd have to eliminate me as a witness. "You don't think I would have mentioned that? At least once?"

"Well... yeah..."

Tick-tick, tick-tick.

"Unless you're saying something else," Saiera said into the growing chasm of silence between us. "Unless you're saying I was trying to keep that a secret. That I knew her but didn't want to say because... because what? It would incriminate me."

So much for my Hercule Poirot act. This wasn't going well at all. Saiera's brow had clouded over, and whatever her earlier expression had been, it turned to pure anger now.

"I found a picture," I blurted. "In... ah... in her things. It was you, and it had hearts drawn all around your face." I was breathing double-time now, but I found I couldn't stop.

Saiera leaned back in her seat. Her foot held the brake. The signal indicator blinked, painting her face like a green flashing strobe light.

Tick-tick, tick-tick.

"My picture," she finally said.

"Yes."

"Show me."

"I found it in her car. In Hixton's barn." *Good job, Brad. Way to paint a target on your back.* I shifted my grip on the door handle. The seat creaked under me. With my free hand, I picked the photo out of my pocket and held it out. "Your picture was there. With hearts."

"Hearts."

"Like lovey-dovey hearts."

"And you think... What? We were lovers?"

I half shrugged. "Anything's possible."

Saiera said something in a foreign language. By the way she spat it out, I suspected it was something nasty, a gypsy curse. She shook her head slowly, as if infinitely saddened by the world, and shifted the gear lever into park. She flicked a switch, and the dome light turned on. Saiera angled the picture to catch the light.

"I don't... No, wait." She sounded puzzled. "I remember this. I hated that turtleneck, and it annoyed me this made the yearbook. This is from a high school yearbook picture, from in front of the school. One of those candid shots they use to fill in pages. You know, like, *Hey look at the kids goofing off and having a great time here at ol' Pottsville High.*"

"High school? How in the world would Consuelo get a copy of your high school's yearbook?"

"And why?" Saiera handed the picture back. "I didn't know her, Brad. I swear."

The overhead light cast her eyes in shadow, but I felt their weight on me. The next few years crawled by as we sat there with the engine muttering and the wipers ticking back and forth. I dry swallowed, my brain activity down to a background hiss of white noise. Intellect was out the window. Instinct ruled.

"Ah hell," I said at last. "I believe you."

"Good." She nodded once, firmly, and sagged a bit in her seat. "Good."

Almost, said the skeptic living inside me. *I almost believe you.* A timeworn phrase came to mind: *Have trust in people, but always cut the cards.* I was ninety-eight—well, ninety-two—percent sure Saiera was telling the truth. However, the question of how her picture had made it into a murdered girl's car remained unanswered. If we solved that mystery, maybe we would find Consuelo's killer.

I cleared my throat. "So. Where do we find a copy of this year-book?"

"I THREW ALL MINE OUT," Saiera said.

"Where else—"

"What does it matter? How is seeing the yearbook—" Saiera's voice grew cold. "Unless you're trying to see if I'm telling the truth. Is that it?"

"No, no, no..." *Well, yes, actually. That's exactly what I'm doing. Think fast.* "No, I'm looking for... someone else from Pottsville. Someone who might want to try and frame you or is... maybe... someone who might have a connection to you or Consuelo. Hell, I don't know. It just seems like a logical place to look for a clue. Isn't that where all the detective shows tell you? *Go look in the yearbook! It's full of clues!* At least, that's what I've seen." I shrugged. "I don't have any better ideas. Do you?"

We played the staring game for a few more years. I could sense the gears turning behind Saiera's eyes. I tried out my best earnest Boy Scout open face.

"Fine." She switched out the light and put the van in drive. "Let's go."

"Go where?"

"The library. Where else?"

The snow wasn't sticking to the streets yet, though they glistened, black and wet and slippery enough to play shuffleboard. The twin beams of the postal van spotlighted heavy flakes an instant before they hit the windshield and were smeared by the beating wipers. Saiera drove with skill on the wet surface, puttering the van along at a respectable clip. We turned on Pennsylvania Highway 68, which became Main Street through town, in under five minutes—a long five minutes as the silence settled thick and tense between us.

We reached the town square and drove past the Route 66 Cafe and the offices of the Pottsville Post-Dispatch before swinging into the library parking lot. I got out. George shook himself and hopped out after me. Saiera got out on her side and slammed the door. I closed mine gently. We walked up the library steps and into the building without a word or look passing between us.

"Oh, dearie me," sang out Thelma Entwistle from behind the counter. "Look what the cat dragged in. And in such foul weather too. Oh, it's you." The last bit seemed addressed to Saiera more than me.

I remembered the librarian had called Saiera a Traveler, aka gypsy, in a disapproving tone. Thelma narrowed her eyes when she saw George, and I thought she was going to order him out. I was prepared with my "you have a dog" argument, but in the end, she said nothing.

"Where are the Pottsville High yearbooks?" Saiera asked without preamble. Apparently the lack of love went both directions.

"Local history, third row in nonfiction, first, second, and third shelf. Fifty years' worth is all we have." Thelma switched her gaze to me. "Bunch of old rubbish, if you ask me. Should have binned the lot years ago."

I winked at Thelma and tagged along after Saiera, who power-walked into the nonfiction section and found the correct shelf. She scanned the spines with a finger, muttering the years as she went. "Ah-ha. Here. My four years of lowest education."

She carried the volumes to a table in the back. A sign reading Quiet, Please—Study Area hung from the ceiling tiles, held up with thumbtacks and string. It stirred in the heat blowing from a nearby vent. The table gleamed and smelled faintly of Pledge. George sniffed around the base of a shelving unit. I recognized the signs as preparation to mark the shelf as his. I called him over, and he flopped at my feet.

We sat side by side, and Saiera handed me two yearbooks. "I don't remember which year that picture was taken, but I think I was a junior. I'll look in my last two years. You check freshman and sophomore."

"Okay."

The fake leather cover of the book in my hand was embossed with the school's name, the year, and a snarling wildcat. The title of the yearbook was *The Trailblazer*. Though several years old, the library copies felt like they had never been opened. The pages were stiff, and they crackled as I turned them. Yearbooks made me melancholy. In the candid shots, all the kids wore happy faces, their smiles grilled with braces. Classroom photos revealed expressions of intense interest as students huddled around chemistry sets or hunched over open books. Football. Homecoming Dance. French Club. National Honor Society. The prom. Cheerleaders. Science Fair. Page after page of youthful, hopeful, shining energy that had yet to be hammered by the responsibility of adulthood. The wonder years.

I had spent most of mine in therapy.

"Here it is!" Saiera pushed her book toward me, index finger stuck in the middle of a page. The scene showed a group of kids hanging around an outdoor picnic table. Five were seated, with a young Saiera standing at the far left of the picture, looking down at whatever was occupying everyone's attention. Two other kids, both boys, leaned over the huddle. The caption read, "The Academic Decathlon Team prepares for Regionals." A long list of names followed. The sixth in the list was Saiera Khosani.

I placed the picture from Consuelo's car atop the yearbook photo and adjusted it so it lined up with Saiera's body in the AcDec photo. We shared a look.

"We have a match," I said.

"We have a match," she echoed.

"A match for what?" asked a man behind us.

I jerked so hard at the unexpected voice that the yearbook slipped under my hand and the cut-out picture swirled off the table. It floated through the air and landed like a snowflake on the toe of a black tennis shoe. I traced upward from the shoe to a pair of jeans, a prodigious belly covered in a Minnesota Vikings purple jacket, and all the way up to the face of Andy Gluck, ace reporter for the Pottsville Daily Dishrag.

Gluck stepped back and picked the picture off the floor faster than a chicken on a worm. He peered at it for a long moment, pinched between finger and thumb, then turned his attention to me.

"Where'd this come from?"

I opened my mouth to answer him, but in a flash, Saiera plucked the photo out of his fingers and said, "What does it matter to you?"

Gluck cast her a fishy stare. "I'm a reporter. I ask questions."

"It came from nunya," Saiera said with flashing eyes. "What do you want?"

"I was having dinner over at the cafe when I saw my favorite gravedigger jump out of a postal van with the famous and beautiful gypsy witch of Pottsville. You looked like you were both on a mission." Gluck's eyes glittered. They seemed fixed on the hand where Saiera held the photo. "It got my reporter juices going. This have anything to do with the dead bodies that keep turning up at the graveyard? Heh. Dead bodies turning up at the graveyard. Sounds like the headline of a story I want to write."

"No story here," Saiera said. "Now go away."

Gluck ignored her in favor of me. "How about you, Langston? Any comment on why you're digging through old yearbooks?"

"Ahhh..."

"No," Saiera said. "He has no comment."

"I have no comment," I parroted.

"Of course," Gluck said. With a last flicked glance at Saiera's hand, the reporter turned away. "Let me know if you change your mind."

After he had moved out of earshot, I leaned over and pitched my voice low. "You really don't like that guy, do you?"

Saiera shuddered through an exaggerated shiver. "He's a creep. He was a creep in high school, and he's been a creep ever since. Look..." She flipped to the index, found what she was looking for, and fanned the pages until she reached the one she wanted. "Here he is."

A young Andy Gluck, chubby as a penguin, stared out of the page from behind round wire-frame glasses. A camera hung from a strap around his neck. Gluck posed with a group of kids on the front steps of what I presumed was the high school. The caption read, "From the editorial and photographic staff of *The Trailblazer*. Good luck and godspeed on the trail of life."

"He doesn't look creepy," I said. "Kind of nerdy, in a harmless way."

"Looks can be deceiving. See that camera? He was always going around with that camera, snapping pictures. Some girls caught him trying to get 'up skirt' shots while they sat at their desks. You know what those are? Up skirt pics?"

"I have a pretty good idea."

"That's right," Saiera said. "You read those German porn rags."

"I—No! That wasn't... I..."

"Relax, Brad. Kidding. Anyway, one of the cheerleaders found a peephole drilled into their locker room. On the other side was the school's old darkroom. The hole was plugged with a stopper, but anyone who was in there... All they had to do was pull it out, and they could see everything. No one used the darkroom much because nearly everything had gone digital at that time. Except..." Saiera held up a forestalling finger. "Some of the photography buffs were allowed access. The one who was in there most?"

"Let me guess."

"Yup. It couldn't be proved Andy was the Peeping Tom, but everyone knew."

"So... a creep?"

"Definitely. For a time, I became the object of his creep. He was always in my shadow for, like, two years. I had to change routes so I wouldn't have to deliver mail to the newspaper offices." Saiera shuddered. "Ugh. Let's talk about something else."

I flipped idly through the yearbook in front of me although there wasn't much point. Saiera had shown me the original photo, and there was no doubt the snippet from Consuelo's car had come from a copy of the same picture. It could have come from any of several thousand graduates from Pottsville High or a teacher or an administrator or even a janitor from the school. Anyone with access to *The Trailblazer* from Saiera Khosani's senior year in high school could have clipped it out, decorated it with hearts, and... and what? Left it in Consuelo's car? Why? Consuelo had come from Kansas. It was damned unlikely she would have come by a print of the Academic Decathlon team from tiny Pottsville, Pennsylvania, developed a crush on a girl she never met, then driven out of her way to try to hook up with her.

"What if somebody's setting you up?" The thought crystallized as I spoke it aloud.

"Glad you caught up, Einstein."

"But why? Why you?"

Saiera bit her bottom lip and stared at the open yearbook. "I don't know," she admitted without looking up, almost as if she was speaking to herself. "I can't fathom why anyone would try and connect me to that poor woman."

We fell silent. I turned my attention back to the yearbook, flipping pages without really paying much attention. I was past the sports and into the extracurricular activity's pages: Drama club, speech club, chess club, French—*Wait, what?* I turned back to the chess club page, and my heart double-clutched, and I sucked in a hard breath. Saiera shot me a questioning look.

"I, uh, I, uh..."

"You sound like a stalled car," Saiera said. "Spit it out."

"We have another suspect." I tapped the yearbook photo of the chess club. "Chess is the clue we needed."

Chapter 27

Saiera frowned and leaned closer to peer at the photo. It showed a group of kids surrounding a single person holding up a trophy the size of the Parthenon. She read the caption aloud, "The Pottsville High Chess Club wins Class 1A State Title."

"Look who's holding the trophy."

"I... know her, I think."

I pointed at the list of names after the caption. "Center: Adamantine Tarwater."

"Addy, yeah. Now I remember her." Saiera's brows hitched together. "But I don't understand. How is she connected to Consuelo Espinoza?"

I leaned back and looked up at the ceiling to order my thoughts. "Consuelo was a chess player in college. She was on her way to meet someone here in Pottsville. Addy played chess in high school—pretty good, too, since the team won state. What if they... connected somehow, through chess, and got to know each other?" I sneaked a glance at Saiera and was rewarded with an expression best described as Are You Nucking Futs? I hurried on with my case. "Okay, so next point. I saw Addy hanging out at the gate to the Hixton property. When I started to go over the fence to get George, she stopped me, saying there were dangerous things hidden in the grass." I swiveled to face Saiera dead-on. "Don't you see? She didn't want me to find the car!"

"Brad..."

I saw the denial coming and threw in my last point. "And you have to admit she comes from a strange family. Have you met the Tarwaters?"

"I deliver their mail. Duh." Saiera chewed her lip for a moment before admitting, "Okay, you have a point about the weird family. But the rest of it is... a bunch of assumptions and guesswork."

"I know I can't prove it yet—"

"Are you going to accuse her like you did me?"

My face heated, and I picked at a loose thread on the worn knee of my jeans. "No. I'm sorry about that, okay? I... I jumped to a conclusion."

"Like maybe you're doing now?"

"Maybe," I said. Then with conviction, I added, "But I don't think so. It's the only connection, Saiera. Why would Consuelo come to visit Pottsville unless it was to meet someone she knew? How else would a Kansas girl meet somebody from this, no offense, podunk town?"

"Wait a minute." Saiera plucked her smartphone from her jacket pocket. "Why are we speculating when we have the interwebs to do the work for us? Let me do a search..." Saiera double-thumbed her typing, her face lit by the screen. "Chess tournaments... Adamantine Tarwater... How do you spell Espinoza? With a *z* or an *s*?"

"*Z*," I said. "Oh, and Addy went to the University of Pittsburgh."

Saiera scrolled and thumbed and tapped and muttered under her breath. I clamped down hard on my urge to ask for progress reports and instead continued flipping through the rest of the yearbooks. Nothing caught my eye, and truth be told, all the young faces blurred together after a while. I found Saiera Khosani's freshman picture and snickered to myself. Dark eyebrows seemed to be eating her brow, and she had sensible glasses too small for her face, a sharp nose, and braces. I turned the page before she caught me looking.

She uttered a profanity and toggled her head from side to side with an audible crackle. "Yeah, I got nothing. No mention of either girl or even a tournament matchup where they might have met. I did confirm the schools have a chess team, but the player names aren't listed anywhere. It's not like football, where they all wear numbers and sign letters of intent."

I glanced at the time. "It's just past five. The GetConnected store where she works is still open. Drop me off there, and I'll... I don't know... do a little subtle questioning?"

"Shouldn't you just go to the police? Tell them where the car is. Let them do the work."

"Yeah, right. Czerniak and Swanson? Come on."

"Oh." Saiera winced. "Yeah, the dumbatic duo. Not exactly NCIS, are they?"

"They're not even Sam and Dean."

"Who?"

"Don't tell me you don't watch *Supernatural*. You should come over one night when Delmont is up and around."

Saiera rolled her eyes. "Focus, Brad. What are we going to do?"

"We? Are you sure you want to get involved in this, Saiera?"

"Somebody left my picture in a dead girl's car. I'm in this as much as you."

The hum of Thelma's electric scooter preceded her appearance. When her mutt, Harrison, saw George, he started barking and tried to wriggle loose. Thelma clamped in one meaty arm on the tiny dog, and he yipped like a squeeze toy. George crawled under the table and hid behind my legs.

"Now, what are you two up to back here in the stacks, hey?" Thelma cooed, all but leering at us. "A bit of snogging, is it?"

My mouth opened, but any response I may have uttered died at birth. "Uh..."

"Hey, how'd you know?" Saiera said. "We've been snogging so hard my lips are chapped. In fact, we've been looking at the sex manuals and trying to decide what position we should try first."

Thelma tittered. "Oooh, a girl after me own heart. Hush, now, Harrison. Quiet. Anyway, I just came to say, I'm closing early. I want to get home before we get snowed in." The librarian looked me up and down and waggled her eyebrows. "Although... if we're trapped here, we'd have to find something to do to stay warm, hey ducks?"

I felt like a mouse caught too far from his hole. I didn't know which way to run.

Saiera stood and took me by the arm. "Come on, hot stuff. Before you melt the chair."

SNOW FILLED THE SKY with white confetti like a frost giant's ticker tape parade. Fat flakes danced through the streetlights, and powdery accumulation frosted all the stationary objects—parked cars, benches, and street signs. A cold, wet wind fingered its way through the openings of my thrift store jacket and sought out my bare flesh.

"Where to, Shaggy?" Saiera asked.

"Huh?"

She pointed at George. "The fraidy-cat dog is Scooby Doo, which makes you Shaggy." She nodded at the postal van. "And there's the Mystery Machine. And before you ask, I'm the hot chick, not the frumpy one. I can't remember her name."

"Daphne."

Saiera rolled her eyes. "Of course you would know that."

"Hey, don't hate on my adolescent cartoon crushes." I shivered inside my coat. Whatever warmth I had gained while in the library had all but evaporated. "With this blizzard setting in, I think my detectiving is done for the day. Can you give us a lift back to the grave-yard?"

We motored along the nearly deserted streets of Pottsville with-out speaking, though the not-speaking this time was much more congenial than the not-speaking from before. George put his paws on the dash and his nose to the windshield. He yipped at the wipers, the driving snow, or for all I knew, the ghosts of squirrels past. Saiera hunched over the wheel and scrubbed the foggy glass with her sleeve.

"It's coming down heavy," I remarked at one point.

"Uh-huh. By morning, we'll be buried."

"Only in snow, I hope."

She looked perplexed for a second then favored me with a twitch of a smile. "Not in the cemetery, you mean? Yeah, let's avoid that."

I craned my neck to get a glimpse of the clouds. "Something I meant to mention. I talked to Stan the other day, and he said that Pippah was gaining power from the moon. When the full moon ris-es, she'll be super hard to tackle face-to-face, so if we're going to try and snatch her bones from the crypt, we should do it tomorrow or the next day."

"What are you talking about, the next couple of days?" Saiera shot me a hard look to go along with her question.

"Before the full moon," I said. "Stan said it would be full in, like, four days. Three now, I guess."

"Stan is full of crap." Saiera turned on Shady Elm, and the van skidded a bit. She fought the wheel and straightened out. She threw another dark-eyed look my way. "The full moon is tonight."

"Tonight? Are you sure?"

"Google it," she said. "But, yeah, I'm pretty sure. They were talk-ing about it on the news because it was going to be a blood moon. The first full moon in October."

I had been feeling a mild anxiety caused by the idea that I would have to—*at some time in the future!*—deal with opening the Brecht crypt, finding, then collecting and removing moldering old bones. That anxiety bloomed to outright dread. My throat clamped shut as if I had swallowed an entire plum, and I found it hard to breathe. With shaky fingers, I opened a web browser on my phone and typed in a search. Weak signal strength, probably due to the storm, meant the web page results loaded as if squeezed through a tiny offshoot of the information highway. I checked three sites to be sure.

"Well?" Saiera demanded after I dropped the phone in my lap.

"You're right," I croaked. "Full moon. Tonight. Rises at eight thirty-six p.m."

"And then? What did you say would happen?"

"Pippah rises."

George looked up at me and whined. The wipers ticktocked. Snow fell.

"Well then." Saiera stepped on the gas, and the van fishtailed a bit before straightening out. "We should get a move on."

The cemetery office materialized from the whiteout, and in front of it sat an idling Datsun truck. A plume of exhaust rose from the tailpipe of the Jimmy Carter–era vehicle. Our headlights washed over a rusted tailgate, a salt-burned paint job, and a pair of mismatched tires on the driver's side as Saiera pulled into a parking space one over from the old truck. We idled in place for a moment, just two cars parked in front of a graveyard at night.

"Late-night visitor?" Saiera had her hand on the key but left the engine running.

"I have no idea." I could see only a vague shape through the Datsun's window. Was somebody waiting on me or lost in the storm and needing a place to pull over? "Hell with it. I'm going inside. Anybody wants to see me, they can come in like civilized people."

I pulled back the sliding door and hopped out of the van. George followed at my heels. The snow was accumulating, and footing was already treacherous. Holding my coat collar tight, I scuffed and skidded around the front of the van, passed through the headlights, and approached the office door with my keys in my hand. Saiera's door rumbled, and she picked her way after me. I kept one eye on the idling pickup while I worked the front door's lock. I ushered Saiera inside and was about to follow her when the pickup's door opened. A small figure in a big coat and a stocking cap hopped out. There was a pom-pom ball atop the cap. In the dim light, it looked like—

"Addy?" I said. "Is that you?"

"You're damn right it's me," said the girl I'd once considered a harbinger of nerdishness. There was no trace of nerdball in her voice or in the way she pulled a shotgun out of the front seat and trained it on my midsection. She stalked toward me, gun leading the way. Her firm jaw and ice-cold eyes reminded me a lot of her father right at that moment.

"Whoa! What the hell, Addy?"

"Shut up," she ordered, "and get inside."

"ADDY? WAIT, WHAT—"

"Shut up and get inside." The shotgun looked about as long as she was tall, but the bore pointed at me represented a tunnel to the afterlife. I had no doubt she could obliterate me with one tiny squeeze, and it wouldn't matter a bit if the recoil knocked her on her ass—too late, game over, insert another quarter.

I backed into the office with my hands held wide. George ran past me and disappeared. I caught sight of Saiera in the corner of my eye, poised with her back against the wall next to the door. Beady sweat popped out on my forehead, despite the chill. Addy stayed back and held the door open with her foot.

"Hey, mail lady!" she called out. "Get over where I can see you, or I blow your boyfriend away."

Saiera grimaced and moved to stand by my side with her hands up. We both backed into the center of the office, near the sofa. The coffee table bumped against the back of my calves.

"What's..." I cleared my throat and tried again. "What's this about, Addy?"

But I desperately feared I knew what this was about. Addy had killed Consuelo and somehow figured out I was onto her. Now she was here to eliminate witnesses.

"Sit down," she ordered. She looked frightened and determined at the same time. Redness bloomed in her cheeks, and her curly hair fell over her forehead. The ratty coat she wore was in worse shape than my thrift store special, and her boots looked as though they had been used to slop hogs once too often. Her voice quavered when she added, "On the sofa. Both of you."

We eased back until we could lower ourselves onto the sofa. Saiera's leg pressed against mine, and although I wanted her to move farther away so as to not get caught in the spray of pellets if Addy fired at me, I also took comfort from the warmth of her proximity.

Addy dug into the pocket of her coat while holding the shotgun grip. The barrel wavered around from the effort of her trying to hold it one-handed but never far enough off target that I for a moment considered rushing her.

"Where did you get this?" Addy demanded. When her hand came free, she held a cell phone up as though displaying a key piece of evidence in our trial. "What happened to Connie? Did you kill her?"

"Did I...?" My jaw unhinged, and I couldn't have been more stunned if I'd been tasered and beaned with a foul ball at the same time.

"Don't lie to me," Addy insisted. "I know this is her phone. When I got it working again, my texts appeared on her screen. So did a lot of others. Did you kill her? Is that how you just happened to find her body? The paper said the cops questioned you for hours."

Saiera and I traded the same expression—confusion mixed with outrage.

"Did I kill her? Are you kidding me? I can't believe this town. I've been here less than two weeks, and everybody thinks I killed a woman who's been dead for over a year. Think, Addy. I found the body, right? Is it a big stretch of the imagination to think I might have found her phone as well?"

I almost added *and her car*, but I bit it off at the last second. Although Addy was acting less like a killer and more like an avenger, a shred of doubt lingered. It didn't seem wise to add that tidbit of information.

And then Saiera threw gas on the fire. "What about you? What's to say you didn't kill her? You're who she was coming to see, right? So what's your alibi?"

Addy slumped against the wall. The barrel of the shotgun drooped. I barely heard when she mumbled, "She never showed."

Saiera pushed off the sofa and marched around the furniture to stand in front of Addy. She gently tugged the shotgun away and propped it against the wall then took Addy by the arm. "Come on, now. Sit down with us. Let's talk about what we know."

"You're right," Addy admitted when seated. She scrubbed her eyes with her palms, leaving them red-rimmed. "Oh, I'm so stupid. Stupid, stupid, stupid. I'm sorry, Brad. I just... I saw her phone, and I went a little crazy."

"That's okay." My voice hardly quavered at all, remarkably. "Tell us about how you know Consuelo."

Addy's story came out pretty much as I'd imagined it. She and Consuelo had met at a chess tournament hosted by the University of Pittsburgh. They hit it off and got together for drinks and kicks whenever their schedules permitted. I wanted to ask if "kicks" meant sex, but I held my tongue—again, remarkably. Then a year before the last July, they made plans for Consuelo—or Connie, using Addy's diminutive—to meet for dinner at the Route 66 Diner in Pottsville when she drove back to Syracuse.

"I was late that night," Addy said then added with a self-mocking little laugh, "Daylight lasts longer in the summer." She shook herself free of the memory. "Anyway, when I showed up, Connie wasn't there. I thought she had given up and gone on, you know? Then she wouldn't answer my calls or my texts. I thought she was mad at me. But then I heard... I heard she had disappeared."

"Until I found her," I said.

"Until you found her."

Saiera and I traded looks again. I interpreted her expression to mean I should tell Addy the rest of the story. I brought out the picture from my pocket. "Look, do you recognize this photo?"

Addy frowned and shook her head. She looked at Saiera. "It's... it's you, isn't it? I'm sorry—I forgot your name. We were in high school together, right?"

"That's right, it's me. Saiera Khosani."

"Addy Tarwater."

"I found this in Consuelo's car," I said, "which is hidden in Hixton's barn, by the way. All her stuff is still in it."

"But... I don't understand..."

"We think the killer planted it there," I said. "To maybe frame Saiera if the car was ever found? I don't know. It sounds weak when I say it out loud."

"Have you called the police?" Addy asked. "About the car?"

"The cops are already crawling up my butt about finding the body—two bodies since Mr. Glatfelter was killed on the property. I'll drop them a postcard or something, but I'm not getting hauled in by those two quacks ever again."

"Two bodies?" Addy's brow creased in a frown. "Who's Mr. Glat-felter?"

"You didn't hear about that?" When Addy shook her head, I filled her in on our gruesome discovery. Her face lost all color.

"Do you think..." She looked at her shoes and spoke in a small voice. "Do you think that's happened to Connie?"

"Actually, no..." I siphoned in a deep breath and said, "I think that Glatfelter was a victim of Pippah Fontenot."

Addy narrowed her eyes and flicked a glance from me to Saiera and back. "Who is Pippah Fontenot?"

"That's... that's a long story."

Chapter 28

"Clearly, you're insane" was Addy's judgment after I brought her up to speed on the supernatural events at Shady Terraces. She appealed to Saiera. "Are you buying any of this?"

Saiera shifted in her seat. "I... don't know. I will say this: This place has a reputation for weirdness. I mean, we've all heard the stories about it being haunted, right?"

"Yeah," Addy countered, "but I've lived next door to it my entire life—hell, I've walked past it a thousand times—and I've never seen a single ghost."

"Something killed Glatfelter," Saiera said. "Something crazy. And not this crazy person," she added, placing a hand on my shoulder when Addy's eyes cut to me. "Brad was with me the whole time. Look, I hate to say this because it just perpetuates the stereotype about gypsies, but my grandmother has The Sight. She's more in tune with the spiritual world than most, and she always said that this place was full of power. She passed some of that down to me, I think. I have felt cold spots and a sensation... like my skin crawling... when I've been on the grounds here."

"You never mentioned that," I said.

She patted my shoulder where her hand rested then took it away. "A girl never tells all her secrets on a first date."

"We had a date?"

"This is cute and all," Addy said, scrunching up to the edge of her seat like she was ready to bolt for the door. I didn't blame her. "But I'm not buying what you're selling."

"You don't have to buy it," Saiera said. Her dark eyes flashed a warning signal, and her tone had turned chilly. "Fact is you invited yourself to this party. Nobody made you come. We have"—she glanced at her phone—"a little under ninety minutes before the moon rises. If Brad's not insane—no offense, sweetie—then we have to find her remains, remove them from the cemetery, and find a way to burn them in hot fire before she rises at full power and goes on a murder spree. Right, Brad?"

She called me sweetie.

"I said, 'Right, Brad?'"

"Huh? Oh, yeah. That's the plan. And Pippah guards her tomb with... with some kind of psychic power. It's like walking into a blast furnace of terror just to get close to where she's buried."

"Right," Addy mocked. "A blast furnace of terror. Are you sure you don't write video games for a living?"

"Look." Saiera stood up and tugged her jacket straight. "Why are we discussing this? We're wasting time. Addy, it was nice meeting you. We'll have to get together someday for coffee. Brad, are you ready?"

I levered myself off the couch with the reluctance of a man on his way to the electric chair. "Not really, no. But it's got to be done."

Saiera rapped out orders like a drill sergeant. "We need flashlights, a big sack of some kind, work gloves... What about tools? What kind of crypt are we talking about?"

"Two big doors. Oak. There was a locked chain, but the lock's broken."

"Okay, then maybe a pry bar and a hammer, in case we have to force the door." She cocked an eyebrow at Addy, who remained perched on the edge of her seat. "You can see yourself out, can't you?"

Addy pulled off her stocking cap, and her curly brown hair sprang free. She scratched her scalp vigorously. "I want to... This is crazy, but I want to go with you." She fixed Saiera with a firm-jawed look of stubbornness. "I have to see for myself, okay? I have to know."

"No," I said. "It's too dangerous."

"Sure," Saiera said. "Come on."

"But..."

"Brad?" Saiera raised her eyebrows at me as though asking the time of day. "Where are the tools, sweetie?"

"I... uh... in the shed."

"Why don't you be a dear and go get those? I have a flashlight in the van."

"And I have one in the truck," Addy said.

"Settled, then." Saiera bussed me on the cheek. "Meet you at the back door? Oh, and I think you should leave George here, don't you?"

"Better idea," I grumbled. "Why don't you take George, and I'll stay here."

"Don't pout, sugar. It makes your face all grumpy."

TABITHA AMBUSHED ME on my way through the kitchen, yowling in the loudest voice she could muster about how I was a failure as a servant, a miserable human being, and the poster child for animal abuse. Her tuna dish was empty.

"It must be embarrassing," I told her as I spooned out her food, "to be such a fierce, predatory beast and yet have the voice of a squeeze toy."

The cat stuck her nose in her bowl and ignored me.

When I stood up to put the tuna away, Delmont was there—or *almost* there. He appeared as insubstantial as a reflection from a cloudy mirror, translucent as weak broth, and if a ghost could be said to look beaten to within an inch of his life, Delmont would have passed that inch about a mile ago.

"We're losing," he gasped. The sound of his voice came to me as if spoken from the far end of a tunnel, weak and echoing. "She's kicking our ass."

"Who? Pippah?"

Delmont rolled his eyes in a *Keep up, stupid* kind of way. "She's sucking up the power like an Eveready battery. We can't stop her. She coming, man. She coming hard." He faded a little more, and I could barely make out his features against the backdrop of the kitchen cabinets.

"We're going for her bones," I said. "You guys hang on."

"Hurry, man." Only Delmont's disembodied face remained, seeming to float in midair. "If she gets it all…"

And he was gone.

I MET SAIERA AND ADDY in the rectangular area behind the apartment that I had mentally dubbed "the patio." I carried a flat wrecking bar and a five-pound hammer in one hand and a twelve-volt flashlight in the other. I had pulled up the hood of my sweatshirt, which I wore under my coat, and had a pair of thick yellow leather work gloves covering my hands. I was still cold. Thick snow was falling, and already, the ground was coated with a half inch or more of accumulation. It crunched underfoot.

"Which way, Brad?" Saiera asked. She, too, had her hood up and was cocooned in a padded silvery coat, thick pants, and hiking boots. She and Addy carried flashlights. I was glad to see Addy had left her shotgun behind.

Saiera cocked an eyebrow when I handed her the hammer and pry bar. "Too tired to carry your own tools?"

"Remember what I told you," I said. "About how Pippah took over my body? If I start acting weird or talking in some kind of odd accent, please get away, as fast as you can. If she gets me again... well, it could get ugly real fast. At least this way, I can't use the tools as weapons."

"You want us to kill you?" Addy asked.

"No, I don't want you to kill me!"

"In the movies, they always have to kill the possessed guy."

"It's the only way to be sure," Saiera added. "And cut off his head."

"Just... no, okay? Jeez." I started off across the patio. Halfway across, I turned and said, "You guys *are* joking, right?"

THE GOING WAS PRETTY easy at first. I led my little band of ghost hunters along snow-covered paths winding through the type of mystical forest seen only on Christmas cards and movies involving magic portals accessed through wardrobes. Then I had to backtrack when I realized I had taken the wrong path, which happened again and again. By the fourth time I had stopped short, positive I was on the wrong trail, Addy and Saiera were close to mutiny.

"Jesus Christ," Addy moaned. She huddled deeper into her coat. "I'm freezing my ass off out here. I thought you would know your way around by now, Brad."

"I do know it!" I said. "It's not me. It's her. She has a way of... of turning me away from her tomb."

I gritted my teeth and forged onward, keeping my mind focused on one goal: the Brecht tomb. It seemed to help, as familiar landmarks appeared out of the snow-capped world, reassuring me that we were on the right path. My blaze-marked tree loomed ahead, its blackened branches dusted white, reminding me of the bones of some long-dead colossal beast. Wind whipped in gusts, changing direction from my left to directly in my face. Flakes pattered against my cheeks, and those that touched my lips tasted bitter and salty. Forward movement became a struggle. Not only did the wind batter and buffet me like a prizefighter trying to drive me back across the snowy canvas, but a sick feeling of dread gathered in my stomach. I felt much the way I had when I realized Tony was still inside our burning house—an awful, inescapable fear that spidered up out of my gut and crawled across my nerves with prickly legs.

Saiera and Addy felt it too. When I glanced back, they were wearing identical expressions of uneasiness shading toward panic.

"Is that... her?" Saiera gasped out.

I nodded.

"I'm beginning to be not in favor of this plan," Addy said.

I turned back around and plowed on. I had to hold an arm crooked across my eyes to block the worst of the blizzard. Never before had I imagined snowflakes as having weight. I mean, weren't they nothing more than fragile, beautiful little drops of crystallized water? Well, when accelerated to supercollider speed, those delicate pellicles of natural beauty became bullets fired from an Eskimo machine gun.

The three of us ooched forward, looking like mimes bent into the wind. The fear in my stomach ate at my willpower. I wanted to go back so badly that my body had turned sideways, and I was crabbing instead of walking. If the two women had not been behind me, there was no doubt in my mind I would have run for it—run for it and never looked back. At least not until I reached California.

The small gap between rosebushes appeared, beyond which, if I recalled correctly, lay a pocket clearing and the Brecht tomb. I had not gotten around to trimming these—*Sorry, Mrs. Perry*—and the wild canes whipped in the wind, a many-legged monster with razor claws, ready to shred us to confetti.

"Follow me! Stay close!" I yelled behind me.

Saiera huddled against my back, and Addy snugged against her, a three-person train. I ducked my head and dove into the gap. Vines snagged and tugged at my coat. Fabric ripped. A flail of thorns razored across my scalp, leaving a burning trail of fire. I slowed, hung up in a barbed tangle, my eyes squinted against the pain. Saiera screamed into my back, a sound of rage and pain and fierce determination. She pushed, and I tore free with an effort. Stumbled. Stayed upright. When I touched my forehead, my gloved fingers came away red with blood. I leaned over from a wave of dizziness.

"Are you okay?" Saiera held me by the shoulder, bending to shine her light on my face. "You're bleeding!"

"Just a flesh wound, ma'am," I joked without much conviction.

She whipped a tissue from her pocket and pressed it to my scalp. "Ow."

"Oh, stop being a wuss."

"Um," Addy said. "Guys? I'm somewhat freaking the hell out right now."

Relief at surviving the cat-o'-nine-tails gauntlet had momentarily crowded out all other sensations. With Addy's reminder, the terror came crashing back. If fear could be weighed, mine would require the combined strength of the entire Ukrainian powerlifting team to get it off the ground. It was unnatural, bone-deep, and paralyzing. From their expressions, I gathered the two women felt it as well. We huddled together, shivering, like three children lost in the woods as the wolves prowled closer.

"It's... it's not real," I said at last. "It's her. She's doing it."

Saiera shuddered. "It feels pretty damn real to me."

"Me too," Addy said through chattering teeth.

"We have to... push through it."

"Or h-head for H-Hawaii," Saiera said.

Addy shook her head emphatically. "China."

We shared a look and managed a trio of weak smiles, which helped push back the fear enough that I could get my feet moving again. I stumbled down the hill to the path below—the path that would lead me to Pippah Fontenot's remains, I hoped, and an end to her evil attacks on the real world. The trees lining the path were dusted with snow, the walkway covered in a thin blanket of white. Heavy flakes slanted from the sky, swatting me in the face despite our change in direction. If it kept snowing at its current rate, we'd be up to our knees by midnight.

Every grudging step tightened the band holding my panic in check. It wouldn't be long before it snapped, and when it did, the next thing Saiera and Addy saw would be a hole in the falling snow the size of Brad Langston. I could tell by the nauseating, heart-squeezing terror flowing through my core that, had I been doing this alone, I would have already bolted. Remaining stalwart in front of Saiera and Addy seemed to be holding my flight response at bay as the shame I would feel at leaving them to face Pippah alone would be life ending for me. I would never recover from abandoning another friend to face death alone.

I realized we were trudging three abreast on the path.

Side by side.

Our hands were linked together.

We came to the clearing where I'd last seen the Brecht tomb. No green radiance lit the snow. Through the thick, hazy curtain of flakes, the crypt doors loomed, a blacker rectangle in the dark hillside. The top of the hill in which they were mounted was lost in the blizzard.

As we stepped into the clearing, the unnatural sense of doom dropped away as if we'd passed through some unseen membrane or brushed aside a supernatural curtain. We traded glances, each of us breathing hard, as if we'd run for miles. Our breath fogged the air like three locomotives stopped at the same station.

"Well," I ventured, "that was easier than I expected."

Saiera snorted and rolled her eyes. "Come on. Let's get this over with."

We dropped our linked hands with the self-consciousness of schoolkids. Addy stuck her hands in her pockets, and Saiera fussed with her flashlight. I studied the snow, cleared my throat, and said, "Well, then."

"Yep," Saiera said.

"Okay," Addy chimed in, "what now?"

I tilted my head toward the crypt. "This way, I guess."

The twin oak doors were as I remembered them. The chain lay in a loose heap on the ground, its massive padlock broken and discarded atop the pile. A simple sliding bolt held the doors together though it had been retracted at some point, and now the tiniest misalignment showed the doors were no longer flush together. They had been opened—not shocking since I had seen Pippah standing in the threshold of the tomb, green light glowing behind her, the first time she had appeared to me. A pair of wrought-iron pull handles waited for one of us to muster the courage to give them a tug.

The three of us shared a look. Addy's expression reflected that her skepticism had become wide-eyed trepidation. Saiera's jaw jutted, and her grim nod gave me courage.

I reached out and clamped my fist around the right-hand pull. My heart thudded with pulse of a Latin dance party, and my tongue buzzed as if I had licked a nine-volt battery. Despite the freezing temperature, sweat broke out on my forehead. Chugging blooms of foggy breath wrapped around my face.

"Here goes nothing," I said.

I pulled, and the crypt door squealed open on rusted hinges.

Chapter 29

The air that puffed out when I opened the crypt door stank so badly a maggot would choke to death. We clamped gloves over our noses and turned away with various sounds of disgust. A warehouse of fish left to rot in summer heat for a week would not have smelled as bad. It wasn't the smell of death so much as a gut punch of every bad smell in the world distilled to its essence and flavoring the air with a stench so wicked I could taste it on the back of my tongue.

And it was colder inside the tomb than outside, like the difference between a refrigerator and a deep freeze, which Saiera commented on.

"How can it be colder inside than out?" she said through her muffled, glove-covered mouth. "That defies physics."

I breathed past my gloved hand. "I have a feeling the laws of physics here in Shady Terraces is really Pirate Code."

Saiera's eyebrows squeezed together. "Huh?"

"More like guidelines," Addy explained, teary-eyed and gasping.

The stench dissipated, either from release into the outside air or because my olfactory nerves were stunned into a coma. Either way, I was grateful. My flashlight beam stabbed into the darkness, revealing brick walls and a slab floor. Blooming algae stained the brickwork, and a layer of gunk coated the floor—dust, dead leaves, and rodent droppings.

Addy squinted in distaste. "Can't you get a disease from powdered rat shit?"

"I hope I live long enough to get a disease."

"You're a barrel of laughs, Brad."

"Come on." Saiera led off, following her flashlight beam. "Less bickering, more grave robbing."

"Yes, Mom." Addy stuck her tongue out at Saiera's back.

Within a few steps, we came to the first burial chamber. A hinged iron door the size of a modest flat-screen TV was set into the brickwork at about chest height. Atop the door, a brass plaque gleamed in light reflected from my flash. "Alberich and Gerwine Brecht," I read with some difficulty. The plaque was so tarnished as to be almost illegible. "Eighteen sixteen to eighteen forty-eight. Huh. Young."

From the opposite wall, Addy read another plaque. "Annadelle Brecht. Died in eighteen forty-four at... thirty years old. Even younger."

More hinged doors lined the walls, a series of Brechts going forward in time the deeper we ventured into their family crypt. We passed from the nineteenth century into the twentieth, following the Brecht lineage forward until reaching Rupert, interred in 1948. Either the Brecht line had died out there, or the family had moved on to a different part of the country.

"Makes sense," I said aloud. "Arlo would have known no one else would be using the tomb."

"Arlo?" Addy shined her light in my face. "What does Arlo have to do with this?"

"Oh, I forgot that part. Pippah Fontenot was the chief suspect in the death of Arlo Weaver's brother. There wasn't enough evidence to charge her, and then she quote-unquote disappeared. I think she was left here when Arlo or his father decided to get a little revenge, vigilante style."

"Oh," Addy said in a small voice. "I always liked Arlo."

I stepped deeper into the crypt. My flashlight beam raked over the back wall, some ten feet farther. My foot hit something that clattered across the floor. Addy screamed when I focused my light on the ground. A loose collection of human bones lay scattered at my feet. Remnants of a rotted cotton dress hung in tatters over the rib cage and pelvis. The leg bones were no longer attached and were strewn about like a macabre game of pick-up sticks. Rodents, I guessed. The object I had kicked turned out to be Phillipa Fontenot's grinning skull, complete with leathery patches of skin and scraggly remains of tightly woven hair.

Black, empty eye sockets regarded me from the floor.

Then they started glowing green.

I'VE HEARD PEOPLE TRY to describe pure terror, typically using phrases like "my hair stood on end" or "I tasted copper" or "my feet froze to the floor," and my all-time favorite was "my heart stopped." None of that comes close to what happened to me when the eye sockets in Pippah's skull came to life. The only way I can describe the sensation is to say it felt like my whole body had licked a light socket.

"*Bienvenu, mon cher.*" The voice slithered into my skull with the raspy tone of a crone trying to seduce a child to come in for a warm nap in her oven. "Welcome to my home. Doan go nowhere, now. I be there quicky-quick."

"She-she-she," I stuttered, "is c-coming."

Addy's voice sounded as shaky as mine when she said, "Wh-What do we do?"

"Gather her bones," Saiera said. She didn't sound all that confident herself, whispering so low I barely heard her.

I tugged the salt sack from my inner coat pocket with a jittery hand. When the skull's eyes lit up, the temperature in the tomb had plummeted. It had been cold before, but now it was deep-freeze cold. Crystalline ice glittered on the walls as condensation froze. The compost-heap stench of the place grew exponentially worse. I sipped shallow breaths through my parted lips to keep from gagging up my stomach contents.

We shared a long, confused moment, each of us waiting for the other to make the first move. The light from our flashlights, held in nervous hands, jiggled around like something out of *The Blair Witch Project*. I knelt and opened the bag, holding the lip of the opening against the floor, next to Pippah's tattered remains.

"Here," I said. "Shovel the bones in with your feet."

With an expression of squeamish disgust, Saiera nudged the rib cage with her toe. It didn't move.

"It's stuck in the gunk on the floor," I said. My guts churned, and I swallowed to keep from hurling. "Or frozen, maybe. Kick it."

Saiera pinched her nose and drew in a deep breath. She stubbed at the rib cage like she was trying to drive in a door stopper. The skeletal ribs peeled loose with a sticky, crackling sound. Three of the ribs broke free and clattered in a jumble amongst the other bones.

"Eww..." she moaned. "So gross. So, so gross."

Addy joined in by toeing a femur closer to the pile then a foot. Slowly, gradually, with evident distaste, the two women swept the floor with their feet, soccer-kicking Pippah into a pile then nudging her into the open mouth of the sack. I cringed whenever a bone accidentally brushed against my hand on its way past me. In minutes, we had bagged up over half the remains, and so far, nothing bad had happened.

I knew it couldn't last.

The crypt bloomed with green light as though the walls had been infected by diseased phosphorous lichen or the air energized by a ghoulish version of St. Elmo's fire. Nausea roiled in my stomach. Pippah's presence invaded the air with malignant hatred that threatened to close my throat with panic. I felt her before I saw her, but when I saw her, I had to fight the urge to pee my pants.

She wore the same simple, shapeless cotton dress as before, her hair still a Medusa's mess of tangles and stalks. She appeared as though conjured from thin air, a malevolent demon sent to rend our bodies and drag our souls to hell.

Pippah materialized in the space between us and the exit. We were blocked in—no escape. She approached without appearing to move her feet.

"Hello, chile," she crooned. "You come back to play with ol' Pippah again, hey? And you brought yo' frens too. Oh, we goan have such fun now, cher."

ADDY SCREAMED AND BACKED away. Saiera took a step back as well. I was kneeling, and I didn't trust myself to stand, so I stayed rooted to the floor. Pippah floated toward us until she stopped just shy of where I knelt. Her froggy eyes narrowed in suspicion when she observed me holding an open sack next to her jumble of bones.

"Watchoo doin' there, you sly devil?" Her voice whisked like the sound of a dagger being drawn from its sheath. "You up to somethin', ain'tcha, pretty boy?"

"Can you see her?" I hissed over my shoulder.

Addy made a noise that sounded like an affirmative.

"Yes," Saiera husked out. "Kind of thin and transparent, but I can see her, all right. Can she hurt us, do you think?"

Thin and transparent? To me, Pippah appeared as solid as a live human. But then again, so had all the ghosts I had seen in Shady Terraces. Since "normal" people couldn't see spirits like Stan and Delmont, it stood to reason that if Pippah could be seen by Addy and

Saiera, she must be projecting some Master-level ghost mojo. The evil woman's lidded gaze slid over to Saiera at her question.

"Can I hurt you, sugah? Now why would Pippah hurt a pretty thing like you? Watchoo take me foah, some kinda boogeyman?" Pippah cackled and turned those freaky eyes back on me. "Bradley here knows. He seen how I do people. I finds me some likely soul..." Her voice dropped so low I could barely hear her, then Pippah lunged and snapped her fingers under my nose. "And I snatches 'em up!" she shrieked. When I fell on my butt, she giggled like a mean girl pulling a prank.

It annoyed me.

"No," I said, levering myself up to stand in front of the women. "She can't hurt you. Not unless she possesses me, and she can't do that anymore. I won't let her."

"Oh, you don't think so?" Pippah cooed.

Then she hit me.

A gale-force blast of her evil, twisted nature slammed into me. I staggered. Bile clogged the back of my throat. Pippah's will hammered against mine. She pounded against my haphazard, untried defenses in a full-frontal assault, a tidal wave of hate. Insidious tendrils of her rotted soul crept under and around the barricades I had thrown up. I could feel her undermining my will, stealing into my mind like water slipping through cracks in a dam. Like the little Dutch boy, I jammed fingers in those holes as fast as they appeared. The stalemate held. The tide receded.

Pippah regarded me with narrowed eyes. Then she grinned. "That was just a test, boy. Now I'm a-comin' for you."

"Bring it, bitch."

Pippah and I went to war.

I lost all sense of my surroundings. The world around me disappeared. I stumbled blindly in the black void left behind. I imagined solid ground underneath me, and to my surprise, it appeared. Shapes materialized out of the gloom as an eldritch light, no brighter than a sliver of moon on a cloudy night, seeped into the void. I stood in one spot and turned full circle. Pippah was nowhere to be found, which was good. I was lost as hell, which was bad.

The smell of earthy loam, like composted leaves, saturated the air. I took a step and barked my shin on a solid chunk of stone and spat a curse. I reached out, and my hands touched rough stone, shaped into a... headstone. I was in a graveyard, of course, so that made sense. Upon that realization, the light brightened enough that I could make out grave markers by the silvering of their outlines under that spectral light. Willows hung low overhead, trailing gossamer webs of Spanish moss. The place reminded me of a pulp magazine cover. *Better Graves and Tombs. Ghoulish Gardens. The Southern Gothic Graveyard Times.*

Wisps of green mist appeared, snaking toward me through and among the headstones as if someone had dumped out a bucket of Kill Brad cobras. The tendrils slipped and twined and slithered, gathering in front of me and braiding together in a coil of mist that grew into a column as tall as my head.

This can't be good.

I cast around for a weapon—a rock, a tree limb... a pine cone. Anything. Nothing but soft, squishy turf. No, correction: the squishy part was writhing worms slithering up through the bare dirt. Earthworms by the hundreds snaked across the soil, questing blindly upward through the earth until they wriggled out, a moving, roiling, slimy shag carpet. And not just worms—creepy crawlies of all shapes, lengths, and multitudes of feet emerged from among the graves. As they broke free of the soil, bits and shards of dirty white bone were disgorged along with them. Remnants of the feast they had enjoyed underground were now discarded like moldy leftovers.

Pippah's raspy voice hissed in my mind. *I'm coming, boy.*

A spider plopped onto my shoulder from the tree above. I slapped it off. Something else tickled my hair, and I shagged at it with both hands.

I backed away from the tower of mist forming in front of me. Whatever it was becoming, I was pretty sure I wanted no part of it. *Wish I'd brought the axe. Or Addy's shotgun. While I'm wishing, a tank would be nice about now.* My feet slipped and crackled over the wriggling mass underfoot.

A zombie tottered from the swirling mass of green. A dead boy, flesh sloughing off one side of his face, revealed a rheumy eyeball in a bare socket and a half grin of yellowed teeth. He shuffled out as if stepping through a curtain onto a school stage. He wore a tattered suit from a discount store, purchased by his parents after his death, the only suit he'd ever worn.

The thing spoke with Tony's voice, hoarse and whispery. "Why, Brad?"

"Hello, Tony," I croaked. My throat constricted, and my eyes watered. "Ah, man. I'm so sorry."

"Why? Why did you leave me there? Why did I have to die?"

This is not Tony. Come on, Brad, you know it's not him. It's that witch, Pippah. Even so, every word he spoke drove a nail into my heart.

"You deserve this, Brad." The Tony zombie stumbled closer. His hands stretched out to me. Bare fingerbones protruded like gloves without the fingertips. Tendons and muscles glistened through black-rimmed gaps in his rotted flesh. "You deserve it for what you did to me."

My legs lost their strength. I dropped to my knees, scattering a flurry of cockroaches. A giant weight crushed the air from my chest as though gravity had tripled in the blink of an eye. I had forgotten how much it hurt. The pain I felt that day, after the reality sank in that Tony was gone, had driven a serrated knife into my chest and twisted it, day after day, month after month. Time had layered the wound with calloused tissue the way a broken bit of shrapnel might be encased in a hardened layer of flesh. Underneath that padding, the pain was still there, just dulled and protected by the salve of forgetfulness.

Pippah's illusion sliced open the callus, laid my pain bare, made me feel it all over again.

She's right. I do deserve this.

"I'm sorry, man," I moaned. "I tried. I tried to reach you."

"You didn't try very hard," the Tony zombie rasped. "It was hot, Brad. And smoky. So smoky. I couldn't breathe. I was scared." He stumble-stepped closer, almost within touching distance. Another step, and those cold, dead hands would wrap around my throat and squeeze the life out of me. Part of me welcomed it. "I thought you'd come, but you didn't. You left me to die."

"I... I tried..."

"Too busy to look after me. Too old to play with a dumb kid like me. I was nothing but a nuisance to you. Good riddance, huh?"

I hung my head. My face was wet, eyes streaming, sinuses filled with mucus. Cold and clammy hands clamped around my throat. The stench of rotted flesh crowded past my runny nose. I didn't react, didn't move. Tony was right. I deserved this. I deserved to die for being such a little shit, for being happy that he was leaving me alone so I could watch TV—a few minutes of peace from his stupid games and his stupid, clinging adoration. Slimy hands tightened and cut off my air. I knelt there on the bug-infested ground and let it happen. If this was it, so be it.

Make it quick, Tony. Please.

DELMONT APPEARED AT the edge of my vision. At first, I thought he was hard to see because I was being choked to death, which tends to make things a little blurry. Then I realized he had appeared as thin and translucent as wax paper instead of his normal solid self. Delmont resembled a ghost as I had always imagined ghosts would appear.

"Dude," he said, "you know this ain't yo' friend, right?"

"Gark," I croaked. Lack of oxygen and a boa constrictor grip on my throat were beginning to send panic signals through my body. Maybe I wasn't as ready to die as I'd thought.

"This is like—" Delmont's mouth worked as he groped for the word he wanted. "Like, ah, what they call it? A smiley? No, that ain't right. Simile, that's it. Like it's an allergy?"

A what?

"A metrofour!" Delmont cried out. "You know, you not really here. This is, like, you know, you came here in yo' subconscious mind." He waved a hand around. "You not really here, here."

The fingers crushing my throat seemed pretty damned *here* to me—no metaphor about it. Yeah, dying was looking less appealing by the second.

"Don't listen to him," Tony hissed. "You need to pay for what you did."

"Naw, man," Delmont said. "You ain't gonna die here, bro. This is that bitch, messin' with your mind. She choke you out here in yo' subconscious, she gonna take over yo' body like she did last time. She take you over, who you think gonna die next?"

Saiera. Addy.

"That's right, them two women you lef' behind," Delmont said. "And then what? Half of damn town could die. You be the Monster that Ate Pottsville. C'mon, man. You need to stand up for those you can protect. That's how you honor yo' friend's memory."

Ah hell. What am I doing? Indulging my own guilt? Trying to make the pain stop instead of being a man and facing my past? Del-

mont's right. I don't honor Tony by letting Pippah take my body to wreak her evil will. I honor Tony by kicking the witch's ass.

Redness had crept into my vision. Delmont was all but gone. My air-starved lungs labored to no effect. I didn't have much fight left in me, but what fight I had, I was going to put to good use.

My hands came up, and I worked my fingers under the vice gripping my throat. I peeled back the little finger of each of Tony's hands and pulled until they cracked. The Tony zombie glared down, his half grin permanently affixed, apparently unperturbed by having its fingers broken. *Well, okay, then. Let's try the next pair.* I peeled back the ring fingers on each hand until they cracked and fell loose. My vision had gone from red to black, and I could no longer see. Thoughts zipped incoherently through my brain, jagged lighting impressions and images from my past. It was all I could do to focus on the middle fingers.

Crack-crack.

The pressure eased enough that I could drag in a breath. Air never felt sweeter. A tiny spark of consciousness returned from the distant shore where it had ventured.

One.

More.

Pull!

Crack-crack.

Tony's hands fell away. I flopped on my belly, heedless of the things squirming under my body. It was all in my mind, right? Nothing to worry about from mind bugs. I breathed and breathed. Deep, ragged gasps blew dirt away from my lips and threatened to suck beetles down my throat. I brushed at the few crawly things close to me. Mind bugs or not, I wasn't having any go down my windpipe.

When I had recovered enough to sit up, the Tony zombie was gone. Delmont was gone. The green mist and graveyard had disappeared. I was back in the Brecht crypt. Both Saiera and Addy crouched next to me with identical expressions of concern.

Saiera had a hand on my shoulder. "What happened?"

"Are you okay?" Addy asked.

"Where's Pippah?" I was surprised to find my voice was fine. I half expected to have a damaged larynx and big purple bruises around my neck. My probing fingers found nothing painful when I felt my neck.

"She blew town," Addy said. "Right about the time you said, 'Bring it, bitch.'"

"Yeah, she disappeared." Saiera rubbed my shoulder. "What happened?"

"I think… I think she tried to possess me again. I, uh, fought her off." *With a little help from Delmont.*

"Is she gone for good?"

"And what now?" Addy said.

"As to the first," I said, "I doubt it. As to what now, I say we continue with Plan A. Let's bag these bones and get the hell out of here."

I had beaten back Pippah's assault on my soul. That had to mean the worst was over. One more step and we would be free of her forever.

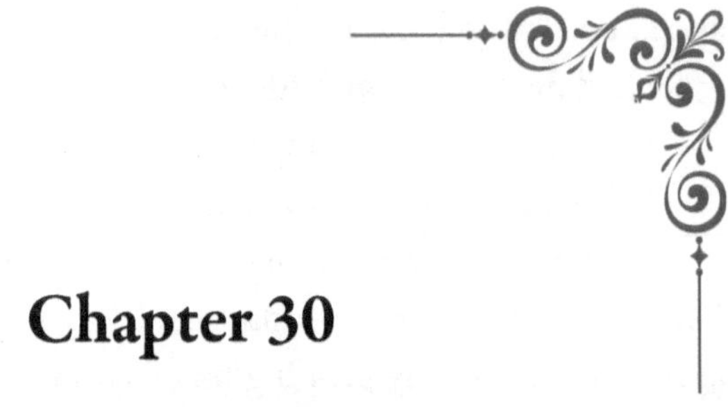

Chapter 30

Addy toed the last of the skeletal bones into the sack, leaving on-ly the skull to be bagged. I held the bag open and nodded at Saiera, who side-footed the skull like a shot on goal. It clattered across the floor and rolled into the sack.

"Goooaaalll!" she whisper-shouted.

I crimped the bag closed and twisted the top into a knot. Addy caught my arm when I tried to stand, and a wave of dizziness washed over me. Fighting Zombie-Tony in my subconscious mind had been every bit as exhausting as I imagined struggling with a live zombie would be. Or, well, not a *live* zombie, as zombies weren't *live* at all, but like, a real zombie.

Man, I'm losing it.

"What?" Addy cocked an eyebrow at me. "Did you say some-thing?"

"No." I shook off the vertigo. "Let's get back to the office. There's coal and charcoal both in the shed. We can load up the car and burn her somewhere far away, preferably under a thousand pounds of an-thracite and Match Light."

"You don't have to tell me twice." Saiera led the way out, with Addy and I right on her heels.

I half expected the tomb door to boom shut as we approached it, followed by Pippah's evil cackle. To my relief, the tomb door remained cracked open. Snow swirled in, and a fine powder had fanned out in a V formation from the gap. Saiera put her shoulder to it, and the door squealed open. I had never welcomed a frigid blast of winter in my face as much as I did right then. Addy muttered a prayer, and Saiera added a quick "Amen" at the end.

That was too easy.

Not that facing Tony's memory and remembering all that pain had been easy—far from it. Having a replica of my friend dredged up out of my memory and turned against me had driven a psychic knife through my heart. A dull, hollow ache remained, and I shivered in short bursts. Pippah had known right where to hit me for maximum damage—no surprise since she'd been inside my head and rifled through all of my anxiety drawers.

However, as battles against evil went, that one was the mother of all duds. I had expected a lot more fireworks, a lot more hands-on, stake-through-the-heart type of action, and what I got was a little grudge match with my own subconscious guilt.

Kind of a fizzle, really.

Conversation was minimal on the way back. Other than the occasional warning about footing or comment on direction, the three of us remained silent—three tired figures, wreathed by plumes of foggy breath, traipsing through the snow. The bag of Pippah's bones clacked against my leg as I walked. A screech owl trilled once, and that was the only sound I heard above the crunch of our footfalls and animal panting of our breathing.

The light shining through my kitchen door appeared ahead, beckoning us onward and filling me with hope that we might just get through this night. After defeating Pippah's supernatural schemes, I could get on with the business of figuring out who killed Consuelo. We picked up the pace at the sight of that yellow glimmer through the trees.

"I'll go..." I had to pause a moment to catch my breath. "I'll go through and load this into the car"—I lifted the sack a bit so there would be no doubt about what I meant by *this*—"then I'll come back and get a wheelbarrow full of coal from the shed."

Saiera nodded. The damp snow sparkled in her hair as if she'd been dowsed by the glitter fairy. "Good plan. Anybody else want some tea? My fingers are frozen."

Addy shrugged. "Why not?"

The smaller girl led the way into the apartment through the back door. I followed close behind her... and ran into her when she stopped unexpectedly. Saiera plowed into my back and said, "What the hell?"

Andy Gluck was sitting at my kitchen table in a black overcoat and a dark suit, with bright-red galoshes on his feet. The reporter's tie hung like a noose around his neck, and his round, doughboy face shone with sweat.

He held a black semiautomatic pistol in one meaty fist, pointed at my belly.

"Come in and have a seat," he said. "We have some things to discuss."

WITH SAIERA BEHIND me, it entered my mind to yell for her and Addy to run for it. Gluck must have read my mind. He lined up the gun sights with my nose and said, "I have, like, a hundred bullets in this thing. Don't even think about trying something."

I thought a hundred seemed far-fetched, but the way we were bunched together, any number over three would be enough to kill all of us. I eased into the kitchen, hands out to my sides. The sack with Pippah's bones felt like a bag of concrete. I didn't believe it was the physical weight that made it so heavy as much as it was the spiritual burden of what I carried.

"Hey, Andy," I said. "What's with the gun, dude?"

Saiera's jaw dropped. "Andy Gluck! What the hell is wrong with you?" I tried sending her a warning glare, which she ignored. "What kind of creepy crap are you playing at now?"

"Sit down, sweet Saiera," the reporter said. "I don't want to hurt you." The look he gave her sent a chill down my back—longing mixed with... something unsavory. He gestured with the pistol. "You, too, Adamantine."

Addy twitched. "You know me?"

"I know all the girls." A faint smile traced the fat man's cupid-bow lips. "All the girls." In a firmer voice, he added, "Sit, sit, sit. Everybody pull up a chair. I need to ask graveboy here some questions."

I pulled out a chair directly across from Gluck. Saiera sat on my left, with Addy to the right. I laid the sack with Pippah's bones next to my feet. A pall of worry pulled at my guts when I realized neither George nor Tabitha had come to greet me. "Where's my dog? And cat?"

Gluck shrugged. "No idea. Now, listen here, Bradley." He leaned forward and rested the gun on the table, its black muzzle not three feet away from my heart. "I'm going to ask this once, and I want a straight answer. Where did you find that picture?"

Picture? What picture? My mind had gone desperately blank. "I... I don't..."

"He means the one of me." Saiera's face was set in grim lines, her tone disgusted.

"The one of..." I made the connection, and the instant I did, a scenario appeared with the suddenness of the last piece of a jigsaw puzzle clicking into place. Dread soaked through me. I stared at Gluck with wide eyes and said, "You killed her. You killed Consuelo."

The reporter cocked his head to the side. Mischief glittered in his eyes. "How do you figure that?"

"That was your picture of Saiera. You worked on the yearbook... hell, you maybe even snapped the original. You... what? Planted it in the car when you were hiding it in the barn?" I shook my head, dismissing the thought the instant I voiced it. "No, you wouldn't be after it if that was the case. So you... lost it, right? I'll bet it has your fingerprints all over it."

Or rather, *had* his fingerprints all over it. Now that I'd removed it from the scene, handled it, and otherwise destroyed any residual prints, whatever value as evidence it might have had was well and truly lost. I had single-handedly ruined whatever chance there was of getting Gluck convicted of Consuelo's death.

Great, Brad. Now when he shoots the three of us, hopefully he'll leave enough clues even Czerniak and Swanson can convict him of our murders. Yeah, right.

"You found it in the car," Gluck said, not a question this time. He shook his head ruefully, like *Ha ha, what a dummy I am.* "I thought you found it with the body." To Saiera, he said, "I thought of you, Saiera. When I was with Connie, I mean. It's always been you I dreamed of."

"What did you do to her, you sick bastard?" Addy jerked upright and fired the question at him, causing Gluck to shift his aim more in her direction. The barrel remained rock steady, but at least it wasn't pointing directly at me. If I lunged... *No.* I'd never clear the table before Gluck pumped me full of lead.

Gluck studied Addy as if she were a curious bug, one he intended to pull the wings off then squash. "I saw her in the diner, by herself. She was waiting for you, as it turned out. It wasn't hard to strike up a conversation. Friendly girl like that. A little something-something in her coffee..." Gluck smirked. "A ride back to my place for a damsel in distress. Some fun and games. You know how it is."

Addy's face had drained of color. Her freckles stood out in stark contrast. Saiera was equally pale, and I had no doubt if I looked in a mirror, my face would be sheet white as well. Supernatural evil was one thing, but this right here... this was pure human evil.

"She was alive when I brought her out here," Gluck continued, as if musing to himself. His matter-of-fact tone sounded like someone recounting the weather. His prissy mouth quirked in a faint smile. "What better resting place than a cemetery, I thought. I dragged her into the woods back there and slit her throat."

Addy gagged and leaned to the side to empty her stomach. I wished she had done it in Gluck's lap. Saiera's eyes were wet, but her jaw was resolute. She was a warrior, and I had no doubt she would go down fighting. Somehow, I had to give her a chance to make it. I owed it to both of them.

"Too bad Arlo saw me," Gluck said out of the blue.

"Say what?"

The reporter sneered at me. "Yeah, the dumbass thought he was going to blackmail me. I showed him the tunnel straight to hell."

"And what about Glatfelter?" I said. "Did you kill him too?"

"Nah, that wasn't me." Gluck pursed his lips and rocked his head like it was on a spring. "At least... not all me."

Saiera and I traded a look. Gluck giggled at our expression.

"I came to the cemetery to interview you, Brad," he said. "After you found Connie's body. I wanted to know what evidence might still be there after all this time. You weren't around, but guess what? I met a friend of yours instead."

Gluck's posture changed. His shoulders drooped, and his eyes became hooded. He shifted in his seat, and when he spoke, it was with the syrupy-smooth lilt of molasses poured over biscuits. "Hello, sugah. Miss me?"

"ARE YOU KIDDING ME?" Saiera demanded. "How many killers do we have to deal with in one night?"

Gluck/Pippah snaked his gaze over Saiera. "I'ma gonna save you for last, sugar pie. Little Mistah Andy wants to play wit'choo for a bit, and I feel like lettin' him have his way. Him being so accommodating and all. Yeah, we make a good pair, he and me. Much better than ol' Bradley there, him such a stick in the mud."

"All right, Pippah," I said. "You got the body you wanted. You can leave any time you want. Why don't you just get out of here and leave us alone."

"Ah, no..." Gluck leaned back and sniffed in a long breath, as though savoring the first scent of spring. "I feel the power comin', chile. The moon ain't riz all the way, yet. Soon, though. A little more time..." Pippah looked at us through Gluck's piggy eyes. "A little more innocent blood... I be unstoppable. Only question is, who gonna die first? You, young Bradley? Lawd knows I'd like to do some special things wit'choo, all the trouble you cause me." He shifted to Addy. "Or this pretty li'l thing. Maybe she ought to be the one."

"Stop it, Andy," Saiera said. "This isn't you. It's the witch. You can fight her off."

Harsh, cackling laughter brayed from Gluck's throat. "Dis one doan wanna fight me, cher. He be liking it down in here wit' me. Ah, the things dis boy done!" Gluck's eyes narrowed, turned sly. "He has him some special pictures of you, princess. From da girl's locker room, yes."

"Ew."

"Yeah, me and Andy, we a pair now. What's that, sugah?" Gluck cocked his head as though listening to a silent voice. Or one inside his head. Gluck's posture changed, and somehow, I knew he had taken back control of his body, "I said we're the new dynamic duo. The Menendez brothers. Leopold and Loeb. Bonnie and Clyde."

I became aware of how surreal it was, sitting around my kitchen table, five people in four chairs, and two of them twisted psychopaths intent on murder and mayhem. The gun muzzle stared at my heart with malevolent concentration. At a distance of three feet, there would be no missing a direct hit on an important part of my anatomy, or if he did miss, the odds were high that Saiera or Addy would take the bullet instead of me.

Here's your chance, Brad. You always claimed to believe in chivalry, honor, duty, and all that male responsibility for the protection of women and children. Well, now's the time. Jump the crazy witch in the madman's body. Take the bullet. Give the women a chance to run for it. Shove the table into his big gut, then do a Batman leap over the table and tackle him. At least it would be over quick, with no slicing and dicing of dangly bits.

I stayed rooted in my seat.

My tongue dried into beef jerky inside a cotton-lined mouth, and my heart capered a manic dance behind my ribs. Sweat soaked my armpits under my winter layers. If fear had another name, it would be called Bradley Langston.

Motion from the hallway caught my eye. A small body crouched near the entrance to the kitchen, belly down, tail swishing, and green eyes swallowed by enormous pupils.

Tabitha. Holy Terror of Ankles. The Graveyard Slasher. One pound, six ounces of hell-bound demon in a fuzzy suit.

"No!" I croaked.

Too late.

The furball streaked across the floor, claws scrabbling. I knew what happened next even though I couldn't see it through the table. Tabitha latched onto Gluck's ankle and balled around it in teeth-gnawing fury.

In Gluck's voice, the reporter yelled, "Ow! What the hell?" He looked down, shoving back from the table. His motion threw the gun off target, its muzzle tracking across the ceiling.

"Run!" I shouted, and with a heave, I upended the table, throwing it into Gluck's face.

Everyone tried to go everywhere, all at one time. Bodies collided.

I tried and failed to put Gluck on his ass by power-driving the table into his face. He fought free though he lost ground, stumbling back into the refrigerator. The box of cereal I had stashed up there fell and bopped him on the head. Too bad I hadn't left an anvil up there instead of Rice Chex.

A flash of tabby fur pinballed between our feet, howling in fury. I danced on my toes to avoid stepping on the cat and fell to my knees.

Of course, instead of running like sensible people, Addy and Saiera leaped into the melee. They both dove for Gluck, who seemed surprised and a little nonplussed at all the activity. He pointed the pistol one way then the other, as if unsure whom to shoot first.

Saiera tripped over me and landed on my back. She collided with Addy as she fell and knocked the smaller woman off course. The goth girl raked Gluck across the cheek with her nails as she lurched past.

That seemed to focus his rage.

The pistol banged out a shot. Addy jackknifed. Her hands grabbed her stomach, and she fell to her knees. A shocked look of dismay registered on her face in the long moment before she fell forward.

"Addy!" I cried. "No!"

By the time Saiera and I sorted ourselves out and regained our feet, it was too late. Gluck had stepped back into the hallway entrance and leveled the pistol at us.

"Stay still," he commanded. "Don't move."

Tabitha had disappeared. *Smart kitty.* I hoped she had joined George under the bed and would guard him with all the power of her feline fury.

"Now what?" Saiera asked in a dull voice. "You kill us too?"

"Shut up a minute." Gluck's expression turned distant, and his head tilted to one side. A silent consultation ensued, punctuated by Gluck's mumbled, "Uh-huh. Yeah. Okay."

I distracted him a moment when I knelt by Addy. He glared at me but said nothing when I felt her neck. It was cold, as cold as the grave. I couldn't find a pulse.

Saiera queried me with her eyes. I shook my head.

"Okay, you two," Gluck said. "We're going out to the shed to get some rope. Have to tie one of you up so we can have our fun with the other." A toothy, self-satisfied grin crept across his face. "You get to choose who we play with first. Now, move!"

I exchanged a glance with Saiera, looking for some plan she might be brewing behind those dark eyes.

She shrugged and lifted one side of her lips in a crooked smile. *Sorry.*

Yeah. Me too.

We shuffled to the back door. Saiera opened it, and I crowded up behind her. An idea took shape in my head. If I shoved her out, I could block the door long enough for her to get away. Gluck would shoot me in the back, but I felt certain I could hold him off long enough for Saiera to get away.

"Don't try it," said Gluck from right behind me as if he'd read my mind. The hard muzzle of the pistol pressed against my back. "I'll shoot right through you and into the woman. She won't make two steps."

We walked out onto the patio, and Gluck held back, opening the distance between us so I couldn't make a try at grabbing his gun like some action hero from the movies.

Fat chance of that.

Snow blanketed the ground. If there was a full moon, it remained hidden behind winter's cloak. Our only light came from a single security fixture over the shed's door, and a lace curtain of powdery snowflakes shrouded its yellowish glow. The cold, wet air razored into my lungs and smelled faintly of wood smoke and pine. A deep chasm of melancholic regrets opened before me, and I fell into it headfirst. *What an awful night to die. What an awful way to die. So much left to do. So much life yet to live.*

I said to Saiera, "Any chance you have a gypsy witch spell that'll get us out of this?"

"Ha. Yeah, I wish. Sadly, my talents run to clairvoyance and fortune telling."

"Too bad you didn't see this coming."

"Indeed. The gifts are spotty at best." She let out a dry chuckle. "I know some great potions. Recipes passed down from my great-grandmother. Given some time, I could whip up a tincture that would have ol' Gluck there squatting over a toilet until his insides ran out."

"Since he's full of shit..."

"Exactly."

"What are you two whispering about?" Gluck demanded.

We had covered about three-quarters of the distance to the shed, about twenty-five feet from the back door of the apartment. I guessed Gluck was about ten steps behind us.

I turned and said, "Go fuuu—"

My voice froze in my throat. From behind Gluck rose the diminutive figure of Adamantine Tarwater. Gone was the shy, nerdy goth girl with a dusting of cute freckles and a quirky smile. In her place had arisen a phantom of nightmares and midnight chills.

She leaped on Gluck's back. Her mouth opened wide, and by the light of the single outdoor bulb, I saw the gleam of twin fangs in the instant before they sank into Gluck's neck.

Gluck screamed and tumbled to the ground. Addy rode him down. Awful, wet ripping noises followed. Crimson spray splattered the snow.

"Oh shit," Saiera said in the tiniest of voices.

"Ah. Yeah," I agreed.

"What's happening?"

"I... I... I wish I knew."

The thrashing mass of Gluck's and Addy's entwined forms stilled but for the horrid sucking noises Addy made as she gurgled and—*Ugh*—swallowed.

The sounds went on for what felt like an hour but, in reality, must have been less than a minute. Finally, Addy looked up. Her black eyes met ours, and a sheath of blood coated her chin.

"We should run," Saiera whispered.

"I don't think that will help," I muttered back. Louder, I said, "Addy? Is that you?"

The goth girl rose and wiped her chin with a sleeve. She looked... embarrassed.

"I really hoped it wouldn't come to this." She kept her gazed fixed on her toes. "But now that you know my secret, I have to kill you both."

Chapter 31

"Jeez, I'm kidding!" Addy smirked. "Seriously. You should see your faces."

Saiera and I exchanged a look. I realized we were holding hands.

"You really have to work on your comic timing, Addy," I managed at last.

"Well, yeah, I suppose," she admitted with a one-shoulder shrug. "Being undead and funny is hard."

Saiera stirred. "So you're a..."

"Vampire, yes." Addy held her hands up and waggled her fingers. In a spooky voice, she intoned, "Nosferatu. Slayer of the Night. Bloodsucker. An exsaguinaphile." She dropped her hands. "I made that last one up."

Shivers racked me from head to toe. *From fear or cold? Both, probably.* I leaned into Saiera and felt her leaning right back. Snow drifted into my hair.

"I'd like to tell you all about it," Addy said. "I've kept the secret so long it's like a truck has been lifted off my soul. If I have a soul, that is." She shook her head, dispelling whatever train of thought she'd been about to follow. "Gluck is dead, but I'm not sure where Pippah went. I suspect she may be temporarily trapped inside his body. Or it could be she was snapped out of it and is trying to make a comeback, even now. We have to get rid of those bones, people. Come on, let's move."

Suiting action to words, Addy spun and jogged toward the apartment door. Saiera and I stood together, huddled together under a wan security light, being dusted by snow and coated with a reality that refused to make sense.

"What do you think?" Saiera asked at last.

I sighed. "I think she's on our side. Addy, I mean. Before I knew about her... situation, I always thought she was a good person."

"So a witch and a grave tender team up with a vampire to vanquish an evil spirit."

"Sounds very heroic when you put it that way."

WE RODE THREE ABREAST in Addy's tired-out Datsun pickup. Pippah's bones and Andy Gluck's body rested in the bed of the truck, along with the charcoal and my bone-burning tools. Addy said she knew a good spot to burn both our problems to ash, well north of her family farm. "It's an old rock quarry with a bunch of pits, ready-made for bonfires."

The little pickup swayed and skidded over snowy roads, but Addy held the wheel like she knew what she was doing. I occupied the middle seat, and occasionally, Addy brushed my knee when she shifted gears. To my own surprise, I stopped flinching after the first couple of times.

"Well, so," I said, breaking the growing silence but with no idea where to go from there. Numerous choices popped up, including, "Think this snow will clear up?" and "How long have you sucked blood for sustenance?" Neither seemed appropriate. *Think, Brad. Think.* "Um. Thanks for saving our lives."

"My pleasure," Addy said. A whiff of iron blood carried on her breath. I wished I could offer her a Tic Tac. She followed that with "I'm really sorry you guys had to see that. I've been, uh, in the coffin, so to speak, for ten years now. Until now, no one knew except my parents."

Understanding struck. "So your dad being overprotective is all about..."

"Keeping my secret, yeah."

Saiera said nothing, but her hand found mine in the dark and clenched it tight.

Twin high beams bored through drifting tufts of white. We all said nothing for a time. The heat in the truck's cab steamed our clothes and humidified the air with the scent of wet dog—my fault, that—and a coppery, meaty smell—which I attributed to Addy—and Saiera's musky fragrance of ginger, cinnamon, and musk.

Addy broke the silence next. "I don't feed on people, you know. Just animals and the... well, just animals. I haven't hurt a person in years and years. Not since after I was first... turned."

I didn't know what to say to that, so I kept quiet.

Soon I found myself nodding off. A combination of the warmth, the hypnotic snow, and the draining adrenaline left me sagging in place. I jerked awake when Addy hit the signal switch and coasted into a turn through an open gate. A bullet-pocked sign read Do Not Enter, Private Property.

"Trespassing," I said. "We're outlaws now."

"Scofflaws," Addy said.

"Degenerates," Saiera added.

"Hoodlums."

"Brigands."

"Pirates. Arrr."

"Arrr."

"Arrr."

We all laughed, and it was good.

IT TOOK ALL NIGHT LONG and into the middle of the day, but we got the grisly chore done. Pippah did not raise a fuss though I fancied I could hear her ghost wail all the way from Shady Terraces. A shudder ran through me, and that was that.

Andy Gluck joined Pippah's bones in the coal-fueled inferno we had built in a shallow, grave-like pit, and I felt bad about that, but protecting Addy's secret seemed more important than providing evidence of his savaged neck for forensic examination. Without Gluck's confession, it might mean the cops would never solve the crimes of who killed Consuelo or Glatfelter, and that was something with which I would have to live.

The heat drove us back, as did the awful smell. We all bowed our heads, Saiera said a prayer, and that was that.

We kept the fire burning for a long time, heaping coal on it whenever it looked in danger of dropping below a million degrees or so. The rock pit acted as a reflector, holding and enhancing the heat until it singed my eyebrows every time I added more fuel.

The snow had stopped by the time we felt the job done, and Addy had taken refuge under the tarp in the truck bed to avoid the weak sun filtering through the clouds.

I drove us back over slippery roads, white-knuckling it all the way, and parked the Datsun in the shed. I closed the shed door to keep Addy concealed in darkness. I joined hands with Saiera and walked into the kitchen. The mess there was the only reminder of the night's terror.

The padding of feet announced George's return to bravery, along with his howling complaint about missing breakfast. He was followed closely by the Queen of Terror herself, with much the same issue regarding household management.

"Oh yes," Saiera told the fur people, dropping to her knees to console them with pets and ear scratches. "Your daddy has been a very bad boy. Why, he's been burning up bad people and hanging out with vampires and even"—she dropped her voice to a whisper—"*trespassing*! Can you believe it?"

I dug out pet food and set it by the can opener. "And all this time, you thought I was a nice guy."

"I know! How can I ever date such a bad boy?"

A warm feeling rushed into my face and... elsewhere. "You want to go on a date?"

"My gypsy senses tell me..." Saiera's eyes twinkled. "Mmm. I see a dark-haired woman in your future."

"You hear that, Tabitha? Competition."

Tabitha growled, sprang at my ankle, and bit me.

About the Author

Scott Bell has over 25 years of experience protecting the assets of retail companies. He holds a degree in Criminal Justice from North Texas State University.

With the kids grown and time on his hands, Scott turned back to his first love—writing. His short stories have been published in *The Western Online*, *Cast of Wonders*, and in the anthology, *Desolation*.

When he's not writing, Scott is on the eternal quest to answer the question: What would John Wayne do?

Read more at snapshooter4hire.com.

About the Publisher

Dear Reader,

We hope you enjoyed this book. Please consider leaving a review on your favorite book site.

Visit https://RedAdeptPublishing.com to see our entire catalogue.

Check out our app for short stories, articles, and interviews. You'll also be notified of future releases and special sales.

9 781958 231005